Aurora Rescue

Aurora Series
Book 1

ROBYN ECHOLS

G

GENEALADY

Winton, California

Published by Genealady
P.O. Box 96
Winton, CA 95388

ISBN: 0615608965
ISBN-13: 978-0615608969 (Genealady)

LCCN: (applied for)

DEDICATION

To my husband, for his patience and support
To Kristine Ball, my faithful-to-the-end reader and critic.

PROLOGUE

On the Monday of Spring Break in 2024, Eddie Burrows took Andrea on a day trip to Dead Man's Drop Mountain. They rode in Eddie's all-terrain vehicle, a two-seater Prowler he used for hunting. The trail grew increasingly rugged as they arrived within a quarter of a mile from the summit. Andrea, tired of being beat around inside the vehicle, finally told Eddie that she would rather walk.

As they pulled off the trail, they saw the sign warning everyone in the area to stay away from the cliffs at the peak of Dead Man's Drop.

"We should not go any further, Eddie," Andrea warned. "There is a bad spirit in this place. It swallows people up."

"What are ya'll talking about, Andi?" Eddie responded with a laugh. "That warning sign is there because of the steep cliff and the winds that can whip up and throw people around if they are too dumb to pay attention to what they are doing. We'll just be careful and there won't be any problem."

"Please, Eddie, let's just explore somewhere else where the spirit of this mountain is more welcoming. I do not want to go any further."

"What is all this talk about spirits, Andi?" Eddie asked, confused. "Ya'll know this Texas white boy doesn't understand all that business about spirits in nature like you folks with Indian blood do. Besides, I thought ya'll were only one-quarter Native American."

"One-quarter Pueblo, Eddie. The tribes are not all the same."

"Okay, sorry. I should know better by now. But, are ya'll sure your fear of heights isn't the real reason why you don't want to climb to the top?"

Without a word, Andrea stared at Eddie, her face void of expression.

"Oh, Sweetheart, future-bride-of-mine, please don't get mad at me for my stupidity on these matter," Eddie teasingly pleaded. "Ya'll come only as close to the cliffs as you want. But, this is too impre of a scene for me to pass up. I want to get some pictures of the canyon and beyond from the top of the boulders."

Ignoring the sign and Andrea's warning, Eddie bolted out of the Prowler and strode towards the top of the mountain. He turned back occasionally to check on Andrea as he climbed the boulders.

Andrea, more cautious due to the dark feeling she could not shake, ventured only a short distance from the Prowler. She stayed as far away from the top of the mountain as she could without losing sight of Eddie. From her vantage point, she used her camera to take snapshots of Eddie. He stood confidently on the rocky outcrop while he captured images of the view beyond the cliff with the camera on his retro Cabela's flip phone.

Eddie walked back to show Andrea the pictures. He could not find one of the snapshots he thought he had taken. In frustration, because it was not on his phone, Eddie shook his head and ignored Andrea's intake of breath as he hiked back towards the boulders.

Eddie changed his mind and sauntered across the flatter surface towards the edge of the cliff. Andrea shook her head with confusion. She should have felt relief at his decision to not climb the rocky outcrop again. Instead, as she watched him move to the left and below the rocks to see if he could capture the image he desired, her feeling of foreboding increased.

In an attempt to distract herself from the uneasiness building inside of her, Andrea turned her camera to video mode and started a holo-video clip of Eddie. She watched him through the viewing window as he stood on the cliff edge. She saw how he centered the scene he wanted in his cell's viewing window. Full of confidence, he ignored the wind that whipped at his clothing and bent back the rim of the brown, wide-brimmed western hat that would have blown away if Eddie had not tightly fastened it under his chin with its leather straps. At this sight of Eddie standing at the cliff's edge, a surge of love for this man coursed so strongly through Andrea that it smothered all feelings of fear inside of her.

After he clicked his phone camera, a smile spread across his face as he checked the image. She guessed Eddie was pleased with his latest picture.

Eddie walked back toward Andrea, his cell phone clutched in his hand. While he made funny faces for the video being recorded by her camera, Eddie's cell rang. He glanced at the caller I.D. screen. The sunlight created a glare making it impossible for him to see who was calling. Eddie stepped back into the shadows cast by the boulders crowing the summit of Dead Man's Drop. He pulled the screen closer to his face to read the incoming number.

Andrea realized the caller must be someone Eddie knew and liked because he grinned before he flipped open the cover to answer the call. Instead of Andrea feeling happy for him, the feeling of foreboding returned and clutched her heart.

Then Eddie disappeared.

CHAPTER 1

Marty could not believe her eyes as she watched Cy's old gray Honda Civic drive into the day-use parking lot. She had invited him to hike with her and their friends at Granite Point Campground even though she knew he was not an outdoorsy kind of person. She had doubted he would come. She broke out in a grin of delight as she watched him pull into a parking space.

Marty knew that this day was a turning point in her life. Tomorrow she would be saying farewell to her family early in the morning. Her parents and younger brother, Jason, were leaving on a two-week vacation to California. Marty's own summer plans were to study the history of the United States most of the summer. Before her scheduled departure with the West Tour Agency on her history immersion tour of key sites east of the Mississippi River for two months, she planned this one last day of hiking in the mountains with her friends.

Everyone but Cy was part of the Granite View Class of 2024 and had attended the graduation party sponsored by the school two weeks before. However, she wanted one last time with them before they all went their separate ways that summer and, for some of them, the rest of their lives. Hiking the Granite Point Mountain Trail high in the Rockies west of the Denver area was one of her favorite things to do. It was a trail she knew well since she and her family had hiked it at least once a year for as long as she could remember. So, when she started thinking about something they all could do that would be fun and memorable—something more than the usual pizza party or hanging out at someone's house—she came up with the idea of a day-hike to her favorite place.

While watching Cy get out of his car, Marty remembered when her parents first hired him to tutor her in trigonometry during her senior year. It had all started when her grades in general and her geometry grade in particular had dropped when she became involved with Brian the last few months of her sophomore year. She put off taking trigonometry during her junior year. She was still with Brian, although their relationship was starting to get shaky, when she started her senior year. By that point, there was no more time to put off taking that last math class she needed to qualify for the university she wanted to attend.

As insurance, Marty's parents hired the tutor that several of her friends used to help them get through their math and science classes.

Cy Riverton was the same age as Marty. Actually, he was a few months older than she was since he turned eighteen weeks before Thanksgiving and she did not turn eighteen until May. He was more than just good in math and science. He was a senior at the university at the same time she and her other friends were high school seniors.

Eddie Burrows, one of Cy's tutoring students at the university, used to call Cy "Genius." Marty remembered meeting and speaking briefly with Eddie and his fiancée, Andrea, a few times since her appointments often followed Eddie's. She agreed with Eddie that Cy was probably a genius even though Cy insisted that he was not. Cy acknowledged that he might be gifted, but he denied being a genius.

Marty resisted succumbing to a feeling of sadness as her thoughts turned to Eddie. *I am not going to get side-tracked thinking about him, not during my hiking party. I might have invited him, too, for Cy's sake, but Eddie is no longer around.* Marty knew Cy struggled over Eddie's disappearance, even though he never said so.

But, this was supposed to be a happy day, a post-graduation celebration for her and her friends. She wanted to keep it that way. For her, having Cy show up made this day a complete success.

Marty was still dating Brian when she started going to Cy for tutoring. Her mind would have capably wrapped itself around the trig concepts except the emotional upheavals between her and Brian ran constant interference.

Everything changed after the first weekend in December. Brian took her to the school's holiday dance. He did all the right things to make it a lovely evening for Marty. But Brian acted like he was distracted the entire time, as if his thoughts were somewhere else that night. Her suspicions were confirmed when he took her straight home after the dance and told her he was breaking up with her for good.

The following week, Marty was the one who was distracted. Preparing for semester finals the first week following the dance felt to Marty like running a marathon in heavy fog. Instead of concentrating on the trig concepts Cy explained to her, she often stared over Cy's shoulder. She found it interesting that she was not really upset that Brian ended things. Unlike past stormy scenes between them, tears never surfaced. Instead, she merely felt disoriented and numb inside.

"Boyfriend troubles still?" Cy had finally asked, waving his hand until he had her attention again.

"I don't have a boyfriend anymore." She did not elaborate and he did not ask for details. "Okay. Then it is time for you to focus on passing this semester class," he said without a word of condolence.

At first his response struck her like an icy blast. Gradually, Marty grudgingly realized he was right. She needed to look towards her future which she envisioned included getting the best grades possible in her senior year so she could qualify for the scholarships to the university she wanted to attend.

From then on, anytime Cy caught her attention drifting, he tapped the book or paper they were working on to get her attention. Increasingly, she found it easier to concentrate. By the time of the final, her brain was operating at full capacity and she aced the trig exam.

Just before Christmas break, Marty tracked Cy down to share her success with him. Rather than enthusiastically congratulating her, Cy surprised her by stating that after he learned she broke up with her boyfriend, he had not doubted that she would do well on her final.

Then, in typical Cy fashion, he used the pointer finger of his right hand to tick off the fingers of his left hand as he listed all the reasons why she could have gotten better grades in school all along if she had focused more on her class work instead of on a boyfriend. He mentioned several logical reasons why it was better if she did not get serious about someone until she was through with her education.

Marty remembered how she had to bite her lip to keep from firing back a sassy retort. But, over Christmas break, she gradually accepted that Cy would never have said something so personal unless he really cared about what was best for her. She also knew that in a way he was right. However, she also wondered if Cy realized that most people cannot turn their feelings on and off like a faucet.

Marty returned to her tutoring sessions in January. She started to see more in him than just a nerdy tutor. She started to stand up to her friends when they belittled him. She found herself pointing out his good traits.

Before long, Marty realized her feelings changed towards Cy. She discovered she enjoyed talking to Cy about many topics, not just trigonometry. Also, she noticed that Cy began to relax around her. As his brainstorms flashed through his thoughts, he started sharing some of his ideas with her. He told her about the classes he was taking, including the advanced astronomy class. He also seemed excited about something to do with the sun and how this year was supposed to be a solar cycle high.

Marty did not understand everything he said. She tried to cover it up by joking. Her subtle humor seemed to go right over his head most of the time. Sometimes she had to bite her lip to keep from laughing at his responses.

However, she never joked about the personal thoughts and plans that Cy shared with her. She knew they were important to him. She felt privileged because she knew he did not talk about these things with his other students. He trusted her to take his interests and goals seriously. The more he opened up to her, the more she realized she was falling in love with him.

After that week, Marty invited him to go with her to parties with her friends from high school. He usually declined with an excuse of a project deadline or work he had to do as a teacher's assistant. Because he seemed so distracted with Eddie's disappearance, she wondered if worrying about Eddie was the real reason why he begged off.

However, when it came to the big event, he did come through for her, Marty remembered with a smile. She kept the picture of the two of them taken that night on her nightstand.

A few times Cy invited her to join him at the internet café by the university when she got off work at the Mile-High Burger drive-through. He bought her sodas and they surfed the net or played video games together. In addition to having fun winning most of the games that required good eye-hand coordination, she picked up some interesting and helpful internet search skills from him.

But, he never asked her out on a real date. He seemed to ignore her attempts to get closer. Was it because his social skills were weak? Was it because he had too much emotional investment in his logical but rigid belief that people were better off if they postponed personal relationships until after they completed their education? Marty did not know. What she did about it was to struggle keeping her own feelings in check. She decided it was better to continue being his friend in order to give him time to see if their relationship would develop into something more.

Cy had declined Marty's invitation to the high school's graduation party two weeks previously. His parents were in town to attend his graduation and to spend time with him. His graduation had been several days earlier than hers and his summer course work, which would give him a jump-start on his master's degree in physics, began the Monday after her graduation.

With that in mind, Marty had invited Cy to the hike. She was hoping that, now their tutoring sessions were over, he would come so they could spend this one last day together before she left on her tour. He had not disappointed her.

Perhaps Cy came only because he wanted a break from his summer studying. But, she hoped the real reason was so he could see her again.

"Be with you in a minute," Marty called out to the others who were gathered at the top of the parking lot. "Cy made it. I am going to go say hi and make sure he knows where we are meeting."

"Cy?" Damien blurted out with a choked laugh. "You invited him? He didn't graduate with us."

"No, but he helped several of us so we could graduate, remember? Besides, he graduated this year from the university. This is his graduation party, too."

"Cy can find his way all over the galaxy, Marty," Ethan observed. "He can surely find his way to this corner of the parking lot."

"I would not be so sure about that," Damien countered. "We did not give him the T-shirt for nothing."

Marty waved off the remarks and started down the hill. She knew what T-shirt Damien referred to.

All of Cy's tutoring students from the high school had pooled their money and given it to him as an early graduation gift. It was solid black and had the solar system printed on the front in vivid color. Between the orbiting planets it read, "Yes, I'm a Space Case. Isn't Everyone?"

The students had meant it as a joke. As usual, the humor was lost on Cy. He thought it referred to the astronomy class he was taking. From that time forward, he wore it so often, it almost became his uniform. The students often snickered and commented to each other that they saw Cy wearing "the T-shirt." No one had to explain what shirt they were talking about.

Only Marty never thought of the saying as a put-down when it related to Cy. She knew from being around him that those times he seemed "lost in space" were times his mind was in a far more complex and expanded universe than she or any of her friends could comprehend.

Charlene slipped away from Ethan's side and caught up with Marty. She grabbed Marty's arm as she huddled close to her.

"Cy, huh?" she quietly asked. "You and Cy have a thing going between you?"

"No," Marty said, shaking her head and rolling her eyes in mock protest. She knew her friend was consumed with curiosity. "He is just a friend. I thought he would enjoy coming with us since he knows most of us and he doesn't have many friends his age at the university."

"If you say so," said Charlene with a laugh as she let go of Marty's arm and rejoined the others. Marty glanced back long enough to see Ethan give Charlene a puzzled look. She hoped Charlene would keep her mouth shut and not start the group speculating about her and Cy.

Cy still had the trunk lid to his Civic open when Marty approached. She opened her mouth to give him her usual small-talk greeting. That impulse ended as soon as she saw the contents of his trunk.

"Is that a pup tent? Oh, and a sleeping bag, too. Um, Cy, maybe you misunderstood. This is a day-hike. We were not planning to stay overnight."

"I know. I decided to rent a space for the night since I am up here anyway. I will have to wait until after 3:00p.m. to get into my campsite, though, so I need to park down here."

Marty blinked, momentarily speechless.

"I wish I had known you wanted to stay over, Cy. We could have planned an over-nighter, although some of our group who are working tomorrow already complained that they had to pull strings to get free just for today."

"Don't you have to work tomorrow?"

"No, my job is over. Once I gave my notice that I was going on the tour and would not be available for two months, they said they no longer need me. They let me go early."

"Oh."

"What is in that other case?"

"My telescope."

"I thought your astronomy class was over."

Cy stared at Marty for a moment, and then shook his head.

"Some of us like to look at the stars even when we aren't taking an astronomy class, Marty. I have had this telescope since I was eight. Up here, I won't be battling the ambient light from the city, so I should be able to get a clear view of the night sky. Once the moon goes down, it could be pretty spectacular."

"You mean you plan to spend the night just so you can look at the sky and then go home tomorrow?"

"No. If you must know, I will probably leave the campground in the morning. I have another area I need to hike. This will work out well with me coming up with everyone today and already being here for what I have to do tomorrow. Tonight with the telescope is just for fun."

"Okay," Marty spoke slowly as she shrugged her shoulders. Then she spotted something else in the trunk that looked familiar. She picked up the nylon canvas case and opened it. Inside was a hand-held GPS unit. "This looks a lot like the GPS my dad has."

"That is because is it the GPS your dad has. I stopped by your house this morning on my way up here to ask him if he had one and if I could borrow it for the weekend. I promised to return it before you left on your trip. He said I could."

"Are you bringing it with you today?"

"No, it is for my hike tomorrow."

"Where are you hiking tomorrow?"

"A little bit further up the road," Cy said with a tone of finality. He took the GPS unit from her and returned it to the trunk.

Marty pressed her lips shut. Her curiosity skyrocketed. It was not like him to be so evasive with her unless the subject had something to do with Eddie Burrows. He never talked with anyone about Eddie. She decided to not push it just yet. If he wanted her to know, he would tell her.

Instead, she asked, "Do you have a daypack or backpack for the hike today?"

"I have a backpack with my camping gear and my clothes for tomorrow. I figured I would just take my shoulder pack today."

She watched Cy pull a couple of small baggies full of sandwiches and cookies out of an ice chest along with a bottle of water. He loaded them into his gray bag with the wide strap that rested on one shoulder. He usually used his shoulder bag to carry his tablet, slab, scientific calculator and other school necessities to and from classes.

She wondered where his slab was. It used to be that she hardly ever saw him without it. It crossed her mind, not for the first time, that she had not seen it recently.

Marty remembered how she used to haul a thick book bag that rolled on wheels back and forth to school when she was in elementary school. Since nowadays just about all reading material for classes, including textbooks, newspapers and internet searching at school, was done on tablets or rechargeable computer slabs—a technology that started with the early electronic readers and tablet computers that came out when she was in pre-school—most students had given up their bulky book bags for lightweight padded shoulder bags.

"Is there enough room in there for your sunscreen, insect repellant, first-aid kit, snake-bite kit, compass, rain poncho and survival kit? You do have a long-sleeve light-colored shirt to protect you from the sun in this high altitude, don't you? How about a hat with a good brim?"

Cy turned and stood to his full height until he looked Marty full in the face. At five feet ten inches, he was two inches taller than she was. His ash blonde hair drooped straight down and covered his forehead almost to his eyebrows except for the strands that floated willy-nilly in the breeze. Because he was standing down-slope from her, they were eye to eye. Marty watched with amusement as he slowly raised his hands and started ticking off a list of responses on his fingers.

"First, this is a day-hike, so I will not need most of that outdoor paraphernalia. Second, I do not use sunscreen. Third, the insect repellant is in my backpack for tonight because that is when the mosquitoes are most likely to be out. Fourth, I do not do long-sleeve shirts in the summer and fifth, I do not do hats ever. A stocking cap in the winter, maybe, but no hats. In addition, as of this morning, the weather channel indicated there is no anticipation of any rain today. Tomorrow, maybe, but not today. So, stop fussing about me Marty. I am not a complete babe in the woods, so to speak."

Cy turned back to his trunk to finish preparing for the hike and securing his car.

Marty did not agree with his reasoning. She forced herself to not laugh out loud at his retort. Then she shook her head as she studied his clothes. As far as she was concerned, Cy did not have it all together as much as he tried to act like he did. For one thing, he was not dressed right for hiking. He wore his usual navy blue canvas Vans with ankle-length socks. He also wore the T-shirt that had prompted Damien's wisecrack. Unfortunately, being short-sleeved and black in color was not good for spending the day out in the sun high in the mountains.

Marty's dad once pointed out how Cy's gray denim knee-length travel pants had been called cargo pants decades earlier. Marty knew Cy loved them because of all the zippered pockets for his techno toys. He also loved his BlackSlab, the successor to the BlackBerry cell phones of a decade earlier. Cy once told her he preferred it to the wrist screen he used to own because of its slightly larger screen size and greater ability to perform math calculations. He used a Bluetooth earpiece for cell calls. Marty did notice he was wearing his Bluetooth, which meant that the BlackSlab must be hiding in one of the pockets.

In contrast to Cy's haphazard hiking outfit, Marty wore a pink fabric hat with a full brim that kept her face and neck shaded. She wore a light pink crinkle-cotton top with loose flowing long sleeves. It was not the latest style, but it worked well for hiking. Her well-used brown leather hiking boots with the mesh liners designed to wick away moisture came above her ankles. They advertized her as a veteran hiker.

In her daypack she had packed a knit top, a light-weight jacket and a rain poncho so she could wear them in layers over her sturdy brown denim jeans in case it cooled off or started to rain. She never trusted the weatherman completely, not when it came to being up in the mountains.

Her thick chestnut brown hair was neatly combed back into a ponytail secured with a strip of heavy tooled leather. Two holes on either end of the leather strip held the walnut-stained wooden pick that clamped her hair in place.

Her one stylish flare was her earrings. The thin gold-plated fishhooks looped through her ears, and dropped in front where each held a polished opal stone separated from a small shaft of lavender quartz by a gold-plated bead.

The light-weight black polyester canvas daypack she used for short hikes was large and sturdy. It had several zippered pockets and a detachable net pouch with a shoulder strap for her water bottles. Along with her extra clothes, she had placed in it a variety of useful survival items. She also packed extra protein bars, jerky and vacuum-sealed packages of fruit and nut mix, just in case. She carried it all with ease on her shoulders.

"Hold your arm out for a second, Cy," Marty said after he slipped his shoulder bag over his head. His back was still to her, but he held his right arm straight out at shoulder height while he used the left hand to slam his trunk lid shut. Marty squeezed a dollop of cream on his forearm.

"What was that?" Cy demanded as he jerked around to face her.

"Sunscreen. Let me put some on your other arm and then you can rub it in. Get some on your face, too, while you are at it."

"I told you, I don't use sunscreen."

"This is not the campus or downtown, Cy. We are up in the mountains and we will not be hiking under the shady trees all of the time. Please just humor me. Rub the sunscreen into your face and arms at least."

Cy grumbled under his breath, but grudgingly applied the sunscreen as he followed Marty up the slope to join the others.

"Hey, look what the cat drug home," Damien heckled as the two of them approached. "And, look everyone! It looks like Cy is wearing his favorite shirt. He must have some really impre friends to give him such a great shirt."

"Yeah, hi," Cy said, ignoring the sarcasm. "I do like the shirt. Thanks again, everyone. I appreciate you getting it for me."

There was a moment of silence. Cy stood awkwardly next to Marty. Marty, afraid Damien would retort with a wisecrack that would embarrass Cy, shot him a warning look. Damien turned red in the face and clamped his lips together so tight they almost disappeared between his teeth. But he kept quiet instead of making one of his usual snide remarks.

"Good to see you, Cy," Charlene broke the tension. "Hey, everyone, are we ready to do this?"

They each shouldered their packs and made last-minute adjustments to their gear before they started up the hill. Cy stayed at the back of the group, studying the area as if he was looking for something in particular. Marty stayed back with him.

Not far from the start of the trail they came to a fairly flat grouping of granite rocks from which the campground took its name. The area was open and about the size of an Olympic swimming pool. It was ringed downslope on three sides by a mix of quaking aspens and evergreens. The group, except for Cy, continued up the mountain past the rocks.

As soon as Cy saw the rock formation, he veered to the right and climbed to a highpoint. Marty followed and watched Cy in silence as he flipped his wristwatch to compass mode. Cy turned to face north and stared straight ahead. Then he turned to the west and studied the treetops that blocked part of the horizon. Within minutes, the rest of the group had retraced their steps and joined them.

"What is so fascinating about *this* place?" asked Damien. It's just a bunch of rocks. They are so flat they aren't even any good for climbing."

Cy ignored him as he continued to check the other two compass points.

"I know you are checking this area out for a reason," Marty finally said. "Are you willing to share?"

"I think this will be a good place to set up my telescope," Cy finally said. "Considering where Mars and Jupiter are this time of year, I don't think the surrounding trees will block them. And, this has a clear view of the northern sky. If there is an aurora further south than usual, I should be able to pick it up.

"Aurora?" asked Charlene.

"You know, northern lights," Marty clarified. She had learned that much from earlier conversations with Cy.

"I thought you only saw northern lights up in Alaska," said Damien. "Where do you think we are, the North Pole?"

"This summer is the high point of a solar cycle," explained Cy. "Sometimes when there is a lot of solar wind, which is more likely during a solar cycle high, we can see auroras in latitudes further south than places like Alaska, northern Canada and other parts of the northern hemisphere. If you are still here after dark, you are welcome to look through my telescope to see if one is visible."

"Maybe later, Cy," Ethan said. "This is morning, so let's stay on track and hike the mountain, okay?"

"Yeah, that would be good," Damien said sarcastically. "Solar high means lunchtime to me."

Marty waited until they were all back on the path before she spoke again to Cy.

"The only problem with setting up your telescope here is the rangers close the trail at 10:00 o'clock. You won't have time to see much before you need to be back in camp."

"I'll work something out."

CHAPTER 2

Lee Hardin reported to work on time wondering if he had made a smart decision. Was it better to get back on a Friday after being away for over two months on a temporary assignment? Or, would he have been better off if he had waited and started fresh on Monday?

The team he was assigned to in New Mexico had pretty much wrapped things up early in the week. Rather than stretch his final reports and debriefings out until Thursday, he had decided to push it through on Wednesday. He traveled home on Thursday rather than hassle the Friday traffic at the airport. But, once he arrived at his apartment permeated by stale air from being closed up for over two months, he decided he did not want to burn an annual leave day just to sit around until Monday.

So, he was back at the office. He acknowledged the few low-key greetings directed towards him as he wended his way through the building to his desk. He did not have a lot of friends in this office, so he did not expect anyone to make a big production of welcoming him back.

That was something he was going to miss about New Mexico. The camaraderie had been good there.

With a reluctant sigh, he parked his bulky body behind his desk and, squirming in his seat, wondered if someone had swapped chairs with him while he was gone. He started the process of clearing off other people's junk that had accumulated on his work area in his absence. He quickly glanced at the subject lines of the written notes and memos scattered across his desktop.

One of the papers on top was a photocopy of a quickly-penned notice about a mandatory meeting at nine o'clock that morning. Hardin checked his watch. There was not enough time before the meeting to get started on anything too time-consuming.

He decided against turning on the computer. He had stayed up on his emails while he was gone, but he was sure there would be a new flood of them once the word was out he was back in town. He would check them later.

Hardin chose instead to read his journal and review what he had been working on before he was yanked out of the office and given 72 hours to report to the field office in Albuquerque. He pulled the brown leather-bound book from his shirt pocket and thumbed back to the first part of April.

The name of Eddie Burrows caught his eye. Immediately his mind shifted back to the case and he focused on his notes about the particulars. No one from the office had sent him an email with any progress updates while he was gone. He had not really expected them to, considering how most of the clowns he worked with on this particular case tended to operate. And, frankly, while he was away, he had put Eddie Burrows out of his mind and focused on the New Mexico problem. Now he was back, he was curious to know if the Burrows kid had been found. He looked again quickly through the papers on his desk. Nothing looked like it might be related to the case.

On the other side of the building he saw Joseph, the lead on that investigation. With his usual air of inflated self-importance, Joseph was walking across the office towards the meeting room. Hardin pulled himself out of the chair and lumbered towards Joseph, turning sideways a few times to avoid bumping into a chair or a cabinet stacked with supplies.

"Hey, how ya doing?" Hardin called out to Joseph once he was close enough to catch the man's attention. Then, in order to save them both the embarrassment of going through the false pleasantries of acknowledging Hardin's return, Hardin launched directly into his question.

"Remember the Eddie Burrows case we were working on before I left? We ever find the guy?"

"Burrows, Burrows," Joseph muttered as he searched his memory. "No, that ended up being a dead-end. Don't think anything is happening on that one."

"What about that other kid that was involved? Ever get anything helpful from him?"

"Not that I recall. That's ancient history, Hardin. Things moved on around here while you were gone. Sorry I can't help you right now. I have to get things set up for nine o'clock. You should have gotten the memo. You'll be there, right?"

"Yeah, I got the memo."

Hardin turned away and started back towards his desk. *Joseph was a jerk before I left and he is still a jerk,* Hardin thought to himself. Hardin had worked with his kind before—the kind who talked the talk but did not always walk the walk. They were often more interested in looking good on paper and impressing the big bosses than following leads through to the end once a case they were working stopped being a career-maker.

Thankfully, most of the Bureau is not like him, thought Hardin. Then again, although the younger special agents entering the field were sharp and efficient, they tended to rely more on technology than good old basic field work. Hardin sensed that he was increasingly regarded as a has-been.

If any of them ever bothered to pay attention, they would see that the old man has still got it.

Lee Hardin checked his watch. He had twenty-five minutes before he needed to report to the meeting. That left him just enough time to pay a visit to the techies and see what they had found out about the Burrows case while he was gone.

CHAPTER 3

"We are never going to get there at the rate you are going."

Marty shook her head as she pushed ahead of Cy. A few moments later, Marty realized that Cy was no longer right behind her. She turned to look back at him, only to see that he had stopped again. He stood about thirty feet behind her studying the small metal box he held in one hand and the compass he clutched in the other. His body twisted and bobbed like a writhing cobra. His backpack flopped from one side to the other while he struggled to get the results he was seeking from the equipment in his hands.

"Are you coming, or not?" she called out to him.

"Wait a second, Marty."

His feet slid on some loose rock and his arms cartwheeled as he struggled to keep his balance.

In exasperation, Marty shook her head as she turned and walked back to where he was standing. She opened her mouth to vent her frustration, but inhaled her words instead as she noticed the deepening red on his face and arms. It was obvious to her that, even with the sunscreen, being out in the sun the last two days had taken its toll on his fair skin.

"On second thought, you really need to get out of this sun for a few minutes, Cy. We need to find a shady spot for you to rest awhile."

"I'm fine," Cy assured her, with a frustrated grimace. "I just cannot get a good reading while I'm walking. Since we are getting closer the top, it is more important than ever to be accurate."

"No, you are not fine, at least not for long. Your face is starting to look like a tomato. Why don't we find some shade and you can sit to take your reading? I see a spot right over there."

Cy huffed out a puff of air and shook his head with annoyance as he joined her on the large flat-topped rock in the shade of a clump of aspen. He had felt okay on the hike the day before, but today he felt the fatigue building inside of him. That was bad, because today was the important day. What he hoped to learn today had been the deciding factor he used to justify the time involved in accepting Marty's invitation to hike in these mountains. He could not give up until he finished what he had come to do.

Marty knew she was handling the heat better than Cy was. For one thing, she continually sipped on her water. She was dressed pretty much the same as the day before except that she wore a loose-weave off-white pioneer shirt instead of the pink crinkle-cloth blouse. Western and frontier cut clothing in natural fibers and earth tones was the popular fashion that year. Marty liked the long-sleeved shirt with its droop-shoulder yoke and loosely-gathered long sleeves because it covered her without clinging. The front V-neck was held together with laced rawhide strings which she left hanging loose rather than tying in a bow below the collarless neckband. The brown knee pants that were part of the same set as the blouse were tucked in her daypack so she could change into them in case it was hot at the mountaintop where they would eat lunch.

From the time Marty had joined Cy that morning she tried to look out for him. He resisted most her efforts. She offered him one of her father's light-colored long-sleeve shirts she brought up, but he refused to wear it. Even after she explained how much easier it was to sunburn at high altitude, even with sunscreen, he acted like it was not important. For someone who knew so much about solar rays, his stubborn carelessness about sun protection surprised her.

Marty had only succeeded in convincing him to carry his backpack with a light-weight rain jacket by pointing out that he could use the pack and his jacket to keep his equipment dry and out of the dust if the weather turned. She had to sneak in the two extra bottles of water and the snack bars.

Other than that, he was outfitted for the hike pretty much the same way as the day before except that he had changed his T-shirt. Now he wore his navy blue Albert Einstein T-shirt with the famous formula $E=mc^2$ emblazoned across the front. In addition, he hauled along a collection of equipment. Marty had no idea what half of the gadgets were supposed to do.

Cy also refused to wear the spare hat Marty brought up. The only thing that helped protect him from the sun was that his windblown hair covered the tops of his ears and most of his forehead. Unfortunately, his nose was already red from the day before. Marty knew it was probably going to blister and peel in spite of the sunscreen he grudgingly rubbed on his face just before they left the car.

"Cy, I thought when you decided to come up here to the mountains you were going to take a break and have some fun," said Marty. "What you are doing looks like work."

"Marty, I enjoyed being with everyone yesterday even though I think some of them considered me just the tutor coming along for the ride instead of me being one of their friends. My interests are slightly different than theirs, but I still had a pretty good time. Even last night was okay in spite of having to listen to the slab with speakers blaring away. Then there was Damien trying to tune in the local stations on his handheld and projecting it on the side of my tent since the VirS would not hold over the campfire. He should have known a virtual screen is affected by heat waves."

"Did you think we were going sit around the fire to sing camp songs and tell ghost stories?"

"That would have been good as long as there were roasted marshmallows and stuff to make s'mores. It would have been a lot more peaceful than bringing the noise and distractions of civilization up here."

Marty leaned closer to Cy with a big-eyed look, trying to figure out his intent. Was he actually making a joke about the marshmallows and s'mores, or was he serious? He was being serious, she decided.

"You amaze me sometimes, Cy," Marty shook her head. "At first I worried you might come with your slab attached to your hip or you would be constantly on your BlackSlab. Yet, as far as you are concerned, we were not outdoorsy nature-lovers enough for you."

"There is nature and then there are natural wonders," retorted Cy, deciding to not point out to her that he no longer was in possession of his slab. "The night sky up here is fantastic. The stars are so much brighter at this altitude than in town. Yet, no one else cared when I set up my telescope on Granite Point away from the lights. I think the only reason they came up and gave a quick look was to be polite. They were more interested in the television."

"I thought seeing the planets and a close-up of the moon was very impre, even if no one else did, Cy. I'm glad you hooked your BlackSlab to your telescope and took pictures. I want that one of Mars for my slab wallpaper, by the way."

"Impre?"

"You know. Impressive! Impre is just the short version. It is faster to say and text."

"Maybe if it was spring we could have caught an aurora, even this far south," Cy continued as if he had not heard her. "It was possible since this is a year of a solar high and auroras can often be seen better in the spring and autumn."

Cy clenched his jaw and stared into nothingness. Marty sensed his dark mood as he continued in a soft, sad voice, "Then, again, under the circumstances, it was a good thing for me that I was nowhere near this mountain last spring."

He is thinking about Eddie Burrows again.

Marty shook her head. She had forced thoughts of Eddie out of her mind the day before, but it was obvious that he was very much on Cy's mind today.

Marty remembered the media coverage about Eddie's disappearance. He was gone without a trace in spite of weeks spent by search and rescue teams combing the area where he was last seen. His parents live in Texas, so she only saw them a few times on local television. But his fiancée, Andrea, was a local girl. Marty did not know Andrea well but was sure she was devastated by the situation, especially since she was with him when he went missing. She wondered if Andrea still kept in touch with Cy.

But, Marty did not ask Cy anything about it. She knew from past experience that Cy would shrug off her questions about Eddie. She decided weeks before it would be better to wait for him to bring the subject up. It was more important that she assure him that she was a friend who understood his loss.

Marty gently nudged Cy's shoulder with hers and smiled at him, but otherwise remained content to share his sorrow in silence for a few moments.

"You are right about one thing, Cy," Marty finally spoke to break Cy out of his reverie. "Our friends are not that interested in astronomy. Unlike you, their dream jobs do not involve learning about space and all that physics stuff you find so fascinating. Did you enjoy spending the night up here alone to study the stars?"

"Yeah, it was a good night. I also spent the time clearing my head for today."

"Do you mean for hiking up this mountain?" asked Marty, surprised. "For someone who cleared his head, you are not very focused on this hike. Why don't you put your techno toys away and enjoy?"

"Trying to gather information from my techno toys, as you call them, is the reason I was trying to clear my head. I am searching for answers to some unexplained phenomena for which I am sure there is a rational explanation. There are a lot of possible factors on this mountain I want to measure and record."

Marty blinked. Cy was talking his scientific mumbo-jumbo again.

"What phenomena? You know, if you need help checking out factors or whatever, Cy, all you have to do is ask. I will be happy to help. It is just that I have no idea what you are trying to accomplish with that machine."

"This is not a machine. It is a meter to detect electromagnetic activity. I am exploring the area so I can compare the meter readings to my compass directions. I want to see if there is any anomaly in the area that affects the directional pull of magnetic north."

"If you say so," said Marty. "Except for the part where the needle on a compass points towards magnetic north, you know I do not understand any of that. I know more about using a compass to keep me from getting lost. "

"I'm sorry if all this is boring you. I am really happy you came back up, Marty, but I did not ask that you come along. You were the one who insisted. I could not believe it when you drove back to the campground this morning with breakfast and lunch packed for us."

"Hiking is like swimming, Cy. You never go hiking alone. If something happens, you need someone with you to go for help. I mean, look at you! You are walking snakebite bait."

Cy rolled his eyes. "You can be such a drama queen sometimes, Marty."

"I am the queen of drama, not a drama queen. There is a difference."

"I was right the first time."

"Why? Because I have ways in which I am smarter than you? Because instead of you always being the teacher, I am looking out for you in my world? You are on your way to a blistering sunburn in case you have not already realized it. And, if you don't get some water down you soon, you risk becoming dehydrated. Once that happens, even a super-brain like yours will turn to mush. I am not telling you to stop your work up here, whatever it might be. I am saying, take a break."

"I don't have time for a break," Cy insisted. "This is something I have to do and it is going to take awhile. You did not have to come."

"I wanted to come!" Marty was just as adamant. Then she shook her head with a snorting chuckle. "Although, I might have thought twice about it if I had known we were going to climb through a barbed wire fence with a 'No Trespassing' sign posted on it. It almost tore my shirt, I hope you know. I thought you plan to work for the government someday, Cy. What is it called, that ocean and sky place in Boulder? If we get caught up here, the only government building we may find ourselves in is one with bars on the windows."

Marty suppressed a laugh as Cy raised his hands to tick off a list of responses.

"First of all, Marty, they do not use bars on windows in the jail anymore. I will not tell you how I know, so trust me on that one. Second, it is the National Oceanic and Atmospheric Administration. But, who knows, I will go where I get a good offer. Third, as for this mountain, it is not a closely-monitored area. It was fenced off and posted because unusual events have happened up here that no one can explain. People have hiked up the mountain and disappeared. Everyone assumes they fell off Dead Man's Drop Cliff, but rescue parties and search drones that have scoured the area below usually do not find a body. The park service decided to close off the mountain to discourage hikers."

"So that is where we are going? You are taking me to a place where people supposedly disappear into thin air? Cy, I always figured your name was short for Cyberspace, but I had no idea you were into the paranormal."

Dead Man's Drop! Marty realized that Cy had shared something important with her. He said nothing specifically about Eddie going missing, but was it not somewhere around Dead Man's Drop Cliff that it happened?

"Cy is short for Cyrus who was a king of ancient Persia," corrected Cy, interrupting her thought. "Mention of him is in the Bible and other records. He was a good king, by the way. He let the Jews go back to Jerusalem."

"Mine is an old-fashioned name, too. Thank you, great-grandmother, Martha Clark," Marty responded with a light-hearted laugh to cover the concern creeping up on her about the direction Cy was venturing into. It was not like him. Maybe this thing with Eddie was getting to him more than she realized.

"Maybe we are just a couple of ancients from the past trapped in this modern, high-tech world," said Cy.

"Did I just hear you make a joke? That is so impre, Cy. But, that does not answer my question. Why are you chasing after paranormal events?"

Especially in the same area where Eddie disappeared. Marty could not help but wonder if there was a connection as kept talking, trying to keep him on point. She wanted to come right out and question Cy if his coming to this particular mountain today had anything to do with Eddie. Instead, she held back, hoping he would bring it up himself if she peppered him with enough questions about what he was doing.

"I'm not!"

"Not what? Making a joke about us being time travelers or chasing after paranormal events?"

Cy jerked his head to study Marty, his eyes searching her face intently. In response, Marty instinctively leaned away from him.

"I told you. I am looking for answers consistent with the laws of physics," Cy finally said quietly, breaking the tension between them.

That was a non-answer if I ever heard one.

"I mean, look at this compass and my EM meter," Cy said, drawing her attention to the gear in his hands.

"Yes, I see it them. After all, that is my compass. I still have no idea why you wanted to use that one instead of yours."

"I wanted a compass that was not right next to the battery that operates my watch. This is a quality compass, by the way, so it is very helpful."

"Of course! In my family, our outdoor equipment is the best," Marty said, wondering what was wrong with the compass on his watch. "That is why you also asked to borrow Dad's GPS with the new holographic topography display. He must really trust you to let you use it."

"And I appreciate that. But, this is what I want to show you, Marty. Look closely at how the compass needle is pointing at what we assume is magnetic north, right? Now look at my electromagnetic meter. It is registering in the lower ranges. But, if I get up and walk a distance due west..."

Cy stood and left the shade of the trees to walk close to the patch of loose rocks where he had stopped earlier.

"Cy, you are back in the full sun again. Please wear the hat I brought for you."

"Come here and see what I am trying to show you, Marty, and I will wear your silly hat."

"Deal!" Marty said as she handed him the light blue fabric hat treated to be water-resistant.

"This looks like my grandfather's old fishing hat," Cy grumbled. He brushed the hair back from his forehead and pulled the soft-brimmed headgear firmly down so it shaded his eyes and nose.

"That just goes to prove that something truly functional does not go out of style. So, tell me. What am I looking at?"

"See how I stood up and walked facing the same direction as I was when we sat on the rock? According to the GPS, we were facing due west, remember? Yet, the compass needle is not pointing north any longer. Instead, it is pointing north-north-east, and the meter is registering a higher reading."

"Let me see that. Show me again."

Cy walked her through it again.

"Interesting," said Marty thoughtfully. "I never would have expected something to affect my compass like that."

Okay, Cy is a physicist. He is looking for answers to something in the field of physics rather than the paranormal, so that is reassuring. The question is, why?

"If you really want to help me, Marty, record these readings on my BlackSlab for me."

Cy twisted his body back and forth as he searched his pockets.

"Oh, let me use my new Sun Access," offered Marty enthusiastically, referring to the combination cell phone and projection computer that was small enough to clip onto her wrist. Like most of the newest wrist screens using cell technology, it was designed to interface with a slab computer. It also came with solar-powered Bluetooth viewing glasses with audio and it could be put in a docking station for use with a standard-size qwerty keyboard.

"After we are finished, I can email it to you," offered Marty. That way, she knew, she would have a copy of what they were working on in her wrist screen, too.

"This is the greatest all-in-one cell phone, Cy," Marty extolled her new wrist screen. "Not only can I text, take pictures, videos and holographs, but I have apps for word processing, voice recognition, GPS, earth maps, sky maps—a whole bunch of stuff. My parents bought it for me because of the solar battery. They did not want to worry about me losing power or misplacing my recharger on my trip."

"May I see that?" Cy asked, as he eyed the new wrist screen that was visible now that she had pushed up the sleeve of her off-white frontier shirt. Marty unhooked the security fastener and slipped it off her arm.

Cy withdrew into his own little world as he studied the unit with its flip-up image screen. He particularly focused on the small solar units on either side of the touch screen that allowed her to recharge the phone using light. So many things had gone solar in the previous decade, but it had taken longer to develop small solar batteries powerful enough for cell units. Cy made a mental note to search for as much information as he could find about how the batteries worked. He knew that would not be an easy task since most of the details were buried behind the heavily-guarded secret walls of proprietary rights and patents.

"Now, that is impressive," Cy said as he finally handed the Sun Access back to her. "Does it come with a keyboard?"

"I can access one on the touch screen but I will use the voice recognition up here. You can format my notes how you want later."

"That would be good. And, if you can manage it, will you please also help me with the GPS?" He unhooked the handheld GPS unit from his belt and handed it to her.

"I told you, Cy. I came to help."

They retraced their path. Marty carried the GPS in holo-topo mode and spoke Cy's readings into the wrist screen's microphone.

"Can you see the differences in the data as we move up the mountain, Marty? The electromagnetic meter is measuring the earth's sub-surface. The earth is formed so that it has something like a gigantic bar magnet in its center. The positive-charged end is near the north pole and the negative-charged end is towards the south pole. The compass needle is supposed to be drawn towards magnetic north. But throughout the rest of the earth, there are patches beneath the surface that have either a positive charge or a negative charge."

"So, are we looking for positive or negative charges?"

"We are in an area of positive sub-surface charges. The Global Positioning Satellite monitor is recording the information sent from satellites in orbit far above the earth," continued Cy. "So the GPS is showing we are walking true west. But, because the compass needle is not reading north like it should, this compass is trying to tell us we are walking west-west-north. Even after factoring in the gradual predictable shift that magnetic north makes over time, something from beneath the earth is altering the magnetic pull of the compass needle."

"Cy, I am not a scientist, but I see what you are saying," said Marty. Then she quickly recorded a summary of everything. She knew he may only want the basic facts, but she wanted to be able to study it later and try to actually understand it.

"It looks like we have a thunderstorm coming," said Marty, hoping it would cool things off. "You may be glad you have that hat for more than keeping the sun off your face."

Cy studied the thunder clouds building far to the west. At the same time, Marty studied Cy. His reddening skin was flushed with more than sunburn. Was he close to getting heat stroke?

"Better make a note of the weather, too, as well as the time of the storm if it breaks. That also can influence what I am monitoring."

"What I am making a note of is your face, Cy. It is time for another break in the shade."

"I have a lot to record before noon. I haven't told you yet about solar winds and the electromagnetic fields that surround the earth. They may factor in this, too. And I need to get this all done before an electrical storm hits the area."

"You are getting ahead of me, Cy. Let's sit down and you explain it to me while you get some water in you. If we run out of time today, I can come back with you another day before I leave on my tour."

"You win," Cy conceded grumpily, inwardly pleased that she was showing such an interest both in him and his project. "How about if we try to find someplace away from this strong positive charge where I can get on the internet and download a few things to show you?"

CHAPTER 4

The two backtracked downhill in an easterly direction about a half of a mile to find a shady area where they could also get internet reception. While they each drank their water and ate a granola bar, Cy pulled up several sites about solar winds and electromagnetic fields on his BlackSlab. Marty found those same sites on her Sun Access and saved them. She also downloaded the available PDF files. She planned to transfer them to her slab computer to study them later.

After Marty finished, she looked up and saw that Cy had gotten that far-away look in his eyes again.

"Are you okay, Cy?"

"Do you know what today is, Marty?"

"Yes, it is Saturday, June 23rd."

"Today was supposed to be Eddie's and Andrea's wedding day."

Marty raised her hand and hesitated only a second before she reached over and gave Cy's shoulder a squeeze.

"I understand now why it is so important for you to be on this mountain today, Cy. What a great way to remember a friend. Thank you for letting me come up here with you."

At last! He is finally talking to me about Eddie.

"Yeah. That is one of the reasons why I needed to be here today. I need to do this for Eddie."

"Do you mean hiking to the place where he was last seen or do you mean all this electromagnetic reading stuff?"

"Both. If you are ready, let's go, okay?"

The spell was broken, but that did not dampen the excitement Marty felt. Cy was opening up to her, trusting her more than ever before.

They returned to where they left off. Using the compass and the meter, Cy zigzagged across the slope leading to the peak.

About a quarter of a mile from the top of the mountain they reached a warning sign that, judging from the rusted condition of the metal, had been posted many years before. It read "Danger – strong winds – falling hazard – stay away from top of mountain."

"There appears to be a strong magnetic spike from the earth's inner core that is close to the surface in this is area," Cy said, "And it is close to noon. The solar winds have their strongest effect on the earth's electromagnetic fields at the equator, and the EMFs are closest to the earth in the middle of the day. I'm curious to see how it relates the overall magnetic charge on this mountain peak."

"Will a magnetic charge wreck our stuff?"

"I hope not," said Cy, studying his wristwatch. He reached in one of his smaller zippered pockets and pulled out a round-faced watch. "Maybe I better check to see if it is really close to noon."

"That looks slightly old-fashioned," Marty said.

"It is. This is a wind-up watch, no batteries needed. I have been checking it against an atomic clock for days now, and, surprisingly, it is quite accurate. I synchronized the watch with my wristwatch and BlackSlab before we left this morning. But, look! They are off by a minute and 17 seconds now."

Marty looked at her Sun Access. The time was the same time that displayed on Cy's BlackSlab. They both were on atomic time and correct to the nanosecond.

"Are you sure the watch was set right?" asked Marty. "If so, then I don't get this."

"You know more than you think you do since you know that magnetic charges can interfere with electronics."

"I guess. But I have no idea why. I just hope all these magnetic charges do not wreck my new Sun Access."

"I honestly do not think the earth's charge is strong enough to alter your wrist screen. The biggest thing we probably need to worry about is if the electromagnetic fields in the atmosphere get really strong. Then they could disrupt our cell signals. And, although the storm looks like it is still off in the distance, having the lightning strike too close to us would not be good for our phones."

"Uh, I hate to tell you this, Cy, but having the lightning strike too close to us would not be good for us. Even though the storm is not here yet, the wind is picking up. I think we should put on our rain gear, just in case."

"You are probably right. What a waste! I suspected we might have a thunderstorm later this afternoon, but not this early. It is important that I get these readings around noon, but not with an electrical storm in the area. I will have to come back another time."

"We will come back together. We can either come tomorrow or any day next week before Thursday," Marty said, cheerful at the thought of having an excuse to spend another day with Cy before leaving on her trip.

"That would be good. I don't think we can do much more today with this storm moving in."

"Before we start back, let me send all this stuff to you," Marty said as she threw her brown nylon rain poncho over her hat and daypack. "I want to see how well this cell works in the wilderness."

"Not a good idea. Besides, I don't know if we can get a strong signal here."

"It will not hurt to check," said Marty as she used the fingers of her right hand to save the document file on her wrist screen. Then she looked at the signal indicator. She could see that the signal was at quarter-strength. She decided to try on the top of the cliff.

While Cy fought the wind to don his jacket, Marty quickly stuffed the GPS in his backpack that was sitting on a nearby rock. Then she jogged with long strides towards the summit of the cliff, scrambling over the jumbled patches of rocks in her path.

Cy resumed analyzing the reading on the electromagnetic meter, distracted with what he was doing to the point that he did not realize Marty had moved from his side. When he looked up a few moments later, he saw her start to climb the boulders that crowned the cliff.

First Cy froze with apprehension. Then he jumped to his feet and ran towards her, panic mushrooming inside him.

"Stop, Marty! Come back!"

Marty waved her arm as she continued to climb. Cy could not tell if Marty was unable to hear him over the wind or if she was ignoring him. As he stumbled on the loose rocks and dirt, he realized he was not the athlete Marty was. He was losing ground. He checked the electromagnetic meter bouncing in his hand as he ran. The closer he got to the boulders, the higher the readings registered.

"Marty, get back here, please! Stay away from the boulders on top."

Marty stood on the rocky outcrop that formed the dome of the cliff. She turned to face Cy. Without any trees or rocks nearby to block it, the wind whipped and snapped the poncho around her.

"Stop worrying about me, Cy. There is no way I will get struck by lightning because the storm is still several miles out. I have a good signal up here. Let me send this to you and then I will scoot right back down."

The wind roared too loudly for Marty to use voice commands. She tapped the screen. Up came the notes that she had saved as a document.

"Marty, please come back! Just wait until we get to the car to send it. This is where the others were when they disappeared."

Marty could tell Cy was panicked about something. If this was where Eddie had his accident, then Cy must be paranoid about this whole area.

"Stop worrying, Cy. I am nowhere near the edge of the cliff."

Marty continued to press the keys to attach the document file to a text message. She brought up the phone pad, hit the shortcut key for Cy's phone number and pressed send.

Marty climbed down off the top of the boulders and moved into a crevice in the side of the rocks, hoping it would act as a wind-break. Once Cy saw that she was no longer standing on top of the boulders, relief washed over him. He grinned as he slowed his pace and sucked air into his oxygen-starved lungs.

Marty stood mere yards away, barely winded. She smiled widely at Cy, her eyes glittering with amusement. Even though she stood next to the boulders that now towered above her, the wind still whipped around Marty. She ignored the flapping of her hat brim and poncho. On impulse, she hit the speed-call key for Cy's cell number.

Marty wanted to tease Cy. She intended to call him to ask if he received her text message. She never had the chance. As soon as she pressed send, a prickly feeling started traveling up her arm, starting from her wrist and hand that were closest to the wrist screen. It then continued up to the back of her neck, then to her head and back down until it enveloped her. She experienced the sensation of her body separating into billions of particles that began to spin with increasing speed. She no longer felt as though she was standing on the ground, surrounded by the earth and sky. Instead, she was falling through space. Small flashes of light spun around her, creating a tunnel of white streaks that wrapped around her like a cocoon.

What is happening to me?

Marty called out to Cy for help.

CHAPTER 5

Marty shook her head as she peeled her face away from the rock. She carefully looked around. It appeared to her that she was on a boulder grouping that was screened from the rest of the world by thick greenery.

Marty clutched her wrist screen protectively to her chest as she climbed to her feet to look around. She saw mostly bushes and trees. The air was warm and humid, but there were no thunderheads in sight. She could not see Cy anywhere.

Marty heaved a sigh. She thought back through the sequence of events before she regained awareness in her current location. She had climbed down off of the large boulders that formed the crown of Dead Man's Drop, but where she stood was still near the edge of a sharp drop-off. She must have slipped and fallen down the side of the mountain after all and been knocked unconscious.

What struck her as strange was that she did not remember falling. She stretched and wriggled her body. It did not hurt anywhere like she would expect it to if she had tumbled down the face of a steep cliff.

Marty scrambled down from the cluster of rocks and pushed herself through the dense growth to reach the crest of the mountain. From what Marty could see, she was close to the high point of her surroundings. There were no cliffs towering over her in any direction. With a sinking heart, she realized that wherever she was, it was far too lush with trees and grasses in varying shades of green to be anywhere near the mountain where she and Cy had been hiking. Something was not right.

Marty checked her cell screen. It showed no missed calls.

Come on, Cy, Marty reached out to him with a silent plea. *I have no idea how long I have been here, but why haven't you called me? Surely once you lost sight of me, you would have tried to contact me on my cell.*

Marty flipped open her wrist screen. In spite of her apprehension after what had just happened the last time she called his cell, she called Cy again. Her call did not go through.

Her battery level was extremely low. Perhaps that was the problem. Marty set her wrist screen on a rock in a patch of sunlight to recharge. She puzzled over what could have noticeably drained the battery. Had she been unconscious that long?

She decided it was time to take serious stock of her surroundings. Marty stood and slowly turned 360 degrees.

She was on a grassy mound with a cluster of rocks not far from the top of the high point. She was surrounded by deciduous trees which created a canopy of green leaves. Some smaller trees were splattered with pink and white flowers. There were a few evergreen trees mixed in. Among the trees was a jumble of low-growing bushes and ferns.

Where in the Rockies do ferns grow thick like this?

Wherever she was, it was pretty country. However, Marty could not ignore the heat and humidity that felt so different than what she was used to. She peeled off the poncho and put it in her daypack. She set the pack on one of the flat rocks and found a seat on another to let the perspiration on the back of her shirt dry. She loosened the neckline of her shirt even more and unbuttoned the cuffs to allow the air to flow under the cloth.

Marty scanned the sky through the tree branches for the position of the sun. From what she could see, it was not directly overhead. She assumed it was to the west. Then again, she might have been knocked out for more than a couple of hours. If she had been unconscious all night, she might be looking at the morning sun.

Marty picked up her wrist screen to pull up her GPS application.

Nothing happened.

She looked at her cell screen with concern. It looked different. Then she realized that there was no time and date reading. There was no signal indicator. She went into her tools to check the clock and calendar. She could not get either to work. She could not access the internet. She tried her compass application.

Nothing.

Something must have jiggled loose inside. How am I going to orient myself?

Marty remembered her old-fashioned folding pocket knife with the compass embedded in the carved bone handle. It had been her dad's when he was a teen. He gave it to her several years earlier on one of the family camping trips. For sentimental reasons, she always carried it when she was out-of-doors. She pulled it from her daypack. Yes, the sun was to the west and the rocks where she came to were to the east of the top of a mountain.

Marty decided to take a picture. She climbed off her rocky perch and searched the area to set up the most descriptive shot of her surroundings. She chose to include the rocky outcrop as part of her picture. She backed away as far as she could without being swallowed up by the surrounding foliage. Her picture included it all: the rocks, trees and ferns.

Marty sighed with relief *At least the camera works.* She saved the image.

Then, hoping there was enough signal for a message to get through, even though her voice-activation did not work, Marty composed a text.

.

Cy called your phone wont work will try to text u dont no where I am gps doesnt work

.

Marty thought of something else she would try, if it would only go through. After all, there was that old saying that a picture is worth a thousand words.

.

will try to send pix please help

.

Marty sent the text with the attached photo. She clipped the wrist screen back on her arm and waited a few minutes for Cy to respond. After considerable time passed with no response, she decided to hike around the top of the mountain to find out if she could see more and figure out for herself where she was. If she was lost, she knew it was better to stay in one place rather than to try to hike out. Let the rescuers come to her. But, she also realized she only had one full bottle of water remaining. The first bottle was almost empty.

Although the crown of the mountain was almost flat, there were some rocks on top. Most were almost flush with the ground, but one of them stood slightly taller than her and pointed up to the sky. Carefully, she climbed up and balanced close to the top.

In the distance to the west, she saw water. Because of the curve of the hill, she could not tell if it was two lakes separated by another mountain, or if it was one large lake that curved around the mountain. Either way, it amazed her to see that much water. She was not aware there were any lakes that large so close to where she and Cy were hiking. She took a holographic image of the scene and sent it to Cy.

Marty looked at the position of the sun. Several hours of daylight remained. She decided to wait by one of the lakes to be rescued so that she was near water.

That presented Marty with another challenge. How was she going to find a way off of the mountain? The lush growth between her and the lake seemed impenetrable. She poked around, searching for a section that looked less dense. She broke into a big grin when she found the narrow pathway. It was either a deer trail or a seldom-used hiking trail. She started down, rechecking her compass readings and the position of the sun to stay oriented.

As the slope of the ground grew less steep, Marty estimated her position to be slightly north and east of the northern shore of the lake. Surely the trail led to water. Whether made by animals or man, there was a universal need to find sources of water.

Marty heard a rustling in the bushes ahead of her and to the right of the trail. She froze in place. She located the general direction of the sound and for a moment listened carefully to identify the source. It was not a small rodent scurrying over dried grass. The movements belonged to a larger animal.

A burst of fear seized Marty. If it was a bear or a mountain lion, she was in serious trouble. Even a deer, if cornered, could be dangerous. She looked around for a tree to climb for safety. Whatever was hiding behind the greenery, she did not want to face it up close.

Marty quickly surveyed the surrounding trees. They either had trunks that were extremely tall before the lowest limbs branched out, or they were not high enough to protect her from a large animal. Back up the path several yards and several feet off to the side she spotted a smaller tree next to a rock. She scrambled up the rock and jumped to grab one of the lower limbs. She swung her leg up over the branch and used all her strength to pull herself up so that she straddled it. Her hat snagged on a short twig and the loose-hanging chin strap almost strangled her. She tore the hat off her head and stuffed it into a side pocket of her pack.

Then, realizing how cumbersome it was to climb with the daypack catching the smaller branches, she quickly shrugged it off her shoulders and hooked it to a short but sturdy branch close to the trunk. She reached for the next branch and continued her climb. She desperately hoped that once she was high enough, she could reach the lower branches of the next tree over and pull herself up into its limbs.

She hoped that she would be able to climb fast enough and high enough to escape.

CHAPTER 6

Cy's breath caught and he froze in place as he stared in horror at the spot where Marty had been standing. One moment, Marty was there, standing next to the crevice carved into the rocky outcrop that formed the crown of Dead Man's Drop. She had been giving him that teasing look so typical of her while the wind tossed tendrils of hair around her face. The next moment she disintegrated into nothingness.

Very faintly, almost so faintly he was afraid he had not actually heard it over the wind, he heard her call out to him.

"Help me, Cy!"

Then there was nothing.

She was gone.

Cy inhaled huge gulps of air. His heart pounded so hard he thought it was going to burst free of his chest. He turned off the electromagnetic meter and pulled his multi-function wristwatch off his arm as he hurried back to the rock where he left his backpack. He turned off the GPS unit Marty had left behind, emptied his pockets of all his electronics and tore the Bluetooth earpiece from his head. He shoved everything in his backpack. Taking only the compass and the wind-up watch, he ran back up the rise.

As Cy neared the top, he fell to his stomach and crawled through the dirt and sharp gravel toward the edge of the cliff next to the crown of boulders. The wind beat at him. He knew the storm would hit before he could get off the mountain, but that did not stop him from taking the time he needed to look for Marty. He kept an eye on the compass needle, noting that it jerked erratically from side to side.

When he reached the edge, he peered over, searching down the sheer face of the cliff to the canyon below. He saw no sign of Marty. He saw no movement of someone sliding down the steep slope. He did not see any sign of a body caught on rocky jags or the few stunted trees that had taken root and grown into the side of the cliff. He saw no clouds of dust billowing up to show where someone or something had disturbed the ground.

Cy was not surprised. He glanced at the wind-up watch and made a note of the time. For the record, he knew he had to check to be sure that she had not fallen. But deep inside of him, he knew that she was not down there.

Cy wriggled backwards a few feet until he was away from the edge of the cliff. Still on his stomach, he collapsed in defeat as a wave of despair coursed through him. He ground his teeth in anger. With his forehead buried in his left forearm, he beat the ground beneath him several times with his right fist.

He, of all people, should have known better. How could he have let this happen?

But, he did. And now she was gone like the others.

Like Eddie Burrows.

Like the ones Cy had learned about after Eddie vanished.

Consumed by guilt, Cy scooted even further back from the cliff edge and pushed himself to his feet. He slowly shuffled down to where he had left his equipment. He tried to think about what he would do next, but his mind was too numb to force it through the usual analytical paces. All he was aware of was that, of all people, Marty was gone.

How could I have let it happen to Marty?

Cy shoved his backpack on the ground and flopped on the rock. He buried his face in his fists.

Focus, Cy, focus! Cy struggled to fight off despair. He cringed under the burden of the mental numbness that gripped his brain.

The dark clouds in the sky above mirrored Cy's mood, but the first few raindrops snapped Cy out of his funk enough for him to gather up his equipment. He did not want anything else to get ruined. He decided to look around for some shelter where he could wait out the thunderstorm. He still had to figure out the next step. But the one thing he knew for sure he wanted to do was to get away from the top of Dead Man's Drop. This cliff had claimed two people who were more important to him than anyone else in his life except his family.

Consumed by incredible sorrow, Cy yanked the straps of his backpack over his shoulders. His feet and legs felt like lead as he dragged them down the mountain.

He was grateful for the hat Marty loaned him now that the storm was breaking upon him. He had accepted the loan of it to humor her. Now, in addition to it giving him some protection from the rain, he considered it an invaluable memento of her concern for him.

As he trudged back down, Cy spotted the place where he and Marty had stopped in the shade for water and a snack while he explained what he was doing. As far as protection from the cloudburst, it was as good of a place as any to wait out the storm. Besides, he hoped it might help him feel her presence. While he huddled on the rock they had used as a bench, sheltered by surrounding foliage, he sipped some of his water and ate an energy bar. He knew she would want him to take care of himself that way.

Cy shook his head in frustration as he obsessed over the situation. Just a few minutes earlier he and Marty were making genuine progress. They gathered and recorded information that, once he had time to analyze it back home, might give him the answers he needed. Up until the moment Marty disappeared, gathering that information seemed like the most important thing in the world to Cy. The entire time he and Marty were working, he thought about how he would use his BlackSlab or the slab computers at the internet café to analyze the data. He anticipated that the solution to the problem of how to get Eddie home would jump out at him.

Now this!

The day's venture had lost its appeal to Cy. He realized that the only thing that mattered to him now was Marty. He wanted her back so much it hurt.

Cy pulled his knees close to his body and pressed against the trunk of tree that hugged his rocky bench. He turned the collar of his jacket up to keep the blasts of rain from running down his neck.

Surrounded by the clatter of the driving rain, Cy forced himself to plan his next move. He dreaded it more than anything he could think of, but he knew what he needed to do, no matter what the personal consequences might be. He needed to report Marty's disappearance to the authorities. He would take the heat for the two of them being in an area closed to the public. That would be bad enough all by itself.

Far worse, he would have to face Marty's parents. How could he tell them their daughter vanished while hiking with him on a mountain known to be dangerous? But, he would tell them everything. He knew that when he told them the truth of what he suspected, they would think he was crazy. Still, they deserved to know.

He nodded his head in confirmation in an effort to convince himself, trying to muster up a courage he did not really feel.

He knew he would need to do it right away, while he still had the nerve. He would not wait until her family returned from vacation, or when they started to wonder why she did not call them or when she did not return from her history immersion trip to the east.

He would no doubt find himself under investigation for her disappearance. After the fiasco with Eddie, the authorities might arrest him—possibly charge him with murder—even though they would not find a body. He feared that circumstantial evidence and the limitations of the reasoning capacity of the normal human brain would seal his fate.

However, his chances would be better that way than if he kept silent and waited for someone to discover his involvement months, or even years, from now. If they thought he was deliberately hiding something from them, he had no chance at all. No, it would be better for him if he followed the same course he had with Eddie. He would find the detective who initially handled Eddie's case and explain everything.

Cy knew law enforcement would send out their search and rescue teams with the helicopters, the search drones and the dogs. They would seek her wrist screen GPS signal. Scores of people on the ground would walk the area in grids to scour every foot of the territory on the mountain and below the cliff. But Cy knew that even if she had gone down there, the rain would soon erase all traces of the fall.

Cy shook his head with the realization that there were no traces of her below the cliff for the rain to erase.

Like the others, Marty was gone. For some of them, like Eddie and the other girl, Brandy Nagles who disappeared a year ago, he knew where they ended up. There were less than a handful of people who knew what he knew. But, like him, if they tried to explain it to others, they were laughed at and branded as being "delusional."

A manic laugh escaped Cy's lips at the thought of the word delusional. Some people would find it easier to believe that what had happened to Eddie and the others was due to magic or the supernatural. Cy discovered that aspect of human nature not long after Eddie disappeared. In one of his more morose moments, he had sardonically snickered at the idea that he could have easily start a cult of believers by claiming people disappeared due to—what had Marty called it? Oh, yeah—paranormal causes. It was harder to convince people that Eddie and the others disappeared due to the application of specific principles of physics. Cy thought it was funny what some people would consider to be delusional.

No one, not even Cy, knew for sure the specifics behind why or how these people vanished. But, he did have a theory. At least he had the start of one, which was why he had been measuring the electromagnetic forces in the area where the others—and now Marty—had disappeared. It had been his goal that day to establish that specific conditions existed on the mountain which, when combined with other certain laws of physics, triggered the disappearances. He was sure that something other than the supernatural was doing it.

Cy knew that even if he found the connection that explained these occurrences, he would have a difficult time convincing the experts in the various scientific fields of his theories. It was not that physicists would think his theories had no valid foundation. The problem was that the physics community operated on the understanding that if such phenomena were possible, we, as humans, were still centuries away from developing the technology to accomplish it. Cy believed that, because he was still a student, the established experts would probably scoff at him for saying it was happening now.

As for law enforcement or Marty's family or the general public, there was no way anyone who was considered credible would ever believe him or give his theories a chance.

The rain stopped as the thunderstorm moved further east. The area around him started to grow lighter as the clouds broke up overhead.

Cy shook the water from his clothes and pulled his gadgets from his backpack. He turned on his BlackSlab. The musical tone that greeted him told him he had a text message waiting. He read the message. Attached to it were the notes Marty sent to him just before she disappeared. He would download the attachment later. He would rather have her back than the information she sent him no matter how helpful the findings that day might prove to be.

Then he heard another tone and looked. It was a missed call. It was from Marty. He looked at the time it was sent.

Cy scrunched his eyebrows as he started analyzing the known information. He had checked the analog wind-up watch when Marty disappeared and noted the time mentally. The time of the missed call was close to the same time that she vanished, allowing for the time difference between his watch and his BlackSlab. Did she try to call him immediately once she arrived somewhere else? More importantly, who did she call just before she disappeared?

Eddie answered his cell phone about the time he disappeared. The other girl was using her cell, also. Not only that, Marty hit the send button for a voice call and disappeared immediately afterwards. Cell phones were involved in all of the disappearances he was aware of. This seemed to confirm what he had already guessed. There was a connection between the newer cell technology and the disappearances.

Cy opened his word application on the BlackSlab and recorded the order of events and his thoughts about it. He saved the document. He punched his BlackSlab off again. Then he checked his watch.

It was still close to the middle of the day. He started back up to the mountain. In spite of the risk, he was determined to get his readings at the top of Dead Man's Drop. He had a feeling that as long as his cell phone was off and safely away from the cliffs, he did not need to worry about disappearing. Electromagnetic readings or not, he had no intention of going too close to the edge of the cliffs and slipping over the edge.

Cy recorded his readings around the crown of Dead Man's Drop the low-tech way—on a scrap of paper he found wrapped around a stubby pencil buried in one of his backpack pockets. The whole time he felt relieved that nothing whisked him away or sent him hurtling over the edge. It also confirmed his growing suspicion that cell phones were a trigger.

The one fact he found most interesting was that the positive electromagnetic readings were slightly higher on the ground next to the large crown of boulders than they were on the rocky top. It was more like the rock acted as an insulator rather than a conduit. That seemed strange. He was sure most of the mountain was formed of granite, so what made the rocks on top different than the rest of the mountain?

Cy made a note to check into the geology of the area, specifically this mountain.

Cy hiked down the mountain until he found another fairly flat rock not far from where he parked his car. He knew he was stalling about reporting Marty missing, but he did not care. He turned his BlackSlab back on. The familiar tone that told him he had a text message waiting greeted him. He ignored it. He didn't feel like interacting with anyone yet, not with Marty missing. Instead, he brought up the document Marty had sent him and quickly consolidated all his notes and observations. He planned to download them to his secure flash drives before he went to the detective that handled Eddie's case. Hopefully, the feds would leave him alone on this incident and he could work on figuring things out after he was finished with his report.

He next checked to see who sent him the text.

The message was from Marty. There was no date or time on the text. With shaking hands, Cy studied the message screen.

.

Cy called your phone wont work will try to text u dont no where I am gps doesnt work will try to send pix please help

.

Cy read the message over several times. He realized it had been sent after she disappeared from Dead Man's Drop. He tapped out a return text to her.

.

Got your text r u ok?

.

Cy sent the message. Then he stared at the BlackSlab for several minutes, willing it to produce a response from Marty.

Nothing.

Cy gazed off into the distance without seeing anything while his fingers tapped his chin in a rapid-fire staccato. Except for the thoughts racing through his brain, the world had ceased to exist for him. The text message from Marty changed everything. She was still alive and had made contact. Maybe he could help her now that he had more data. But realistically, once he reported her disappearance, he risked being under such close observation by law enforcement that he might have trouble going places and gathering any additional information he needed. Worse yet, did he dare risk being stuck in jail while the officials searched in vain for her?

After what seemed like an eternity, Cy sent the message again. He waited. Minutes passed, although they seemed like hours to him. There still was no response.

Maybe it is like it was with Eddie.

Eddie sent several messages to Cy after he disappeared. Some came through hours after they were sent, some not. Cy discovered that there was better success sending and receiving text messages at night. It made sense. Texting uses sound waves, and they tend to travel further and stronger at night because there is less atmospheric interference.

The power level on his battery registered dangerously low. Cy turned his cell off. He would recharge it in his car on the way home. Maybe he would have better luck getting his text through to Marty tonight. Maybe he would get the pictures she said she sent.

He sipped water from the second bottle Marty had insisted he bring along. He could not afford to get dehydrated and have his brain turn to mush, as Marty had put it.

He needed to think the situation through. He needed to develop a course of action to get Marty home, one that did not involve anyone, especially law enforcement, running interference on him.

He started by reviewing in his mind the situation with Eddie.

CHAPTER 7

Eddie was four years older than Cy even though they were both seniors at the university. He majored in agricultural engineering with a focus on animal husbandry management. Eddie loved animals, especially the kind that roamed in herds. He struggled with the scientific coursework. He had saved his toughest classes for his senior year and then hired Cy to help him get through applied physics and calculus.

Eddie was a big, blustery guy with brownish hair that bleached out in the summer. He often cracked jokes and gently poked fun at people in his booming voice. At first, being Eddie's tutor had been awkward for Cy since he was more comfortable tutoring students at the high school closer in age to him.

Eddie often wore camouflage clothing. Cy remembered asking Eddie if he was planning on going into the army after college. Eddie had laughed hysterically. Then he informed Cy that he was wearing woodland camo, a favorite pattern worn by hunters, which is much different than the pattern the military used.

Eddie masked his discomfort over being tutored by someone younger than he was by jokingly calling Cy "Genius." Being addressed as Genius intensified Cy's concerns that his fellow students at the university did not feel he belonged. He repeatedly told Eddie that, although he had a natural aptitude for math and science, he was not a genius. Eddie ignored Cy's claim.

After several weeks of tutoring, Eddie must have decided his tutor was okay for a nerd because he started to open up to Cy. He shared with Cy his visions of where he wanted to go in his future. The majority of his plans involved Andrea and their upcoming wedding in June that would follow Eddie's and Andrea's graduation. He also told Cy of his and Andrea's expectations once they moved to his home state of Texas.

Cy had met Andrea and briefly talked to her a few times when she joined Eddie at the close of some of the tutoring sessions. She let Cy know she preferred Andrea to Andi because her last name was Jackson. On one occasion she had sardonically asked Cy if he could imagine any parents naming their daughter Andy Jackson.

Eddie did not care about the Andy Jackson comparison. He just liked the name Andi. It was his name for her. His thinking was that she would not be a Jackson for much longer.

Cy grew to admire Eddie's appreciation for nature, his sense of humor and his intuitive ability to solve practical problems. He was not sure when it happened, but long before Spring Break, Cy realized that Eddie had become a close friend instead of just a tutoring student. He no longer minded Eddie calling him Genius.

The world as Cy had known it changed on the Monday of Spring Break. Eddie and Andrea went on a day trip to Dead Man's Drop Mountain. Only Andrea made it home. While he was on the cliff, Eddie disappeared.

That Monday, Cy had been down in town alternating between being cooped up in his apartment or stuck at the university library while he worked on his semester project for Advanced Astronomy. He first became aware that something happened with Eddie when he received a text message from him that night.

.

cy im lost. i think im in amish country no modern anything. 1st im on the mtn, next im here. cant call. pls help me get home. tell andi luv u 4 me. ttyl ed burrows

.

At first, Cy puzzled over the message. He shrugged it off as one of Eddie's jokes until he read about Eddie's disappearance in the newspaper the next day. He reread the text message from Eddie and knew he had to share it with those who were searching for him.

Cy also wanted to keep a record for himself, just in case. He transcribed the text message onto paper. Afterwards, he downloaded the message from his wrist screen sim card to his slab computer. He charted all the information, including the time received, as well as the technical information that might help law enforcement find Eddie.

He also realized that once he told what he knew, the detectives might write him off as a nut case. Worse, they might think that he was involved somehow in Eddie's disappearance. He had watched enough detective shows on television to know he could not afford to barge in naively in an effort to be helpful. He needed to protect himself first in case some over-ambitious detective got the wrong idea about him.

Cy made sure he backed up Eddie's message in more than one place. One copy he put on his vault drive, a flash drive for which only he had the combination.

He sent one copy on a DVD to his grandparents in Seattle. They had never owned a computer and claimed they found no need for one at their stage in life. However, the one piece of equipment that was almost as important to them as their holo-television was their DVD player. They loved to receive family videos that they could play on their holo-television. He created a program with some photos and holographic shots and added some narration and background music. Hidden in the files on the DVD where his grandparents would never find them, and where others also would not unless they knew what to look for, were his back-ups.

As he suspected, once he took his wrist screen with the text message to the police station, the detectives confiscated it as evidence. He assumed they turned it over to their technical experts for them to try to determine the location from which the call originated and to verify that his claim was not a hoax.

The detectives kept him in a room for hours. They peppered him with the same questions over and over again. He knew they were looking to see if each round of questioning dredged up new memories with additional details. They also wanted to see if he changed his answers. They were trying to draw him out and possibly trip him up. After several rounds of the same questions in slightly different forms, he began to suspect that they were trying to get him to confess that he was involved in the disappearance.

All Cy knew was that he was tutoring Eddie in one final class of calculus so Eddie could graduate that May. All he knew of Eddie's plans for the week of Spring Break was that he and Andrea were going to be working on the upcoming wedding. They also planned to get away for a day in the mountains to take a break from everything. Cy had not seen Eddie for over a week, not since their last tutoring session. As far as the text message, he had nothing to tell the detectives other than what was on the wrist screen itself.

The detectives finally let him go home. He fumed over their insistence that they keep his wrist screen for analysis. He knew they could have downloaded the information from the sim card the way he had. Instead, they left him without his phone numbers for his professors and tutoring students. The saved photos, holos, videos, holo-vids and internet files were gone, too. He would have to get a new phone and download them from the cloud.

Afterwards, Andrea had come to see Cy. It was so late when she knocked, he almost decided to not check to see who was at his door.

CHAPTER 8

Once Marty climbed high enough to see beyond the rim of the hill, she looked in the direction where she had heard the noise. Over the tops of the bushes, she saw a small clearing carpeted with grasses and low-growing plants. A woman wearing a fringed leather skirt with a matching pull-over tunic searched among the knee-high greenery in the meadow.

Marty sighed with relief. She reversed her climb, ready to cheer with excitement. Someone was close by who would know where she was and how to get back to civilization. Once free of the tree branches, she quickly trotted down the trail and pushed her way through the bushes into the clearing.

The woman jumped back, startled by Marty's sudden appearance. She dropped the herbs she had been cutting with a short-bladed knife as she immediately turned to face Marty and she assumed a defensive stance. Marty threw her hands up and took a step back.

Marty eyes grew wide with amazement as she studied the woman further. She was not sure what to think of the costume worn by the person standing in front of here. She knew the mountains were full of "back to nature" people whose philosophy leaned towards an older, simpler way of life. They tended to avoid others who were not like them. However, the woman before Marty seemed to have taken that approach to excess. In addition to the leather skirt and top, she wore beaded moccasins. A necklace of shells circled her neck. Her hoop earrings appeared to be cut from shell or bone. Her hair was parted in the middle and worn in a single braid down her back. Dots of red makeup adorned the front of her hair part as well as her cheeks and her earlobes.

Except for her coloring, the young woman appeared to be Native American. Her hair was light brown with ash tones. Her eyes were grey. Although she was tanned, her skin and features spoke of European ancestry.

Pits and scars marred the woman's face. Marty guessed she had suffered from severe acne when she was younger. Marty felt bad for the young woman. It was a shame that her parents had neglected to get her to a dermatologist when she was a teenager. If they had, the doctor could have prevented a lot of the damage to her complexion.

The two of them made no move as they studied each other silently. The woman's eyes never left Marty's face. Only after Marty glanced toward the baby in a cradleboard that was hanging from a tree branch on the opposite side of the clearing did the woman carefully side-stepped until she put herself between Marty and the child.

"I mean you and your baby no harm," Marty said with a quivering smile, still keeping an eye on the knife in the woman's hand. When the woman gave no indication she understood, Marty asked, "Do you speak English?"

The woman stood erect once she was in front of the baby. She continued to study Marty in silence.

"I speak English. It no longer flows swiftly over my tongue," she finally said. "My Lenni Lenape family hid my English away many years until I was adopted into the Turtle Clan."

"Oh, good," said Marty with relief. "I hope you can help me."

"I help none but those who come in peace," said the woman. "I choose to hide my English words from those who will harm the Lenape. My English ears now hear only the talk of the British when they treat with the sachems. I tell my people in my own language if the British hold the Lenni Lenape close to their hearts or if their words are noises in the bushes."

Marty hesitated before she continued. *Noises in the bushes? Lenni Lenape?* She had no idea what this woman was talking about. She did not know of any British embassy or businesses in the area. But, if there were businesses nearby, there were people who could help her get back home.

"I am so lost. Will you please help me find a ranger or show me the way out of here?"

The woman's eyes sparked with hatred.

"Rangers! Do you mean the Mohawk raiders sent north by Johnson to fight the French and their Algonquin allies where they suffered great defeat? I will not help you find rangers. The warriors of our band will drive them away if the Mohawk come to the Ohio to reach the French along the great river. We are ready to treat with the British so that we may trade with them, but we want no more for the British to bring their war with the French to our towns."

"Okay," said Marty slowly, feeling not only lost, but confused. *British and French? Mohawk in Ohio? Is this lady even sane?* "Never mind the rangers. Please, let me start over. Let me introduce myself. My name is Marty and I just need a few directions if you are familiar with the area."

"Greetings to you, Marty." The young woman said. Marty guessed she must have decided that Marty posed no danger to her because she lowered her knife. "My name means Green Corn in your tongue."

"What an interesting name," said Marty, thinking that whatever cult this woman belonged to, they evidently liked to follow the Native American practice of taking their names from nature.

"It is a name of much power," said Green Corn with pride.

"It is? In what way?"

Humor her. Maybe then she will stop treating me like I am an enemy. If she decides she trusts me, she may help me find my way out of here.

"I am the future of my adopted family. I had smallpox as a child before I came to the Turtle Clan. When I was captured during a mourning raid, my new family saw my scars. They knew I will remain healthy when the white man's death comes to our village again. Because of my blood, my children may also live. This will help our clan to survive and grow. My name speaks of the Lenape green corn celebration in spring. It promises that life will continue and there will be a good harvest. Because I will live through the smallpox, many families wanted me to marry their sons."

"That is interesting," said Marty politely while her mind raced.

Smallpox! They got rid of that disease decades ago. But maybe smallpox explained the scarring on her face. Marty felt like she was talking to someone from a bygone age rather than to a woman of the twenty-first century. Marty's curiosity got the best of her.

"What do you mean by a morning raid?"

"It is when our women suffer a great grief for those in our clans who have died. We send our warriors to capture new people to take their place. The Lenape have lost many to war, but many more have died because of the great sicknesses brought by the Europeans. The captives we know will weaken us we torture and kill for revenge. Others who will strengthen us we adopt so our clans grow big again."

"Oh," said Marty, regretting she had asked.

"It was good for me to leave my English home and be adopted by the Lenni Lenape," said Green Corn with a tone of confidence and pride. "My adopted family loves me. I bring our clan much strength."

"But, from what you just said," Marty responded cautiously, "if you were captured by this Lenni Lenape group, did it also mean that some of your family and neighbors were killed and maybe tortured first?"

"My English parents and my oldest brother were killed but not tortured. Once I understood the Lenape ways, I learned why it must be that we drive the Europeans from our land. I learned to put away my sadness for losing my old family so I could be happy with my new life. Many English who are young and strong when captured learn it is better the Lenape way, especially if they were child slaves to the British."

"Child slaves? Do you mean black people?"

"They are English. They have a piece of paper they bring from across the great waters that says for many years they must be a servant to the person who buys the paper. Often, the Lenape treat them better than their English masters. Many choose to be adopted and not go back among the British."

"Oh, it sounds like you mean indentured servants. I don't know that I would call them slaves. But, you weren't an indentured servant, were you?"

Marty started to feel like the conversation was getting way out of control. She knew that there had been no indentured servants since the time of the Revolutionary War.

"No. I lived on the frontier with my English family who is no more," Green Corn continued.

"Do you ever wish to return to your own people?" Marty decided to play along for the time being. She really needed this woman's help.

Green Corn's eyes hardened with conviction.

"The Lenni Lenape are my own people. It is better for me here where I have more freedom. The Lenape value my words. Among my clan I am a woman of power."

"But you would have these same things among the British, right?"

Green Corn gave a snort of derision.

"European women are weak, the French as well as the British. Your men claim too much power and put themselves above women. They force your women to be weak."

"What on earth are you talking about?" Marty demanded. "Women are not weak. Well, okay, as a rule we do not have the large muscle strength that men do. But, we are stronger than men in other ways. It all balances out."

"I was English once. I know how your men think they are better than their women. English women are not free. They must submit first to their fathers, and then to their husbands and obey them. But now I am Lenni Lenape, I do not have to obey my husband. If he mistreats me, I can leave him and choose another husband. English men own their children. Our children belong to the clan of the mother who gave them life. English women must give up their lands and all they own when they marry. Our women govern our clans and we own our houses and land. English women may not speak in council or help choose their sachems. The voices of our women are heard in council."

"It does sound like you do things a little differently than what I am used to," Marty responded carefully.

"The Lenape way is better than the English way, especially for women. The British tried many times to ransom me, but I hid and refused to go back. Why be ruled by men when I can stay and have my own power among my people, the Lenni Lenape?"

Marty was unsure of what to say. The claims made by this woman could not be true. Marty was well aware that American women speak in public and many are prominent in community and government affairs. They do own land and they have as many rights as men. Green Corn was either crazy or was coming up with excuses to promote a new world order of some kind.

Then again, Marty realized, women did not always have equality with men. She remembered how annoyed she used to get in her high school classes when they studied about women struggled for many years in order to obtain equal rights with men. She knew the nation was already making plans for a big celebration of the 250 year anniversary of the Declaration of Independence in two years. Yet, she was starting as a high school freshman in 2020 when the nation celebrated the centennial of women gaining the right to vote.

Marty decided that whether she needed help or not, she did not want to debate the issue anymore. If Green Corn chose to live in what she obviously considered a backwoods utopia instead of in modern society, that was her choice. What Marty needed was directions on how to find her way home. Surely Cy was starting to worry about her by now, even if no one else knew she had taken a misstep and now was missing. She changed the subject.

"Do you know how to get to a nearby town? If you will just point the way, I will be very grateful."

"The great hunting grounds of the Ohio Valley have many towns. Kuskuski, the town of my family, is to the west. The Pennsylvania village of Logstown is several suns to the north."

Here she is talking about Ohio again, and now Pennsylvania. Has nobody told this woman that she is in Colorado?

"Where are you going?" Marty asked her tactfully.

"I go with my husband and others back to my village to speak again to Conrad Weiser. The Haudenosaunee have sent Tanaghrisson to be half-king to speak for us. The words of the Haudenosaunee say our people are now changed to women who wear skirts because we gave away our lands peaceably. They will be our uncles and only they may speak for us at council. Only they will brighten the Covenant Chain with the Pennsylvanians. But we listen to Tanaghrisson with half an ear and speak with our own mouth."

Marty blinked her eyes in confusion. *Here we go again. What does she mean by all this skirt talk and half-kings?*

"Okay, help me out here. What land did your people give away?"

"The land was by the Chesapeake and the great island where once we allowed the Dutch to live. We did not give it away. The Europeans gave many gifts to share our lands. We let them build their villages and plant their crops. When we returned to our own lands we agreed to share, they said the ink on paper captured words of a treaty that say the land is no longer ours, but only theirs.

"How can that be?" she continued. "We came out of the ground there. How can it belong to the British who came out of the ground across the great waters? The ships of the British carried more of their people to take our land that Lord Baltimore and others claimed with the trick of the talking ink and paper. We could not fight for our lands then because the European sicknesses killed too many of our people and our warriors were too few. The Haudenosaunee were stronger than the Lenape and made themselves our uncles to speak for us. Their hearts were full of anger because we treated with the Europeans without them. They sent us west and say that now only they may treat with the British."

"Lord Baltimore?" asked Marty, picking up on a familiar name. "As in, Baltimore, Maryland? I know where that is."

"Yes. Lord Baltimore in Maryland. But is it often after Lord de la Warr that our lands are called by the Europeans."

Marty gave her head a slight shake. She never heard of him.

"Then our fathers treated with the round hat, William Penn," Green Corn continued. "The council between the Quakers and the Lenni Lenape spoke of allowing his people to share some land, as much land as a man could walk in a day and a half. Penn understood the Lenape words and knew what land he spoke of with our sachems. He also knew there was only talk to share, no treaty to give it away. The round hat's sons do not honor the words of their dead father. Their ears are deaf to the words of our sachems. They point to the words some man wrote on paper and say our land is theirs by treaty. No Lenni Lenape sachem put his mark on paper. But the sons of the round hat Penn sent their fastest runner in direction of the best land. By fraud they stole land from the Lenape we did not agree to share."

Green Corn's story triggered a memory in Marty. She remembered that during her history class she studied something called the Walking Purchase. She could not remember if it happened during the Revolutionary War or before.

Whenever it was, though, it was long ago. That surely could not have anything to do with whatever Green Corn was talking about, not after all these years. This must be something entirely different.

Then Marty decided there might be one way to find out if Green Corn was making up a story out of her imagination.

"Have you heard of a man named George Washington?"

Green Corn's eyes grew hard with contempt.

"Yes. George Washington is one of the Virginians who claim the Lenape and Shawnee hunting grounds along the Ohio River. The Virginians asked their great king across the waters for our land. This king claims to be the great father of us all, the British and the tribes who came out of this ground. However, words have reached the Lenape that it is in the hearts of the Virginians to break their treaty with the Haudenosaunee. Their paths do not intend to stop at the mountains east of the Alleghany River which are named after the old Allegewi tribe. They want our lands further west. The Haudenosaunee claim this land by right of conquest because they drove other tribes out many summers ago before they sent us here. Their words are noises in the woods. They never built their longhouses here. It is the Lenni Lenape that has filled the land after we were driven from our lands to the east."

"Okay, wait! You lost me," said Marty, confused. "You keep saying Haudenosaunee. Where are they from again?"

Green Corn studied Marty.

"You are not from here or you would know the six nations of the Haudenosaunee. Their longhouses are mostly in the land the British call New York. The British call them by their Algonquin name, Iroquois, the enemy ones, because they are not Algonquin like the Lenni Lenape and the other tribes who live close to the great waters. The Haudenosaunee say they do not choose between the French and the British, yet they stay close to the British to trade with them. They claim to be the uncles who speak for all the tribes driven from the eastern lands. It is in their hearts to speak first for the Haudenosaunee.

"The Iroquois?" Marty asked with surprise, remembering them from when she read *The Last of the Mohicans*. "But, if you have a treaty saying that all the land west of those mountains is for the tribes, how can the Virginians take it away from you or the Iroquois?"

"The Virginians did not come to the council in Lancaster four summers ago to hold the Haudenosaunee close to their hearts," Green Corn explained. "The Virginians once again asked for a talking paper treaty saying they may have all the land that was given them by their great king. The sachems believed their words spoke of brightening the old treaty where the land of the British ends east of the mountains the British call Alleghany.

"The Virginians went in the bushes, away from the Haudenosaunee, and wrote the treaty words claiming for Virginia all land west of the Alleghany Mountains to the great waters far in the west. The Virginians even claim that the land west of Pennsylvania belongs to them. These new words were not spoken to the Haudenosaunee sachems. The sachems believed the Virginians spoke with a true heart about the old treaty where the paths of the Europeans are stopped at the mountains. The sachems gave their *Yo-heng* and accepted presents to once more brighten the old Covenant Chain. They made their marks on Virginia's new treaty. Now the Virginian's have gone across the great waters to their king. They use their new talking paper to steal the lands of all the tribes who live along the Ohio."

Marty knew from studying history that there were many times the British, and later the Americans, broke treaties with the native tribes. They took advantage of their lack of understanding of the European legal system and concept of land ownership. It almost sounded like Green Corn was talking about one of those occasions. The woman obviously felt very passionate about the situation she was describing. It was also pretty apparent that she was not a fan of George Washington.

Then again, she may be talking about a different George Washington than the nation's first president.

"Conrad Weiser speaks for Pennsylvania. He has been to our towns," Green Corn continued. "He is counting our warriors and knows our fighting strength. He knows we in the west grow strong. He has told the Haudenosaunee that it is time to take the skirt off of the Lenni Lenape and give us back the breechcloth so we may treat for our own lands. We will not allow the half-king, Tanaghrisson, sent to us by the Haudenosaunee, to speak for us. Our own sachems will speak for the Lenape. We will form our own circle of friendship with Pennsylvania and make our own covenant chain."

This is more information than Marty asked for, but she could tell there was no stopping Green Corn now.

"We will first hear the words of Pennsylvania's Conrad Weiser in Logstown after harvest," Green Corn continued intensely. "The wife of Elkhorn will stand in the shadows and her ears will hear the words of the British and the Haudenosaunee. We will not let the Virginians or the Haudenosaunee take our land from us. We will send the wampum belts of war to the Shawnee and Twightwees and fight for it if we must."

"I agree that it is important to fight for your rights," said Marty diplomatically. "After all, that is why we have laws and the court system. Does your group have a good attorney?"

Green Corn's brow wrinkled with confusion.

"I know not what you mean by attorney, Marty. But I do know the Lenape have many strong warriors in the west. Our warriors are ready to fight now but will wait until our sachems talk to the English in Lancaster. We will trade with the British if they treat in peace and stay far from our lands. But if the Virginians or any of the English try to take our land, we will drive them away and leave none alive."

Marty was not sure what to say. All she knew for sure was that the longer she listened to Green Corn the greater a feeling of apprehension began to build up inside of her. Whatever was going on, this woman was convinced there was a real possibility of violent fighting involving those close to her. Maybe Green Corn's group was hostile to anyone who looked European.

Marty was no longer interested in getting directions from this woman.

I need to get away from Green Corn and her friends—now!

CHAPTER 9

After Cy let Andrea into his apartment that night, she told him her first-hand account of the day Eddie disappeared. It was the same story she had previously told the detectives.

Then, he disappeared, Andrea told Cy as she finished. There was no other way she could describe it. He did not get blown down by the wind. He did not lose his balance and fall over the cliff. One moment, he was there. The next split-second, he was gone.

"I told Eddie that the place had a bad spirit and we should not go there," Andrea explained to Cy. "But, you know Eddie. He could not see anything wrong, so he went anyway."

Cy looked at Andrea, but did not comment. He understood the predictability of math and the laws of physics. He felt uneasy when conversations turned to the topics of the spiritual or the super-natural. He encouraged Andrea to continue with the facts surrounding what happened to Eddie.

Andrea explained to Cy how she continued to record the holographic video for a few seconds before it registered in her brain that she could no longer see Eddie. She looked over the top of the camera. He was nowhere in sight. She ran up the slope. When she was within a few feet of the edge of the cliff, she dropped to her hands and knees. Terrified at what she might see, she crawled to the edge, calling Eddie's name. There was no sign of him. She backed away quickly, scraping her knees. Then she stood and ran back to the Prowler. She drove as fast as she could to get help.

The sheriff's detective detained her for hours while she repeated her story multiple times. She was so shaken, though, that it was not until she arrived back home that she remembered her camera. She transferred copies of the pictures and the holo-vid she had taken of Eddie onto her computer. Then she made several digital back-ups of everything before she took a back-up copy to the detectives. They let her go home, but they asked for and kept the camera.

Andrea gave Cy a copy of everything from the camera that she had given the detectives. Cy and Andrea played the holographic video of Eddie disappearing. They repeated it several times. Cy used a program to review the holo-vid frame by frame. He found the point where one frame showed Eddie standing on the cliff next to the rock and the next frame showed the cliff empty.

Cy had no idea what had happened. But, of one thing he was sure: Eddie did not fall.

Andrea also received a text from Eddie earlier that night. She showed Cy her cell screen so he could read it.

andi received 3 of your text msgs 2nite. im ok. lost in time warp??? its 1857 here in franklin pa no joke. find cy n tell all. if any1 can help me he can. luv u eddie

Cy felt fortunate that she brought the message to him before she took it to the detectives. She did not know how to save a copy from her cell to her computer and hoped Cy could help her. After what happened to her camera, she knew they would take her cell phone memory, too.

After hearing her story, Cy's analytical mind switched into high gear. He asked her detailed questions about times and the weather on the mountain that day. Did Eddie still have the same camo-colored hard shell flip phone with the Cabela's emblem on the metal compass cover? Were there any other calls or messages from him?

The text to Andrea arrived Wednesday night, two days after Eddie disappeared. He received three of her text messages, but only at night. He sent his message at night.

Cy asked Andrea to bring her cell phone to the roof of his apartment complex. Some of the tenants had container gardens there, but at that time of night the area was deserted. He asked Andrea to send Eddie a text message. Afterwards, they waited almost a half an hour for a reply.

Nothing.

Cy begged Andrea to excuse him if he acted paranoid. The truth was, he confessed, he felt paranoid. She accepted his comment with a shaky smile. He felt bad for Andrea and he did want to help. But after the hassle he had been put through at the sheriff's station, he had already figured out that they were looking for a suspect. He did not want to invite more trouble if he could avoid it.

Careful to not handle her cell phone or let it come in contact with anything in his apartment, Cy made two lok-stik back-ups and handed her one using a towel to keep from touching it.

It was well past midnight when they finished.

Cy asked Andrea to wait until morning before she took her cell phone to the detectives. He told her he wanted time to go over all the data he had collected so far. But, he knew he also needed time to make preparations.

As soon as Andrea left, Cy combined his files and copied off several back-ups including one to his vault drive. He prepared a new narrated photo DVD for his grandparents with his complete Eddie file embedded. He left his apartment long enough to drop it into a mail collection box three blocks away, making a point to avoid known cameras along the path.

Back home, he searched his apartment for a waterproof container so he could hide his vault drive, plus the back-up lok-stik and the USB drive with the information from Andrea's cell.

It was early in the morning when Cy finally went to bed. He sighed as he threw his arm over his eyes. Even though he was exhausted, anxiety prevented him from falling asleep right away. He figured he could expect the detectives to show up at his doorstep later that day. As much as he wanted to avoid more involvement with law enforcement, he knew he was probably in for another grilling.

Eddie had named him by name in the text message. With no other explanation than what the average person would consider logical, he suspected that the detectives would probably focus back on him.

CHAPTER 10

Nervously, Marty laced her fingers together, turned her hands palms-out and cracked her knuckles.

"So, Green Corn, are you here alone with your baby?"

"No. I travel with my husband and three more of our warriors. Conrad Weiser has asked for a stick for each warrior of our band so that he may count our strength. We return from our towns east of here with warrior sticks."

"You are traveling with warriors, huh? Okay! You know, it has really been nice meeting you, Green Corn, really impre. But, I think it is time I move along."

"You are leaving?"

Marty started to back up towards the foliage that formed a thick hedge around the meadow. She realized she was chattering nervously as she moved to make her escape.

"Yes, I really would like to find someone before dark who can get me turned in the right direction. So, I will let you get back to what you were doing. I enjoyed our talk, though. It was all—very interesting."

"You were not searching for us? You did not run away to join the Lenape?" asked Green Corn, puzzled. "You would not travel alone disguised as a man if you were happy among the English. I have never seen such leggings and moccasins as yours, but I know the British do not allow their women to dress as men or go without covering their heads."

Come on! Women have been wearing pants for decades. And hats are optional—well, unless you are going to be out in the sun a lot.

"You will run the gauntlet," Green Corn continued. "The people will take their revenge for those who have died by the hand of the British. If you are strong and show no fear, you will be accepted. Have you lived through the smallpox and measles?"

"I will not get sick with either one of those diseases."

Green Corn studied Marty with renewed interest.

"That is powerful medicine for you, Marty. The European diseases kill more of our people than the British soldiers. You will live when many will die. Come with me. I will speak for you. When you are adopted, you will add much strength to your new clan and will be much sought after as a wife. You will have a better life with the Lenape than as an Englishwoman."

"I appreciate that, Green Corn, I really do. I would like to be your friend but as far as joining your group, let me think about it awhile, okay?"

I really would rather have her as a friend. She is very nice even with her strange ideas. I know I sure do not want her and her companions as my enemies.

Marty heard squirming noises coming from the cradleboard. The baby was starting to wake up. Green Corn gave a quick glance in the baby's direction. Then she turned back to face Marty.

"Your eyes speak that you still fear my people," Green Corn said. "But when you speak to me, I heard words of friendship. We shall treat to hold each other close to our hearts."

Green Corn pulled a leather pouch beautifully decorated with red and blue beads from her waistband and brought it to Marty.

"Marty, I give you this medicine bag with the purple flower herb that heals the sickness of the lungs and stomach. There are also sticks of the willow that drive away fever and the pains in the joints. This is my token of our treaty of friendship."

When Marty looked closer at the leather bag, she saw that the beads were dyed quills. It was beautifully crafted and must have taken Green Corn or someone else hours to make.

Marty wondering what she had that would be of equal value to give this woman in exchange. Nervously, she brushed a lock of her hair behind her ear. Her hand touched an earring. She quickly pulled the wire hooks free of her ears and gently placed them in the young woman's hand.

"Green Corn, I do not have much. I hope you will accept these earrings as a token of our friendship."

Green Corn lifted her hand from the shadows and wiggled her fingers. The motion caused the sunlight moving through the facets of the lavender quartz to sparkle. The quartz was even more beautiful to Green Corn than the purple wampum beads that were so valuable to her people. Her eyes glowed with delight.

"This gift speaks with much power of your friendship, Marty," said Green Corn. Then she looked Marty in the face as she spoke again. "I hope someday you choose the path of the Lenni Lenape. When you do, I will speak for you among my people. But if not, I will still hold you as a friend in my heart. You will be my friend even if the Lenape and the British take up the hatchet of war."

"Thank you, Green Corn," said Marty, grateful for the offer of friendship but still feeling uneasy because of the talk of war. "I hope all goes well for you and your people in Logstown. I also will try to help you any way I can."

Marty did not pay attention to the bird call until Green Corn turned sharply in the direction from which it came. She quickly turned back to Marty and shoved her towards the bushes.

"Go now, Marty. Quickly! Hide and stay still until we are gone. If you do not wish to join with the Lenape, you must return up the tall mountain. I will guide the men west to Deer Lake so they do not find your tracks. Fare thee well."

The baby howled impatiently.

"Good-by, Green Corn," Marty mouthed to Green Corn just before the woman turned and hurried to her child. Marty also turned and buried herself in the bushes that separated the meadow from the path that led back up the mountain.

Marty glanced back and caught a glimpse of Green Corn lifting the cradleboard and untying her little one. Then she froze in place as she caught another movement out of the corner of her eye. She held her breath, fervently hoping she was far enough back into the foliage so that she could not be seen. A man about Green Corn's age with the distinct coloring and features of a Native American stepped into the clearing close to where Green Corn stood with the baby. From the look in his eye and the softness about his face, Marty guessed it was her husband.

Marty did not dare take any chances. Her back and hips were twisted. Her knee that was bent at an awkward angle was starting to hurt. Her arms that she had lifted up to keep the brush from flipping back into her face grew increasingly heavy. She did not think she could hold her position much longer although she knew she must. She was afraid to move even the slightest bit. She did not dare chance rustling the leaves or snapping twigs beneath her feet. Green Corn's husband—what did she call him? Elkhorn?—might hear her and come her way to investigate. Marty knew that even if she was well-camouflaged, his peripheral vision would pick up any movement.

Marty hoped to be found, but not by these people. Too much of what Green Corn said about this group she called the Lenape bothered Marty. Whatever their agenda was, Marty wanted no part of it. If the men found Marty, she could be in real danger.

Marty noted the man's fringed leather leggings, tunic and beaded moccasins. His head was bald except for a scalp lock that was decorated with shells and feathers. His face appeared to be painted.

He must really be into this back-to-nature thing big-time, too.

Although Marty could not hear them, she knew the two were talking and smiling about something. She also noticed that Green Corn subtly shifted her position so that, as her husband continued to face her, she maneuvered him so he had his back to Marty. A few moments later, the couple with their baby walked through the brush on the other side of the clearing.

Only after several minutes had passed did Marty cautiously untwist her body. She silently sighed with relief as the pain eased when she was able to stand almost straight. Marty carefully pushed through the bushes and started toward the path. She found a branch with leaves and used it to brush out the distinctive tread of her hiking boots.

Protectively clutching the leather bag to her chest, Marty quickly hiked back up the trail. She took a detour only long enough to reclaim her daypack and hat. She did not know where the Lenni Lenape were camped, but she guessed that it was next to the lake where Green Corn said she would guide them.

Marty felt thankful that she still had a full bottle of water. She would wait another day before she worried about finding more if she was not rescued before then. She would stay at the top of the mountain and give Green Corn and her friends plenty of time to leave the area.

Reaching the summit of the mountain in the dimming light, Marty leaned against the rock at the top and studied the intricate beadwork on the leather bag. She used the drawstrings to tie it securely to her belt loop. Then she finished off the last of her partial bottle of water.

Marty checked her cell again and began to wonder where Cy was. Why had he not called her or at least sent a text? There were so many cell towers around in even the most remote areas these days that surely this was not in a dead zone.

As the sun started to sink into the western sky, Marty decided she needed to find a place to spend the night. She felt too exposed on top of the mountain, especially since the path led straight to the summit. She stumbled back to the rocks where she first gained consciousness. There, she found a cave-like hollow facing east. She decided it was an excellent hiding place for the night. She almost hit her head on the rocky ceiling as she crawled in and pulled the shrubbery back in place to cover the opening.

Marty looked at her boots.

Like that really matters. If these are really Native Americans, even modern ones, they can track me no matter where I go even if I try to brush away my prints.

Avoidance was the key, Marty realized. She hoped that Green Corn would be true to her word and steer her companions away from the mountain.

To be safe, Marty decided against lighting a fire. She found the lunch she had packed for her and Cy in her daypack and slowly ate half for dinner. She pulled back the sleeve of her frontier blouse and saw that there had been no incoming calls or texts. She sighed as she covered the wrist screen back up. Then she found the tightly-folded emergency solar blanket and shook it out to its full size. She found that if she scrunched up her knees in the fetal position, the blanket covered most of her body. She squirmed around to get as comfortable as possible before she concentrated on trying to fall asleep.

Cy, where are you? Did you call out the rescue squad to come find me?

***

Marty was almost asleep when she heard the trill that told her she had received a text message. She threw her solar blanket aside and shoved her sleeve up her arm to read the I.D. screen.

Marty sighed with relief. The message was from Cy.

CHAPTER 11

Cy fought the hypnotic trance he felt himself sliding into due to the afternoon heat. His eyes strayed to the sun moving west. I am delaying the inevitable, he admitted to himself. Then he forced his focus back to the events that followed Andrea's visit to his apartment.

The following morning, the Thursday of Spring Break, Cy was awakened mid-morning by a handful of FBI special agents with a search warrant. Since the email to Andrea stated Eddie was in Pennsylvania, the case was then classified as "an abduction across state lines." The feds went through everything in his apartment and his car.

They also had a search warrant for his office on campus. As a teacher's assistant at the university, he shared a cubby hole room that also served as overflow storage in the back of the science building. Much to the dismay of the university, the feds confiscated the ancient all-in-one desktop computer he used on campus.

The special agent in charge asked him several questions which he answered honestly. To his surprise and relief, they did not arrest him or take him in for further questioning. Perhaps the local sheriff's detectives had already checked his activities of the past week and knew he was nowhere near the mountain where Eddie disappeared. But, he also knew that if the suits found anything they considered suspicious, they would be back.

One fed in particular caught Cy's attention if for no other reason that that he gave Cy his business card.

Lee Hardin was older than the other special agents, although he was younger than Cy's own father who was almost 50 years old. But, this man was not in charge of the team. In fact, Cy noticed that although there was a lot of discussion between the others, they tended to ignore Lee Hardin. Hardin looked out of place with his slightly thicker middle on his large, tall frame, his rumpled business suit and dress shirt and his dark brown hair combed back from what Cy's father jokingly liked to call a "high forehead." Cy guessed that the man had been an athlete when he was younger. Now he looked like a college football player that had gone to seed.

"Still like the old-fashioned paper and ink books, do ya?" he had asked as he quietly sifted through Cy's collection of books and papers. Since most young people downloaded their books, magazines and newspapers to their tablet readers or slab computers, the man seemed to find that noteworthy.

Cy remembered shrugging in reply, not sure why that would be relevant to anything.

"So, tell me about Eddie," Lee Hardin had asked. "He a good friend of yours?"

Once again, Cy repeated to Hardin the story of how he met Eddie and how they had become friends. He described the last day they had seen each other.

It was the other special agents who scooped up his equipment, old DVDs, lok-stiks and flash drives, all the while vocally recording notes on their cell phones. Special Agent Hardin quietly who took out a pen and a pocket journal with paper pages and wrote notes about what he found on Cy's desk and bookcase, including some of the things that the feds did not take. The special agent in charge was the one who told Cy they may be back and to stay in town. It was Special Agent Hardin who wrote his cell number on his business card and told him to call if he thought of anything else about Eddie.

Cy assured Hardin he would call if he learned anything about Eddie. But, Cy knew he had no intention of contacting anyone in the FBI for any reason, especially after they took the equipment that he needed to function.

After the feds left, Cy slumped into the second-hand upholstered chair he used for reading his books and readers. Not only was his wrist screen gone, they took his tablet and his slab, too. School was due to resume the following week. What did they expect him to use?

It was a small comfort to Cy when he thought about what he had kept from them. What the feds did not find was the flash drive and lok-stik with the Eddie file. They did not find his vault drive, either. These were in the baggie that he had stuffed in an empty waterproof first aid pouch and taped to the bottom of one of the garden containers on the roof.

He still had copies of all his files and documents close at hand. He just had nothing left in his apartment that he could use to access them.

Cy called his parents and asked them to mail to him his old notebook computer he kept in his room back home. He would need to use it until the FBI returned his things. That is, if they ever did.

He did not plan to tell his parents what was going on. He decided that as long as his involvement in Eddie's disappearance did not make their local news, he did not want them to worry. He definitely did not want his parents to descend upon him at the university when there was nothing they could do to help. Thank goodness he had turned eighteen the previous November and was legally an adult.

He soon found out it didn't matter. The FBI contacted them. His mother called Cy back to ask him why the FBI wanted to know information about his mental and emotional state, such as, if he was prone to depression, had a drug or alcohol problem or had trouble socializing. Since he went to the university with students several years older than he was, the feds wanted to know if he tended to be a loner.

That infuriated Cy. He suspected that being a loner was a classic description for people who had personality issues, sometimes associated with people who turned violent against others. Cy believed the feds were trying to profile him as a loner so that they could move him to the top of their suspect list.

Why did people think that just because he was smart and ahead of most students in school that he did not get along with people? Granted, a lot of people did not share his interests and there was a certain amount of rivalry among the other students in his field. But that did not make him a loner.

Albert Einstein was a genius, yet he was known to be very sociable, Cy reminded himself. His contemporaries thought he had great sense of humor.

At that point Cy was especially happy that he had decided to earn extra money by being a teacher's assistant and by tutoring. Even though not everyone considered him a best friend, he did get along well with several people. He realized then he especially got along well with Eddie and Marty, even though it annoyed him when Marty teased him about not having much of a sense of humor.

Okay, Cy acknowledged to himself, maybe I'm not big on quips and corny jokes. But, still, I have friends. The feds cannot justify labeling me as a loner.

Cy assured his parents that the whole thing was routine. He was considered a "person of interest" only because he had been tutoring Eddie. The feds were investigating everyone who knew Eddie.

Cy suspected that the reason the FBI had not picked him up for more questioning was because they planned to watch him instead. He felt it was in his best interests to continue to be paranoid. If he was going to do anything to help Eddie, he had to stay free of further suspicion.

And, he had to stay out of jail.

Cy could not sit at home and do nothing while he waited for his old computer to arrive. He had to get to a computer.

Cy purchased a multi-pack of flash drives, a small role of white cloth tape and some latex gloves. Thursday afternoon he went to the internet café a few blocks from his apartment and set up an account. Rather than trying to hide from anyone who might be observing from the outside, he sat where his use of the touch-screen computer could be easily watched. He hoped that if, for some reason barely comprehensible to him, the suits had a warrant to monitor his transmissions, using the internet café to search for information would provide some protection. The old-fashioned units were hard-wired to the service provider and the minutes online were paid for by a tap card. No air waves to capture.

Cy chose a computer that allowed him to face the shop entrance with his right shoulder towards the front window. He adjusted the screen so that what he was viewing could not be seen by passers-by. What was also blocked from the view of anyone watching was his use of the USB port on the side of the projection devise connected to the left of the screen. He accessed the internet using the touch screen commands, opting to not use a holographic display projected onto the tabletop. Then, rather than use voice commands, he typed in the search terms on the hard-wired keyboard attached to the pull-out shelf below.

When he first logged on, Cy made a show of inserting one of the flash drives. He accessed a site that would help with his astronomy class. However, he later switched to a site with information that he hoped might help him with Eddie. When he found something useful, he did his best to be inconspicuous about switching the flash drive to one he would sync with the Eddie file on the flash drive hidden on his rooftop.

The one flash drive he would carry out of the café at the end of the day. It would contain files he saved only from those sites that he would have visited for fun or schoolwork. The other would stay hidden in the building.

Cy visited the men's restroom. A quick swipe of the back of one of the toilets with a paper towel assured him that the college help hired to clean the restrooms did not worry about surfaces that did not show. Before he left, the other flash drive would be wiped down, wrapped in plastic and taped to the back of the toilet.

As he searched the web, the first type of information Cy sought in order to satisfy his curiosity was news stories about people disappearing. He wanted to determine whether or not Eddie's situation was a unique event. He had heard of people vacationing in the mountains and getting lost. Before Eddie, he had not followed the stories to their final outcome. He assumed most of the hikers had either been found alive or had fallen to their deaths.

Cy was amazed at what he discovered.

A year earlier, a high school student from Oklahoma City visiting with a school field trip had disappeared from the same cliff at Dead Man's Drop as Eddie. An older couple celebrating their retirement set out to tour the eastern United States and hike part of the Appalachian Trail. They never returned to their motor home. Their bodies were never found. Their children had put out several pleas for help. Two high school sophomores, riding their dirt bikes near the mining ruins above Salida, Colorado the previous summer never came home. Their dirt bikes were found close to a mountain peak by the mine shaft.

Then there was the MIT grad whose idea of celebrating receiving his diploma was to hike the Continental Divide Trail starting at the Mexican border until he reached the Canadian border. He disappeared somewhere in New Mexico.

One thing Cy recognized about the locations where these strange disappearances were reported was that they were in mountainous regions. He made a note of it on a file he kept on the flash drive he would leave at the café.

Cy invested in a calling card after he left the café that first day. He telephoned the sister of the missing girl. From her he learned where Brandy Nagles ended up, the era and that the sister had received text messages even though she did not live in the mountains. But, like with Eddie, text transmissions were more successful at night. Neither Eddie nor the missing girl could make a voice call back to this time.

Cy used some of the money he had earned from tutoring to buy another cell phone on a pay-as-you-go plan. He had little hope that he would get his old one back. The store had a special on a BlackSlab model, so he chose that rather than another wrist screen. It would help ease the loss of his newer slab. He downloaded his textbooks from the cloud and his most important files from his vault drive.

Cy found Eddie's cell number among his notes. Later that evening, long after most people were in bed, he climbed the stairs to the apartment rooftop. Staying in the shadows, he moved away from the satellite dish and found a spot where he would not create a silhouette. He dimmed the light on his screen to read mode and hunched over his phone to block the glow.

He thought it was unlikely that the FBI considered him so important that they were still watching him at this hour. Cy seriously doubted that they had gotten a warrant for listening equipment. Still, he would tap the text rather than use voice. He knew they could retrieve messages from his cell provider, but he would take the chance. He had nothing to hide. Still, if he could avoid it, he just did not want to be questioned anymore about what he was doing to try to help Eddie.

.

New cell no 405 555 1212 text at nite one hour only then cell off to save battery. Andi sends her love. Cops took our cell fones n feds all over me. Will try to help no answers yet.

.

In three minutes, Cy sent the message again. He repeated the transmission every three minutes. After the fifth try, he received a reply.

.

u r my bff. ucdi if any1 can genius. its 1857 here no joke. horse n bugy daz. good i can shoot n ride working on farm. miss andi tell her i luv her. Please help me get home.

Cy quickly composed another text message.

Got good info today. Hope to figure all out to get u back soon. Think solar flares affecting cell transmissions but how? Y mtns n not everywhere? How to reverse? U ok?

Before three minutes were up, Cy received another message from Eddie.

ok so far. sleep in barn. worked 4 clothes. no zippers or tshirts back here. hid modern stuf or wud freak em out but hat n knife works. solar flares sure mess radio waves.

A few more text messages later, Cy found out exactly where Eddie first landed. It was on another mountain with a rocky peak like Dead Man's Drop Cliff. Eddie's battery power indicator showed he still had three out of five buttons left. They agreed to make contact every third night.

It was after Eddie's disappearance that the forest service decided to install the barbed wire fence and post the "No Trespassing" sign. Cy discovered this the following week when he went to the location where Eddie's disappearance had taken place. He drove up the access road to the base of the mountain. But, when he saw the area blocked off and a forest ranger truck parked not far away, he kept driving south. He would not do Eddie any good if he was picked up and detained for trespassing.

Besides, if the feds were watching him, they would think it was suspicious if he showed too much interest in the place where Eddie vanished. Cy decided instead to stay home to do more research.

The night came when Cy no longer received a reply from Eddie. He assumed Eddie's cell phone battery finally went dead.

Cy studied maps, read everything he could find on physics, sound and light waves and time travel. He reviewed everything from Newton to Maxwell to Einstein to Mallett to everyone in the field who had come since. He crunched numbers, then changed them around and crunched them again, looking for the patterns that would give him some answers.

Even after his folks sent him the old notebook computer, he continued to use the internet café for most of his web searching and data analysis. He occasionally brought his flash drive and his vault drive from the rooftop hiding place only long enough to add the information he had found while on the café's computers. He never put critical information onto his notebook's hard drive or in his BlackSlab memory. Once the text messages from Eddie ended and he had saved them several other places, he scrubbed the BlackSlab's memory drive. He kept multiple back-ups of everything, but not where they would be easily found with a search warrant.

Cy never knew if the feds would come after him again. He did not receive any follow-up contact from the FBI after the day of the search warrant. By the end of the week following Spring Break, it seemed like everyone had gone back to school and work and forgotten about the missing student. Cy assumed that once the search in the mountains had produced no results, Eddie's file was probably consigned to the bottomless depths of unsolved missing persons cases.

The feds might forget about Eddie but Cy had not forgotten. He still searched for a way to get Eddie home. When Cy was not in class or working as a T.A. or a tutor, his time was spent on his secret research project that he did not share with anybody.

CHAPTER 12

Cy swallowed the last of the water. His entire purpose for coming to the mountain this day was to look for more information to help Eddie. He had not intended for Marty to come along. But, when she showed up, he had felt so excited about having her with him, he could not bring himself to ask her to go home.

Now she was gone. Like Eddie and the other girl, she vanished from the cliffs that top Dead Man's Drop Mountain when she pressed the send button on a cell phone. Like them, she made contact by texting after she disappeared.

Unlike them, he realized with a burst of excitement, Marty had a new Sun Access wrist screen with her. It used light to recharge the battery. As long as the cell unit did not get damaged, she could keep the battery charged. He could stay in touch with Marty.

The cell technology had to be a key element in transporting people to the past. Cy had suspected as much, but now he felt it was confirmed. The only thing that bothered him about relying on that theory alone was that cell technology had been around for decades. So, why did people start disappearing just in the past few years? Cell technology alone was not the whole answer.

Still, it had to be a factor. The question was, could whatever sent these people to another era also bring them back to 2024? He felt confident that the answer was yes. He obsessed over how to do it. Especially now, he had to find out how to do it. He needed to bring Marty home.

Cy made another decision. He was not going to report Marty's disappearance. Not yet. He had two weeks until her family was due home from their vacation to California. He had two months before she was due to return from her history immersion tour back east. As long as she could text her family, they might not become suspicious about just how immersed in history she probably was. That is, assuming she had gone back in time like the others he knew of, not forward or sideways. That would give him two months to find a way to bring her home.

He would take the chance.

***

That night in his apartment, Cy turned on his BlackSlab to see if Marty had been able to send an image. He hoped it was there but knew he had to be realistic. There may be no internet where she was which meant that she may not be able to send it as an email attachment. Even though a text message got through to him, a picture or holograph may be too large of a file to send with a text.

Cy opened the text attachment and squinted at the screen. He guessed that Marty's wrist screen normally took good color images. What he saw was a far cry from a quality photograph. There was little to suggest much color. The mostly black and white image was very grainy.

There appeared to be a rocky mountaintop. The trees were not the kind found in the mountains they hiked in today. There was a valley in the distance. None of it looked familiar.

The second image was a holograph, but a very sketchy one, of a mountain surrounded by a lake. The 3-D looking image lacked a lot of substance. He inhaled deeply and shook his head. What a challenge to figure out where the images were taken.

Using his notebook computer, Cy tried to match Marty's photo to a place. Even if the FBI found his search history later, he did not think that anyone would tie his place search to anything to do with his missing friends. He would tell them about the advanced geography class he was scheduled to take in the fall.

Hours later, he flopped back in his chair, exhausted and dazed with amazement. In spite of the poor quality of the images Marty had sent him, he had identified the location. The shape of the lake, or lakes, as he finally figured out, was the key clue.

The BlackSlab still had a strong charge when Cy checked outside his window and saw that the sky was fully dark. It was time to try again to contact Marty.

CHAPTER 13

R u ok? Got your pix. Pretty sure u r on top of the Negro mtns in western Pennsylvania. They r part of Appalachian mtns

.

      Marty blinked several times when she read the message. She read it again. Cy's message made no sense to her.
      She wondered if she dare use her voice mode to respond to Cy. Just in case Green Corn's friends were nearby, she decided against it. She tapped out her return message.

.

Im ok what r u talking about how could I get to Pennsylvania from Colorado I must have fallen r the rescue squads looking for me yet I want to come home if u cant find me please send help

.

      A few moments later, she received another text that baffled her even more.

.

U went back in time like ed burrows. He went to Pennsylvania in 1857. I was working on how he got there n how to get him home while we were on mtn today

.

What do u mean how could ed go back to Pennsylvania in 1857?

.

He was on Dead Mans Drop n disappeared when he answered his cell n that is where he ended up. Later he sent a text. Dont no how or y but working on it. Same thing with u now

.

Marty slumped back against the rock, feeling stunned. She was elated that she finally received text messages from Cy. However, she shook her head with disbelief over what he was saying.

This has to be a joke.

Marty flung her head back and rolled it along the rock as she thought back to when she heard about Eddie's disappearance. One news report said that Cy was a "person of interest" in the case. When she asked Cy about it, he merely shook his head and refused to say anything. She knew there was a big search effort for Eddie. She remembered thinking at the time, how awful! Not only did he vanish but they never even found his body. Cy behaved like he was distracted so often after that she knew it weighed heavily on his mind.

Marty reread the text. No, she realized, Cy could hardly joke about anything. He certainly would not joke about Eddie's disappearance. He was serious. If Cy said Eddie was living back in 1857, then that must be where Eddie was. And it happened when he answered his cell phone while he was on the same mountain where she stood when this all happened to her.

Maybe that explained why Cy had yelled at her to stay away from the top of the mountain even though she was not close enough to the edge to fall over.

If Cy said she was someplace in western Pennsylvania, she must be. But, even if somehow she had been transported back east, could she really be back in time, too?

Marty thought about her conversation with the Lenni Lenape woman, Green Corn. She remembered Green Corn's unusual speech patterns and how strange the lifestyle she described sounded. Maybe Green Corn and her husband were not part of some modern back-to-nature cult. Maybe they were the real deal from an earlier time period. Marty shivered at the thought that she may have actually come in contact with native people from several hundred years ago.

Still, Marty could hardly believe what Cy told her, even though everything was starting to point in that direction. Marty slowly composed her next message.

Y am I just now hearing about eddie in pa in 1857 y didnt u tell me before

Would u have believed me?

Marty had to admit the truth.

No

No one else has except Andrea n one girl whose sister disappeared like u n ed. Feds were all over me n took my tablet slab n cell fone. Thats y I had to get a new cell number

.

It all started to make sense to Marty. She now realized why the man from the FBI came to the house to talk to her parents about Cy. It was Spring Break and she had not seen Cy that week. One thing she remembered telling the agent was that she knew for sure that Cy was not the outdoorsy type. She could not imagine any reason why he would have gone to the mountains with Eddie and Andrea.

When Cy told her he had a new cell number and she found out he was using an old notebook computer, she had assumed his others had been stolen or were sent out for repair. Now she realized that they had been taken as evidence because the FBI thought he had something to do with Eddie disappearing. They thought Eddie had been the victim of foul play and somehow Cy was involved. How awful for Cy.

.

I believe u now do u still text with eddie

.

No his battery died. U have sun access n your battery will recharge so I hope to get u home before anyone knows u r gone

.

Am I back in time too am I close to eddie

.

Donno. Do u c any buildings or people?

.

I saw one woman n baby in a cradleboard shes English but adopted by lanne lenape turtle clan going with warriors to her town kuskuske west of here French n British r at war n something about

.

Anything else?

.

Something about conrad wiser of pa counting sticks for each warrior going to meet at logstown north of here after harvest they wont let Iroquois half king talk for them anymore Iroquois let British trick them into treaty saying all land west of Alleghany mtns to great waters in west belong to England not tribes where r Alleghany mtns?

.

I will investigate n get back to u tonite stay by your cell. U think of something else text me. Brb

.

Sure, Cy. Like, I am really going to pack up my things and take off to somewhere else. I do not even know where I am now.

Then she thought of something else to tell him that might help.

.

I remember she said something about geo Washington n Virginians going to king cross great waters to ask king to take Ohio lands from tribes

.

Good info

.

Please get back to me soon this is scaring me ;(m

.

Marty's entire body shook with fear as she clutched her wrist screen to her chest. Her confidence to handle situations in the wilderness had evaporated. She was in uncharted territory in more ways than one. Not only was she not at the bottom of Dead Man's Drop in Colorado, but she probably was not even in 2024.

If Green Corn had been talking about the same George Washington Marty knew about, she was now living somewhere in the 1700s. What if Green Corn's tribe really hated white people? Because she spoke English, Marty would be mistaken for being British. If the warriors traveling with Green Corn had found her, who knows what might have happened.

If only she had listened to Cy and stayed away from the top of the cliff.

Suddenly her hiding place between the rocks and bushes felt too confining. She had to walk around while she waited for Cy to get back to her. Marty decided that for her own sanity she must trust Green Corn's word that she would keep the men off the mountain. Although the moon was not visible, there was enough light for her to see to climb the rocks. She carefully worked her way up the rough, uneven boulders until she was on top. It allowed her a better view of the sky above the treetops.

It was then that Marty noticed the glow in the night sky to the north. It was faint, but there appeared to be a wavy streamer of aqua green moving across the sky. She wondered what it was. Could it be northern lights? At the campground yesterday, Cy said if there was a lot of solar activity, it was possible to see auroras further south. Was that a good sign that she was at least still in 2024? She studied it in wonder for several minutes before she decided to climb back down to her campsite.

Relieve flooded Marty when she finally heard the tone announcing an incoming text.

.

Lenni Lenape aka Delawares settled Ohio valley aka western PA n Ohio with Shawnee n Mingos after 1742. Mingos were from two Iroquois tribes that settled south of Lake Erie. Alleghany mtns was name used for all of Appalachian mtns til mid-1800s. Virginia was trying to form Ohio Company to sell Indian land for profit. Geo Washington was part of that

Marty shook her head with frustration and quickly fired off a text.

Forget history lesson cy when n y am I here?

She no sooner sent her text than she received another.

Conrad Weiser visited Delawares about August 1748 n took Indian census of warriors. King Georges war Brits vs French fought until Oct 1748.

Marty swallowed hard. Cy was warning her that she might be in the middle of a war. Okay. But that still did not answer her question. With shaking fingers, she wrote her next text.

Y in 1748? Y did I end up in boonies and not where its civilized?

Donno u r in highest mtns in PA. Solar cycle one started 1755 peaked 1758-60? Cycles each 11 years so 1748 makes sense as a solar hi before that. Do u c an aurora in northern sky?

I c something aqua green moving in north sky kinda wavy its pretty but rather c u so please get me outta here n back home

Not sure but think electmag fields n solar winds involved with u n eddie. They create auroras when strong. Try calling me tomorrow when sun is overhead. Em fields closest to earth at noon

Y did I end up here when I called u today y not somewhere in colorado y not in 1857 at least with eddie

Donno. Was sun overhead when u got there? How much battery power?

It was later afternoon n battery was low

Go to high point of where u landed tomorrow at noon w full battery n try to call me. No guarantees. I will wait for u on Dead Mans Drop. Stay safe

Sounds like a plan.

Then, another concern popped into her head.

.

Ok but if u cant get me home tonite can u at least get my car home? :)m

.

She had paid for a weekend parking pass at the campground Friday and had decided to make good use of it. She left her car in the parking lot at the campground when she and Cy traveled together in his Civic to the mountain to hike. She would feel better if she knew her car was sitting at home in its place on the side of the driveway while she was away.

.

Yes tomorrow. Too late now park closed. Need key

.

No key all pushbutton code to unlock is your six digit birthday code to start is your six digit birthday backwards

.

My birthday?

.

Yes dates n numbers for my family r too ez for someone to figure out I got car for Christmas n remembered your birthday which was month before so I used it no one would ever guess not even u :)m

.

In spite of her apprehension about her current situation, Marty enjoyed catching Cy by surprise about her car.

.

Will get your car home. I will text u each nite til I figure this out. Send texts at nite because radio waves travel better then. If text does not go thru first time wait five minutes n try again

.

What should I do I dont have much food n need water tomorrow if natives find me they might want to kill me ;(m

.

U r resourceful u will think of something. If u dont make it back home try to find a British town to the east or south.

.

That should work well I will just show up on their doorstep with my hiking gear n I will probably get shot

.

Just be yourself u will b ok. Btw b sure to text your mom to say u r ok n having fun etc but dont tell where u really r yet

.

Dont like keeping something this big from my parents

.

Im in danger if people no u r gone. Feds watching me because I tried to explain about ed n they thought I did him in. Cant help u if I go to jail. Please buy me time to get u back. Ttyl

.

Marty did not like it. But, the more she thought about it, the more she realized that Cy was right. Without experiencing it for themselves, her parents could not believe this anymore than she would have if Cy had told her everything about Eddie from the beginning. No one she knew of had ever heard of people vanishing only to end up in a different time and place. Not for real, anyway.

.

Ok I wont tell anyone I will give u time but please dont take too long thanks cy u r my bff :)m

.

With trembling hands, Marty turned off her wrist screen and carefully wrapped it in a bandanna she pulled from her daypack. She put it in the zippered padded pocket inside her pack. She could not let it get broken. It was her lifeline to home.

She thought about what Cy had told her to do. Text her family to tell them everything was wonderful and she was having fun. It was way too late now. Maybe tomorrow night she would send a text to her mother. Maybe by then she would be home and things would be all right. Tonight she was not up to it. This definitely was not wonderful and this was not her idea of fun.

She pulled the solar blanket back over her and wriggled around to get comfortable. Her thoughts raced many directions at once. Cy was never able to get Eddie back. He was counting on the solar unit to recharge her wrist screen battery in order to allow enough time to figure out how to help her get home. He also said "no guarantee." That meant she might be here for awhile.

Marty involuntarily shivered. Maybe she was stuck here for forever, just like Eddie was now stuck where he ended up. Only she was surrounded by hostile people.

Cy said I am resourceful. I am! I'll survive here just fine.
Marty just wished she felt a little braver.

She knew she had to trust Cy. He was so smart about these things. If anyone could figure out how to get her back through time and space, he could.

After what seemed like hours, Marty finally dropped off into an exhausted sleep.

CHAPTER 14

The next morning Cy woke up early to the sound of his alarm. His entire body ached. Even though he constantly walked around campus and the surrounding area, he spent much of his time each day in a chair with a tablet or slab. After two days of hiking in the mountains, including hauling extra electronic gear the previous day, his shoulders and legs, especially, let him know they were not used to the workout they had received.

He took a long, hot shower to help loosen his muscles. He dressed in his usual tech tacky style and grabbed his last two stale store-brand donuts for breakfast. He finished off the orange juice in the gallon jug and tossed the empty container in the trash. Then he drove to the campground parking lot.

Once there, Cy quickly found Marty's car. It was a cute little hydrogen cell domestic compact bright red in color. It suited Marty. He parked his own fourteen year-old clunker with its chipped gray paint a row over and down from hers.

His car suited him, too.

Two years earlier his parents decided that he should have a car while at the university in case he needed it for his tutoring jobs. He made it clear to them that he did not drive very often. Therefore, he wanted any extra money from them to go into his technical equipment rather than a pricy car or one that used a lot of gas. The old stick-shift his parents decided on for him got gas mileage almost as good as some of the hybrids the same age.

After he parked, Cy walked up to the five button security lock on the driver's door of Marty's car and unlocked it. He shook his head at the thought that she had used his birthday. He chuckled with the realization that her brother Jason, at fifteen and eligible for his driver's permit, may have been the biggest reason why she chose a combination he would not guess easily.

Cy settled into the driver's seat and found the touchpad for the ignition. He punched his birth date numbers in backwards and pushed the ignition button. The car immediately started. On the drive back to town, Cy found he focused more on how the car handled compared to a gasoline model than he did the scenery.

Thanks to several tutoring sessions at her house, Cy knew where Marty lived. He pulled Marty's car onto the concrete pad on the side of the main driveway and locked it.

Cy yawned and wriggled his back as he started down the sidewalk towards his apartment. He figured it was about four to five miles away. He was acutely aware of the continued ache in his legs. He had already figured out that the Vans were not designed for hiking great distances in the mountains or on the concrete sidewalks in town. He wished he had brought a bottle of water. It was going to be a long walk back to his home.

***

Cy arrived home and ate a quick snack of peanut butter and crackers. Now that he had Marty's car back at her house, he needed to figure out how to get his own car home to his apartment.

He checked the bus schedule. The bus system did not go to the campground. He thought about calling a taxi and then decided against it. A cap company would keep a record of his name and address and where he was dropped off. Under the circumstances, that was not a good idea. He did not want to call anyone who had gone camping with him and Marty. They might ask questions.

Cy ended up calling another teacher's assistant from his department.

At first the guy was reluctant to give up his afternoon to help Cy. Only after Cy explained that he was having trouble with the Check Engine light coming on did he finally agreed to give Cy a lift in exchange for gas money plus ten dollars for lunch.

To make it look good, Cy decided he needed to take some oil. Before he left his apartment, he grabbed his empty gallon orange juice jug out of the trash and rinsed it out. As soon as he climbed into the T.A.'s car with his empty jug in hand, he asked the driver to stop at the auto parts store so he could buy the oil. The guy did not ask Cy any questions about what might be wrong with the car. Cy guessed that he, like Cy himself, probably was not very mechanically inclined and did not want to feel obligated to help work on the car. That was fine with Cy.

Once they arrived, Cy waved his ride good-by. He decided that since he had carried the charade to that point, he might as well check his oil and the water level in his radiator.

Cy had the hood up and was unscrewing the radiator cap when he realized he was not alone. He straightened up and turned, almost bumping his head on the edge of the hood.

The fed—the one who had snooped through his stacks of books and papers while the others grabbed his computers and digital media—stood directly behind him. The man wore wrinkled trousers, a rumpled knit shirt with a collar that was unbuttoned at the neck. It took Cy a moment to remember his name.

"Hello, Special Agent Hardin. I did not see you coming."

"That's good. It means I haven't lost my edge," Lee Hardin said with a lopsided grin. "I'm impressed. You remembered my name after all this time."

"You left your card," Cy reminded him. "You were the only one who gave me your cell number."

"Are you having car trouble there?" Special Agent Hardin asked, changing the subject.

"Appears that way," said Cy, striving to sound casual. "I don't think it is that bad."

"What seems to be the problem? Maybe I can help."

"I doubt you want to get your clothes dirty on this old car. Besides, I think it might just be low on fluids or something."

"What makes you think that?"

"The Check Engine light keeps coming on. I did not want to drive it all the way home and risk having a major break-down that would cost a lot of money. So, I decided to leave it here and come back with some oil and a jug to haul water."

Lee Hardin stepped forward and looked into the open radiator.

"Water level looks good. Have you checked the oil yet?"

"If you have been watching me for any length of time, then you already know I haven't." Cy said, his voice edged with irritation. As soon as Hardin broke into his sideways grin again Cy realized he had made a mistake by letting his annoyance show.

"I was just getting ready to," Cy mumbled.

Cy searched until he located the dip stick. He pulled it out and checked it. Lee Hardin stepped forward and also looked.

"Looks okay from here," Hardin commented. "Of course, you know that to do it right, you really should wipe it clean with a rag and dip it again."

"Well, I did not bring a rag, and I really do not want to wipe it on my clothes. I think it is safe to assume there is enough oil in the car after all."

"Then what do you think was the problem?" asked Special Agent Hardin, pointedly.

Cy looked him full in the face. He could tell the fed was baiting him. He took a deep breath.

"I am not a car mechanic, so I do not know for sure. Maybe it is the car's computer that is broken. I hear it happens a lot in these older cars. The computer says there is something wrong with the engine. But after people spend thousands of dollars trying to find out what it is, it turns out that the only thing broken is the computer."

Lee Hardin's laugh was genuine.

"Well, you seem to be the computer whiz-kid, from what I hear," Hardin said with a hint of sarcasm. "Maybe you can fix it."

"Except I do not work with those kinds of computers," said Cy, refusing to get riled up. "I am a math and physics major. I tutor some students who plan to become engineers. Some of them may learn how to fix the computerized systems in cars, but not me."

"I see. So, it looks like you are all set to take your car back home. Of course, this whole situation leaves me with a big question mark in my brain."

"I am sorry if you remain puzzled, Special Agent Hardin," Cy said, struggling to keep the sarcasm out of his voice. "But I really should get back now that it appears the car is okay to drive home."

"The big question mark is this," Hardin continued as if he had not heard Cy. "Why is it here in the first place? I've heard a lot about you but nothing to lead me to believe you're an outdoorsman."

"Well, I guess you learn something new every day," said Cy flippantly. Then more seriously, he asked, "Of all the things you have heard about me, did anyone tell you I am interested in astronomy and that I just completed an advanced class in astronomy this last semester?"

"It was mentioned, yes."

"I came up here with my telescope. It is too hard to see the stars clearly in town with all the street and building lights. I was studying Mars and Jupiter. I was hoping to see some auroras, too. They should be pretty strong this year."

"Auroras, huh?" said Hardin. "You mean like the northern lights?"

"Yes, but when there is a solar high like there is this year, they sometimes can be seen further south. Although they are usually seen more around the spring and fall equinoxes, I was hoping that by getting up high and losing the city lights I might get a glimpse of an aurora."

"Any luck?"

"I saw some threads of light far to the north, but it was hard to tell."

"So, is that what you were doing up on that mountain yesterday? The one where Eddie Burrows disappeared? Setting up your telescope to look for auroras?"

Cy froze and stared at Hardin. How did the man know he was on Dead Man's Drop Mountain yesterday? He watched the lopsided grin appear on the agent's face. Cy knew he had to be very careful.

"You said you can see these auroras best during the spring and autumn equinoxes," the agent continued. "So, were you up on that mountain with your telescope looking for auroras over Spring Break when Edward Burrows and his fiancée were up there?"

Cy took a deep breath and slowly let it out.

"Agent Hardin, have you read everything the local sheriff's office had in their files on the Eddie Burrow's case about me, including everything that took place before the FBI became involved?"

"Yep," Hardin responded, watching Cy closely.

"Then you know that I was nowhere near that mountain or any mountain the week Eddie disappeared," Cy said. "I was working on a big semester project for Advanced Astronomy. I was on or near the campus all week, up until the time I *voluntarily* went to the detectives with a text message Eddie sent to me. They have a record of where I was every day because I have to use a tap card to get in and out of my department building and the library when school is officially closed. They even found security video of me eating at one of the local food joints that day about the time they estimate Eddie disappeared."

"Pretty defensive about all this, aren't ya Cy?"

"What do you expect?" retorted Cy bitterly. "I was nowhere near Eddie when he disappeared. When I became aware he was gone, I tried to help. What I got for my efforts was to have my wrist screen, tablet, slab computer and most of my digital records confiscated—*stolen*—by the very people that are supposed to protect the public from theft. People like you, Special Agent Hardin."

"I can understand why you are unhappy about that, Cy. Unfortunately, it was all legal and determined to be a necessary part of the investigation so we can solve the case."

"Well, they should have gotten everything they need off of my equipment long ago," snapped Cy. "They could have made copies of my hard drive, flash drives and all my media and had all the information they need so they could return my stuff to me. Instead they kept it, forcing me to use my old-and-slow piece-of-junk notebook. I also have to pay off my old cell contract while at the same time I have to pay for a new service so I can have a phone. It is theft, no matter how you want to spin it, Special Agent Hardin. And you want to know why some people, like me now, do not want to help law enforcement?"

"You will get your things back after it is no longer considered possible evidence in the case," said Special Agent Hardin quietly.

"Sure," Cy said with a grimace. "By then, everything will be obsolete. I had to finish my classes without my tablet for my textbooks. You know, it would have been one thing if taking my stuff had helped Eddie. Instead, it only made things worse for him. So why are you here? Are you going to take more of my stuff as 'evidence'?"

"Is there a reason why I should want to take more of your stuff for evidence, Cy?"

"No reason I know of. I came forward because I want to help find Eddie. I just do not like losing what I need in order to do so."

Cy looked off into the distance. He felt Hardin study him in silence. He willed himself to calm down, even though he felt anything but calm inside. He hoped Hardin had not caught what he said about how law enforcement taking his things had made it harder for him to find Eddie because he was not sure how the suit would interpret that. Cy looked back at Lee Hardin, expecting to see his smirky grin again. Instead, the man wore a thoughtful expression.

"Sounds to me," Lee Hardin started slowly, "like you are not as concerned about us having your digital information as you are that we took your equipment and information so you no longer have it for your work."

"That is about the size of it. I keep trying to tell you people I am not trying to hide anything."

"If that's the case, then maybe you could give me some information to clear up a few questions I have."

"Sure, why not. It does seem a little funny to me, though, that I have not seen you for over two months, not since you and the others came and cleaned out my apartment. Now, all of a sudden, you show up in a campground parking lot to ask me a bunch of questions."

"Well, that is part of what I have questions about, Cy," the special agent said casually. "To answer a question for you, the reason I have not been around is that not long after I was at your place, I was sent out of area on a temporary assignment. When I got back a few days ago, I find out that other than the lab techs, no one has done much on this case. Not really giving up on Edward Burrows, mind you, but after not finding anything following the initial search, other priorities got in the way."

The manner of speech Special Agent Hardin had slipped into reminded Cy of his one grandfather who liked to tell tall tales. His grandpa moved his stories along at a leisurely pace, drawing out his listeners so that they must wait in anticipation for the end. Sometimes his grandpa's tales were riddles. Cy knew this grandfather liked to watch him to see how long it took for him to understand where the story was going. It was all in fun.

Cy knew Lee Hardin was leading up to something, but it was not all in fun. Cy forced himself to listen closely. He knew he had to pay attention to what the man was really saying. He braced himself inside so he would not over-react or respond in a manner to give this man a reason to suspect him of any wrongdoing.

"So, I pull out my notebook," Hardin said, as he slipped the bound journal with the leather cover from his shirt pocket. "Now see, they call those portable computers notebooks still, don't they? But to me, this is a notebook. Pen to paper, bound and stitched. Those high-tech types like you that I work with—well, maybe not as good as you can be or will be someday—they like those digital recorders on their cell phones to take their notes. Some of them wear them on their wrists and walk around talking into them like they think they are Dick Tracy or something. But, then, maybe you're too young to know about Dick Tracy."

"I am aware of the cartoon character named Dick Tracy. When my parents bought me my first wrist screen, my grandparents were quick to comment about him."

"That's good. Then you know what I'm talking about. But my point is, digital recordings can be altered and corrupted. You know all about that, though, don't you? You probably know how to do it."

Cy sensed that the fed watched him closely for a reaction. Cy offered no indication that he agreed or disagreed.

"On the other hand," continued Hardin as he waved the bound journal, "these babies have saved my bacon more than once. They are a permanent record of my notes, dated and initialed in the order taken. The pages are stitched together so I can't add a page or tear one out without it being noticeable. If it has to, my notes hold up in court, no problem. Right here in my pocket, handy as any cell phone. As long as I don't let my pen run out of ink, I'm good to go."

Hardin paused and looked around the campground parking lot. Still Cy refused to move.

"So, when I get back and find out no one was actively working on the Burrows case, I decide to catch myself up on the investigation. You know, see what developed while I was gone. The boss thinks other projects have more priority, so he puts me off about it. Since I have no family at home and nothing much else to do on weekends, I decide to drive around a little on my own time, just to get a feel for things again. Yesterday, I came to see the mountain to see if it had anything to tell me. I had no intention of climbing up to where Burrows disappeared, mind you."

Cy instantly felt himself tense up, but he forced himself to appear calm. Lee Hardin was by the mountain yesterday, the same day he and Marty went for their hike. Did he see Cy's car? The FBI special agent's next words answered some of his worst fears.

"Well, the mountain told me quite a few things, Cy," Hardin said in his rambling style so opposite from his intense look that bored into Cy. "I saw a car parked at the base of the mountain. Of course, I wondered why it was there, especially since the forest service has fenced off that part of the mountain to keep people away from where those kids disappeared."

Cy's jaw involuntarily clinched. Special Agent Hardin said "kids." As far as Cy knew, he had only discussed Eddie Burrows with the feds and the local detectives before them. Did Lee Hardin know about the other girl that disappeared from the same place last year? Was he trying to build a case against Cy for everyone who vanished in these mountains without a trace?

"So, I called the plates in. Don't have all that many buddies in the Bureau anymore, but the one I needed worked dispatch yesterday. Guess who the license plate came back to Cy? You!"

Lee Hardin paused and studied Cy intently. Cy shrugged, his eyes avoiding the intense stare.

"That all you got to say, Cy?" the Hardin pressed him. "Just a shrug? What were you doing there yesterday?"

"The mountain calls me, too," Cy responded carefully, turning to look Lee Hardin full in the face. "I still think about Eddie quite often. He started as my tutoring student but we became pretty close friends. I miss him. I was up this way anyway, so I decided to go to the mountain and walk around."

"You willing to say that on a lie detector test, Cy?"

"Sure, if you need me to."

Cy watched Hardin consider his response. The special agent pursed his lips and nodded.

It was all true, thought Cy. It was not the complete truth, but it was true. He did not dare tell the agent everything, not with Marty gone and depending on him to help her get back home. Cy wondered how long Hardin watched his car. Did he see him and Marty start up the mountain together? Did he see him come back without her?

Relief flooded over Cy as the fed continued.

"Well, then my curiosity kicks in about you. So, with nothing better to do today, I decide to keep an eye on your place. Sure enough, this morning you climb in this car here, the one you say you have mechanical difficulty with, and I follow you as you drive it here to the parking lot. Then I watch as you lock it up, walk over to another car and punch in a security code like the other car is yours and you drive it away. I follow you to a house where you park it in the drive, lock it up and walk home.

"So I check my notebook here," Special Agent Hardin said as he waved the pocket journal in his hand, "and sure enough, the address turns out to be for one of your tutoring students, Martha Clark. I run the plates on the car. Turns out it comes back that it belongs to the same person. I go to the door, but no one is home."

Lee Hardin put the journal back in his pocket and folded his arms.

"So, I catch up with you and follow you the rest of the way home," continues Hardin. "What do you have to say about that, Cy?"

"If you were following me, you could have offered me a ride home. It was a long walk and hot, too. I could have used a lift."

"You got a cell phone, Cy. Why didn't you call your friend who brought you up here to come pick you up?"

"He is not really my friend. He is another teacher's assistant in the Physics department. We are not friends enough for me to feel comfortable asking him to come pick me up from Marty's house. Besides, when I started, I did not think it was that far to walk or that I would get so hot. I did need a ride to come get my car here at the campground. He agreed to bring me out here in exchange for gas and lunch money, which was cheaper than a taxi."

"Okay," said Lee Hardin slowly. "Then what's all this dog-and-pony show about you having car trouble?"

Cy shook his head.

"It was stupid, I guess, but he really did not want to help me at first. I gave him the mechanical problems sob story so he would give me a ride—that and the money. Since I had the oil along and a jug to haul water, I decided I might as well check things out while I was here. I do have trouble with the Check Engine light, just like I told you."

Lee Hardin pursed his lips, never taking his eyes off Cy.

"So, where is your girlfriend?"

"What girlfriend?" Cy answered, surprised. "I don't have a girlfriend."

"What about Martha Clark?"

"Oh, you mean Marty? We're friends, but we are not boyfriend-girlfriend or anything like that."

"You unlocked her car like it was your own and drove it to her house. You do that for just anyone?" the special agent pressed.

"I do if that person is my friend and asks me to it as a favor," Cy said carefully.

"You still have not answered my question. Where is your friend, Martha Clark?"

"When she asked me to drive her car to her house, she was back east."

Lee Hardin twirled his hand in a circle.

"Back east? Back east is a big place. Where back east?"

"Western Pennsylvania."

"Western Pennsylvania?" a surprised Lee Hardin asked, shaking his head in disbelief. "According to her mother, she went hiking this weekend with friends, one of them being you, Cy, at this very campground."

"We did go hiking," Cy said. "The whole group of friends that she invited went on a day-hike Friday. After the campfire, everyone but me went home. I was the only one who stayed over until Saturday."

"To look for auroras through your telescope with no one around to bother you," Hardin concluded.

"It was not exactly like that. I set the telescope up early on Friday and invited everyone to take a look. Most were not that interested. But, yeah, it was pretty great to study the night sky after everyone left. It was quiet and dark enough to see more stars than are usually visible."

"Did Martha Clark leave with everyone else?"

"Yes, as far as I know. At least she left my campsite with everyone else."

"But you stayed over and that is why you were still in the area yesterday when you decided to drive up to the mountain where Eddie disappeared."

It was a statement, not a question. Cy nodded in agreement.

"Did you see her car in the parking lot the next morning when you left?"

"Yes."

"What did you think when you saw it was still there?"

"I assumed she went with a friend and left it here, intending to come and get it later," Cy said carefully, knowing it was a stretch of the truth. He was the friend.

"Her folks say she is supposed to leave on her tour to go back east later in the week," Hardin said. "Until then, she is supposed to be at her house. They said nothing about her going to Pennsylvania this weekend. And you have no idea why she ended up there?"

"No, not really. I had no idea she was going. I found out where she is when she sent me a text."

That last statement was definitely true.

Cy almost sighed with relief when Special Agent Hardin spoke again.

"Okay, Kid, good luck in getting your car home without any mechanical problems. You have my number if you think of anything you think I need to know."

Cy nodded to the fed, forcing himself to appear relaxed as the man turned and walked back to his truck.

Cy would have felt happy at the man's departure except he was too annoyed. The reason why the special agent showed up to question him was bad enough, but that was not caused Cy's face to grow hot with anger as he watched the fed saunter back to his truck.

Cy hated it when people called him "Kid."

For years Cy had been so much younger and usually smaller than the other students in his classes. Too many times, when the other students, or even a few teachers, could not outthink him, they resorted to belittling him. A favorite method was to call him "Kid," to rub it in that he was younger and smaller. It set him apart from everyone, as if to say he did not quite belong.

Cy decided that Lee Hardin's remark was intended to keep Cy off-balance. He refused to let it work on him. He wriggled his shoulders to symbolically shrug off his annoyance.

Mostly, Cy hoped Hardin was satisfied that Marty was okay and there was no reason to search for her. He also hoped Hardin would not question the rest of Marty's friends who went on the hike. Cy suspected that Marty's decision to return the following day, yesterday, was a last-minute impulse that only she and Cy knew about.

But, he did not know that for sure.

CHAPTER 15

The next morning, Marty climbed on top of the rocks that had sheltered her through the night. The temperature was already climbing. She ignored her thirst because she knew she must be very conservative about how much water she drank. Assuming she arrived back on Dead Man's Drop at noon, she still needed enough water to last her while she hiked down to the road.

Marty stood on top of the rock where she first regained consciousness. She had everything packed into her daypack which rested on her shoulders. Her hat was secured tightly to her head. She slowly turned in a circle in an effort to absorb the beauty of her surroundings. She studied the emerald garden created by the sun shining through the trees. She said a silent farewell to the mountain.

She was ready.

The sun was overhead. Marty took a deep breath and briefly closed her eyes while she wished herself luck. She pressed the speed-call for Cy's cell number.

Nothing happened.

She tried again.

Still nothing.

Marty gulped air as the panic seized her. Why was it not working? Why was she not going back home? Was she really stuck here? Was she going to be forced to travel through this unfamiliar forest alone with no one she knew waiting for her at the end of her journey?

Stay calm!

Being careful to not lose her footing due to the added weight of the daypack on her back, she climbed back down from the top of the rocks. Next to the hollow in the rocks where she had spent the night, she hugged the stone formation that formed a wall on that part of the mountain. She positioned her wrist screen in what little shadow was available at the noon hour in order to see the screen clearly. She went through her call memory. It showed the failed call she had made to Cy the previous day, but nothing since.

Marty was not sure what she did wrong. She decided she must have been so excited about getting back home that she had been in too big of a hurry and missed a step. Still in the shadow of the rock, she slowly tapped the speed-call button on the touch screen to call Cy. She carefully pressed the send button.

The tingling sensation traveled up her arm as the swirling cocoon of light enveloped her.

***

Cy waited for Marty by the cliff at Dead Man's Drop for over three hours. Even though he expected Marty to return to the top of the boulders, he could not bring himself to stand on the outcrop itself. He sat on a rock further down from the crest where he had an unobstructed view. He had hoped that she would return to the same location. However, the longer he waited, the more his doubts grew. It was not going to be that easy after all. He could not quell his disappointment.

Along with working at solving the physics involved, he had also tried to better prepare himself on a personal level. After he had returned to town with his car, he had gone shopping. He invested in a good pair of hiking boots. He had plastered bandages on his feet in every location where he thought he might get blisters. In addition, he wore two pairs of socks. Yet, that afternoon as he sat at the top of the mountain, he knew without looking that his feet would be raw in spots by the time he got home.

He wore a new pair of stone-washed blue Levi's he had purchased that morning. On top he wore a long-sleeved off-white cotton shirt he had found in the back of his closet.

On his head Cy wore the hat Marty had loaned him. He knew Marty would comment on it. He practiced the words he would say when he handed it back to her. He hoped she would find his quip humorous.

He took a sip of water from one of his two bottles topped with sports caps while he double-checked the analog watch on his wrist. In his mind, he calculated the range of time in which the sun was overhead in June back in Pennsylvania.

Cy looked to the west. There was no sign of a thunderstorm that day in the Colorado Rockies. That worried him. He did not know whether or not a key element of success was having a thunderstorm with its attendant electrical charge close by. Then again, there was no electrical storm when Eddie disappeared.

He knew the sunspot activity was high. All over the internet the radio buffs were commenting about it. He hoped it meant that there was enough of an electrical charge in the electromagnetic field surrounding the earth for her to get back.

He checked his BlackSlab. It was on, ready for its signal to pull her back to him. It was only a theory, but since the cell technology seemed to be the key to the disappearances, he hoped that the radio waves moving between the cell towers was a means of helping Marty travel back to Dead Man's Drop Mountain. Even if she was transported back somewhere in the area, she could contact him to come get her as long as she was in the current time period.

He realized he should have warned her to text him if she ended up somewhere other than Dead Man's Drop Cliff. If she tried to call him, she might be transported away again.

There were so many factors to consider. There were so many things that could go wrong. There was too much he still did not know.

Cy waited until the sun began to sink towards the western horizon. No Marty. He checked his cell. There were no texts or missed calls.

Cy decided it was time to leave the mountain and drive his car away before the rangers made their nighttime rounds. They would spot it parked on the side road even if people driving along the main highway did not see it. He did not want to be caught hiking in the restricted area.

Then there was the other problem: Mr. FBI Special Agent Lee Hardin. Cy hoped that the man was not going to start following him full-time. He knew if Hardin saw him by the mountain again, there would be more questions. For some of them, he did not have answers.

The only thing he knew for sure was that he had to stay out of jail and under the radar of suspicion in order to help Marty.

CHAPTER 16

About the point that Lee Hardin was desperately wishing that he had brought more water, he saw Cy hike back down the mountain towards his car.

After the scene in the campground parking lot with Cy, Hardin decided to squeeze in more surveillance time on him. He left Granite Point before Cy did and went home to change into more comfortable clothes. Then he had half-heartedly turned on the television to see what it had to offer that afternoon. While he had flipped through the program guide, his mind mulled over his conversation with Cy. There was no ball game on that afternoon and none of the other programming held his interest. That was when he decided to check on the kid to see if he made it back to his apartment.

Hardin had swung by Cy's apartment building. The Civic was in its assigned slot. Hardin searched the street for the right parking space to keep an eye on both the entrance to the complex and the parking area. On the seat next to him was his lunch—a chicken box meal and a bottle of water. Since the university was not open Sundays, Hardin did not expect the kid to leave unless he went to the internet café. He was surprised when, as soon as he shifted his truck into park, he saw the kid with half of a sandwich clutched in his mouth come barreling out the side door of his apartment building towards the parking stalls.

Instead of the multi-pocketed travel shorts and beat up slip-on shoes Hardin had seen the kid wear earlier that day, Cy was dressed in blue jeans and what appeared to be new hiking boots. He had a backpack tossed over the shoulder of a long-sleeve shirt rather than the smaller shoulder pack most students used to carry their slabs and loose papers. Hardin had thought to himself that except for the goofy hat he wore, Cy was dressed like a regular guy for a change.

It did occur to Hardin that it was too hot for a long-sleeve shirt. He had wondered what the special occasion was.

Hardin had already figured out that the kid was smart, but not necessarily alert to his surroundings. Still, he followed Cy carefully, staying far enough back to not draw the kid's attention. Not long after Cy left the city, Hardin realized the kid was driving to either the campground or the mountain leading to the cliff at Dead Man's Drop. There was no need to take any chances that Cy would notice that he was being followed. Hardin dropped far enough back so that in case Cy looked in his rear-view mirror, his truck was not visible.

Sure enough, Cy drove past the campground until he came to the mountain. The kid did not park in the same spot he had the day before. Instead, he pulled into a dirt fire access road and stopped several hundred yards from the main highway.

It was a bit tricky for Hardin to find a place where he could park without being seen but he managed it. He was far enough away that he had to use the field glasses he kept in the glove compartment. He watched Cy start up the mountain.

Hardin sat there for hours waiting for Cy to come back down. He finished his chicken meal, sipped on his water, reviewed the notes in his journal, and wished he had brought more water.

When Cy returned to his car, Lee Hardin studied him carefully through the binoculars. He finally realized what was so noteworthy about Cy's appearance.

When Cy had started up the mountain, he had walked with a spring in his step. His body language spoke of someone who was happy and enthusiastic. Coming back down the mountain, it was an entirely different story. Something had happened that involved more than heat, fatigue and blisters because of the new hiking boots.

The kid looks like he just lost his girlfriend or his favorite dog.

That is when Lee Hardin realized his hunch was right. There was something more going on with the kid than what the case file showed. Cyrus Riverton, math and physics genius, required watching.

CHAPTER 17

Marty shook her head to clear it as she sat up and looked around. The first thing she realized was that she was not back in Colorado. The trees were wrong. She fought back tears of disappointment.

The damp rocks reflected evidence of a recent rainstorm. Overhead, the low ceiling of gray clouds that had produced the shower was thinning and moving across the sky. Marty stood and pulled the knife with the compass from her jeans pocket. The clouds were moving to the east in a slightly southerly direction.

Marty slowly turned in a full circle, surveying her new surroundings. Mostly she saw treetops aflame with the autumn colors of orange and brown. She guessed that there was a valley to the east. She could not see much because of the haze from the storm that clung to the treetops like thick cobwebs.

After walking around the cluster of boulders, she found a jumble of smaller rocks that she used as a staircase to climb to the bottom. She walked away from the stone formation as far as she could and looked back. The tan and gray stones seemed to have deep fissures that created narrow and dark crevices. It was as though some giant hand had set them on top of the mountain, stood them on end and then gathered them together like a cluster of pick-up sticks.

As the clouds thinned and the sky lightened, Marty took a holo of the boulder formation with trees in the background. She sent it to Cy.

Then she shook her head in frustration. It was too early in the day. He probably could not receive it. She would send it again that night. She took a regular picture in case they transmitted better than the holos.

Where am I now? Marty was almost positive it was not the Rocky Mountains. It was more like the mountain she just left. However, she definitely was not on the same peak. As for the season, she was positive it was later in the year. Was it the same year as the one when she met Green Corn?

Marty knew she had a few hours of daylight left. Her battery was low again. She set her wrist screen in the soft sunlight to recharge. The earliest she could expect to successfully contact Cy was that night. The soonest she could try again to get back to Colorado and her own era was tomorrow at noon. Until then, she needed to make a camp for the night.

Concerned that another storm might come through, she inspected the crevices to see if one offered good protection from the rain. She spotted what looked like a cave. Marty noticed faint traces of ash in the ground close to the entrance. The tall, narrow cave had been used before. One particular flat-sided rock close to the opening looked like it had served as a wind deflector for fires in the past. Towards the back of the fissure, there was a deep and narrow pocket that was the right size for her to stash her daypack.

While scavenging for wood, Marty also searched for berries and other edible plants, preferably juicy plants, to supplement the remaining partial lunch she planned to eat later. Since her bottle was only half full, water was still an issue. She knew she must conserve until she was home or found a spring or a stream. She did not dare wander far for fear of stumbling upon people. Before she met up with anyone, she first wanted to be able to observe them to see if they were friendly or hostile.

She took inventory of the food in her daypack. She still had two energy bars, two packets of trail mix, the package of jerky and the rest of the lunch she had packed. Her resources were dwindling.

Marty decided on a plan. If she could not get home by tomorrow, she would hike down to the valley to the east to search for water and maybe someone to help her. A lot depended, though, on what Cy had to say tonight.

Once she set up her camp, discouragement and loneliness descended upon Marty. She sat on one of the rocks in the weak afternoon sun and held her wrist screen. While bent over with her elbows propped on her knees, she used both of her hands to read through the text messages she had saved.

Some were received before her hike with Cy. They seemed like they were from so long ago. They struck her as terribly insignificant. She devoured the more recent ones between her and Cy. They kept her from feeling completely alone and abandoned. Now that she was away from Green Corn's time, she found the historical information Cy had sent her about Green Corn's era more interesting.

Before the sun completely set, she climbed back on top of the rocks and looked to the east. The haze had lifted and she could see the valley more clearly. Although she could not see buildings among the trees, there were patches of cultivated fields. A few plumes of smoke floated heavenward. Marty took a picture.

The approaching darkness brought out the mosquitoes which swarmed around her. Marty put on her jacket. She found a cylinder of fibrous fire-starter in her survival kit and pulled it in half. She set her laser to intense beam to focus the heat on the fire-starter. Within a few seconds, it burst into a small flame. She watched it spread, slowly drying out the surrounding wood as the kindling burned. Even though she smeared mosquito repellent on her exposed skin, Marty hoped the smoke would keep most of the mosquitoes away. She held her hands to the flames to ward off the chill. She hoped it did not get too cold before morning since she had not come prepared for cold weather camping. She ate the last of the lunch she had packed as she watched the dusk turn to full night.

Marty donned her poncho and shook the emergency solar blanket out of its folds. She squirmed to find a comfortable position free of small rocks and twigs that was still close to the fire. Her wrist screen was once more firmly strapped to her arm where it could be protected by her jacket sleeve.

Marty flipped open her Sun Access. The dual screens glowed like a beacon in the dark. Marty decided to first contact her family. She switched to voice recognition mode but discovered it did not work. She carefully tapped the onscreen keys to use proper grammar and spelling since she knew her mom disliked reading texting lingo.

Dear mom and dad. Having fun. I hope you are having fun in California. Wish I was there but looking forward to my tour. Will text again soon. Love Marty

Marty shot her message to her mother's cell number. *That was trite and non-detailed enough.*

Marty did not want to think what their reaction would be if her parents knew what was really going on. She tapped out her next text to Cy.

Uno by now I did not go to dead mans drop im not on same mtn its very humid leaves with fall colors im in a rock cave in mtns with a valley east of here will send pix

Marty found the two pictures she had saved from earlier in the day to send to Cy since she was not sure if the holo made it through the first time. Before she finished attaching them to a new text message, she received a response from Cy.

Im so disappointed u did not get back home. If hot n humid fall colors n mtns u could b anywhere in eastern no America or any continent with deciduous trees. R u ok?

Marty shook her head. It was just like Cy to get a little bit of information and then shift his brain into analysis mode. She only hoped that he would be able to identify her new location like he had the day before. She responded.

Im ok so far dont see any people yet but at least I no its not dinosaur days because there has been a fire before by my cave did u get holo do uno y I didnt get back home?

Not long afterwards, she heard the text tone.

No holo. No thunderstorm in mtns today n I dont no if thats y u didnt make it back here or not. Dont no what went wrong. Working on it. What kind of trees n rocks r there?

Not many evergreen trees mostly broad leaves kinda like where I was before I picked berries didnt take geology so rocks r rocks to me but not like in Colorado will send pix

Marty sent the pictures she had taken earlier and waited.

Try to find people maybe get a pic if not modern times. Your car is already home but FBI wants to no where u r. If u r back in 2024 I will come n get u wherever u r

Uno I will call u if im back in 2024 but nothing works on my screen so I dont think so thanks for bringing my car home what did u tell fbi

I said u r in western PA. The fed says u leave on your trip end of this week

I may not b in western pa now do u no where I am btw I do leave on my trip Thursday morning early what else can I tell u to help u get me home

Got pix. Donno where u r but will check. U look for weather n houses n auroras at nite. U r my bff. Im so sorry I got u into this mess. Tty tomorrow

Marty felt her face stretch with a big smile. Good old Cy. He was always so serious and responsible. He seemed awkward and aloof most of the time at home. She suspected he never would have told her to her face that he considered her his best friend forever. Yet, he felt safe saying it to her in a text message while she was far away. She hoped he meant it. No matter what, she knew he would not give up on her. She sent another message, hoping she could catch him before he turned his cell off or went out of range to receive her text.

.

This not your fault its mine I shud have listened to u at dead mans drop but I didnt believe people cud disappear in thin air til now

.

Comforting warmth descended on Marty as she read Cy's reply.

.

Not your fault but mine. I should have told u everything sooner. I should have trusted u

.

Thanx for all u r doing to help me if I c auroras tonite I will text asap if not ttyl u r still my bff :)m

.

Marty wrapped her wrist screen in the bandanna and put it in the padded pocket. She moved to sit on the rock that reflected the heat from the small fire back into her cave. The warmth of the fire felt good on her back. With relief, she realized that the mosquitoes were gone for the night. She studied the night sky. The moon faded out the stars closest to its light while other stars further away twinkled brightly. As she felt the cold night air chill her legs, she knew it was time to settle next to the fire and try to sleep. She moved to the space between the fire and the high rocks of her cave, added more wood to the flames and wrapped the solar blanket around as much of her as it would cover. The fire kept her company until she fell asleep.

***

Marty's eyes popped open. Something was different about the night sky. She rummaged in her pack until she found her flashlight. The beam played across the rocky stairway as she climbed to the top of the stone formation so she could see the sky more clearly.

Her mouth dropped open in awe. To the north, colorful sheer draperies of pink and green light shimmered in waves across the northern sky.

Marty stumbled down to her cave and pulled her wrist screen from the zippered pocket. She then climbed back up on the rocks and found a spot with a clear view of the incredible scene. She snapped several pictures and saved them. She found the one she liked best and sent it to Cy with a text.

.

Sending u a pic of northern sky most impre site ive ever seen :) yes I c auroras I hope that helps tty tomorrow nite :)m

.

She hoped he would get it that night.

Marty did not know why, but the sight of the aurora lifted her spirits.

95

CHAPTER 18

Cy yawned and rubbed his eyes with the palms of his hands. He decided to call it a day. He knew he promised his physics professor he would finish the summer project by the first of July. He struggled to stay interested in it, but his mind kept wandering back to Marty. The stress of needing to focus on both was getting to him. He plugged his BlackSlab into its charger. That was when he noticed the icon telling him there was text message waiting for him. He wondered why he had not heard the tone announcing its arrival.

The picture that downloaded on his screen was dark and grainy, but he could tell there was something in the sky. Then he smiled as he read Marty's text.

Yes, Marty, that definitely helps, he thought. The presence of an aurora narrowed down the possible locations and years in which she was trapped. Most likely, she was in the more northerly latitudes during the months of a solar cycle high.

Cy was aware that before the solar cycle that peaked in 1894, there were no records of the months and years of the solar cycle highs. He only knew when the cycles began and ended, with Solar Cycle 1 starting in 1755 A.D. By tracking the years and months the known peaks had occurred after the beginning of each cycle from March of 1890 to present, he could extrapolate the information to figure out the probable peaks for the century and a half before then.

But he was too mentally exhausted to work on it right then. He promised himself that at the first opportunity in the morning he would go back over his notes on auroras and solar cycle activity. In addition, he needed to check his websites to stay up-to-date on what was happening in the current cycle.

Cy shuddered as he remembered that Marty had come in contact with a woman who was part of a frustrated tribe of Native Americans who were growing increasingly hostile to the British invading their lands and driving them west. If Marty had met one of the men first, she may not have escaped. He hoped Marty came forward in time, not back. He hoped that she could find someone in this new era who would tell her the date and her location. He did not know yet how much it mattered knowing that information. In case it proved to be a key factor to getting her back, he wanted to know.

Most importantly, though, he wanted her to stay safe.

CHAPTER 19

As she woke up the following morning, Marty rubbed her shoulder where it had pressed against the hard rock. She felt the chill of the autumn air and was grateful for the reflective emergency blanket she had packed. The fire was mostly dead. She used some of the left-over tinder she had saved from the night before to get it started again.

Marty kept the fire small, just enough to warm her hands as she ate one of her fruit and nut packs for breakfast. She shook the water in her water bottle. Only a couple of swallows remained to wash down her food. Especially with dehydrated food, she needed more water. She knew that she must find water that morning.

As the sun rose, Marty cleaned up her camp area. She did her best to make it appear like no one had stayed there recently. She brought some more branches and twigs near the summit and scattered them under the trees so that they did not look like they had been gathered by a human. She carefully put out her fire and scattered the ash. She hoped it looked like the way she found it the night before. Unfortunately, she could still smell the soot on the rock.

Before she left, Marty once more climbed to the top of the rocks and looked to the east. The morning mist shrouding the valley below had burned off and she could see small streamers of smoke rising in the distance. It was too far for her to clearly see any details that would identify the time period.

Marty realized the smoke could mean one of two things. She was further back in time and the only way to provide heat and cook food was over a wood fire. Or, it could mean that she had landed in a resort area in fairly modern times where people went to a cabin in the woods to "rough it" and relax. Her parents told her they could remember when atomic clocks became widely available, so, if that were the case, that would explain why she still could not get any readings on her wrist screen even if she was in the twentieth century. Then again, she figured, if it were more modern times, the area would be dense with cabins.

No, she realized with a sinking heart, she was probably in an earlier era when the population was sparse.

The autumn sun dispersed the chill enough for her to shed her jacket and put it in her pack. Just in case someone should come to the mountaintop before she could get back, she decided she better move her daypack away from the cave where she spent the night.

The top of the mountain was covered with numerous rocks and crevices. After about twenty minutes of searching, Marty found what she wanted. The spot, deep in a narrow crack in the boulders, was covered with a solid granite ceiling that would protect her pack from rain. A few well-placed large rocks in front with leaves and dust scattered over them to create the appearance that they had been not been moved in years would conceal it from view.

Before she hid her pack, Marty took a few minutes to decide what to take with her. She hoped she was back in more modern times. However, if she was not, she knew explaining twenty-first century clothing was going to be a problem. She did not have a long skirt, which was the most acceptable style of clothing for women in earlier eras. Green Corn had mistaken her pants for leggings. They were too modern-looking and clung to her uncomfortably in the rising heat and humidity. She changed to her knee pants and hoped they would pass as breeches, which were worn for hundreds of years. She tied the medicine pouch to her belt in case she came across another native tribe. Her boots were too modern, but, along with her frontier blouse, they would have to do.

Hopefully, she could observe and take pictures without being seen herself.

With her mouth as dry as sawdust, Marty could no longer ignore her thirst. It did not matter if she could see what was in the valley. She had to find water. She took two water purification filters from her survival kit and screwed them into the necks of her two water bottles. She put the bottles in her detachable nylon net carrier with its wide polyester shoulder strap and draped it across her chest. She would refill them at the first stream or river she came to.

Marty also took the knife with the compass in the handle and her Sun Access. Before she wrapped her wrist screen in the bandanna and shoved it into her front pocket, she clicked a picture of her hiding place to help her find it more easily when she returned. Feeling as ready as she was going to get under the circumstances, she buried her pack behind the rock cascade.

Before Marty left, she used some leafy branches to brush away her boot prints. She tried to scatter leaves and twigs on the ground so that it looked undisturbed. That completed, she checked her compass heading and started down the southeast side of the mountain. She saw another rise to the south of where she was and hoped that between the two slopes she would find a stream that emptied into the valley below.

Marty broke into an exultant grin when she heard the sound of water splashing over rocks. Soon she saw a clear stream moving swiftly down between the two mountains. Branches from the broad-leafed trees bordering the stream arched over the water like an orange and brown tunnel, shading it. She knelt on a rock next to the stream and filled her water bottles. She drank deeply, patiently waiting for the water to trickle through the filter on her bottle. It was cool and refreshing. She refilled her bottle, checked her compass direction again and made a mental note to help her find her way back. She followed the stream down the mountain.

Marty did not know how many miles she walked before she reached the edge of the clearing. Ahead of her was a cabin with mud chinked between the squared-off logs. At the far end of the cabin she saw the top of a wide chimney made of stones. The steep roof was covered with weathered thatch that curled over the edges of the narrow eaves like fringe. She could not see any windows.

She saw no movement in the yard between the cabin and the large log barn that was off to the left and close to a field of some crop Marty did not at first recognize. After smelling the scent carried to her by a few gusts of the breeze, she recognized it as tobacco. A small field of wheat between her and the cabin had been partially harvested. Large bundles of straw were piled at the end closest to the cabin. Another field to the left of the wheat field was dotted with dried corn stalks and old vines.

Marty cautiously moved through the trees and across the field, using the clumps of cornstalks to hide her from anyone looking out of cabin. Streamers of bean vines coiled up wooden stakes. She stepped carefully to avoid tripping on the pumpkin and squash vines growing between the cornstalks.

The view from the new angle revealed two cows grazing in a pasture on the other side of the barn. It was partially fenced with a stone wall and partially with a wood rail fence. There was a smaller structure between her and the barn. She also saw a pen on the back side of the barn in which there were several pigs. That explained the strong manure smell she had detected as she moved closer to the farm.

Marty decided to creep toward the side of the barn where two large trees with thick trunks shaded both the outbuilding closest to her and the barn. She hoped she would have a better view of the front of the cabin without being seen. It seemed to her like it took an eternity to cautiously move from one hiding place to another as she worked her way forward. Finally, she stood behind the larger of the two trees.

As she peeked around the trunk, she saw that there was a small door in the long wall of the cabin, but still no windows. The fireplace covered almost the entire end of the cabin. Across the small yard there was a lean-to with what looked like a fire ring and work bench. She had not seen it earlier from the edge of the field because it had been blocked by the cabin. Beyond, between the lean-to and the cabin, towards the south, she saw a large vegetable garden close to the stream.

Marty pulled her wrist screen from her pocket, unwrapped it and quickly took pictures of the cabin and the yard. All hope that she was in more modern times evaporated. She realized that she was looking at an authentic log house from a bygone era. Her only question was, how bygone?

Marty decided she did not want to approach anyone and talk to them. In case they found her, though, she decided she better hide her boots. She remembered reading that they did not start making shoes for left and right feet until sometime in the mid-1800s. Before that, all shoes and boots were cut the same. That alone would make her boots stand out. However, unlike the smooth soles of older footwear, the soles of her boots were of a synthetic material with a distinctive tread pattern. The metal eyelets and hooks at the top for her laces also looked out of place.

Marty backed away from the trees and found a stack of hay and corn stalks behind the barn. She guessed it was feed for the animals. She wrapped her knife in one sock, and stuffed her socks in one of the boots. She definitely needed to hide the pink hat. She stuffed it into the other boot. She hid the boots and nylon carrier for her water bottles deep in the hay.

Marty tucked her bandanna in her pocket and kept the wrist screen set to picture mode in her hand. She circled around the back of the barn towards the tree on the other side with the hope that it would give her a better view of the doorway to the cabin or any activity between the cabin, the barn and the lean-to. All she needed was to take a picture of someone in period dress. Then she would slink away to her hiding place on the top of the mountain and wait until she could contact Cy.

Just as Marty reached the tree on the opposite side of the barn, she heard a dog bark. She closed her eyes and turned, pressing her back to the tree trunk.

I never even considered that there might be a dog.

Marty knew the dog would hear and smell her long before any people were aware she was there. She held her breath and hoped that the dog would think it heard a squirrel running through the trees. Maybe he would decide to ignore her after a few minutes.

The barking grew louder. Marty carefully peeked around the trunk of the tree. The dog was running straight towards her. A sturdily-built middle-aged woman followed with a quick walk, a large pitchfork gripped tightly in both hands. The woman looked like she was prepared to lance someone with it. Marty did not know what era the woman's attire belonged to. But, with the pitchfork held like a weapon and a scowl spread across the woman's face, Marty knew the woman was in no mood to welcome her with open arms.

Marty quickly powered down the wrist screen and wrapped it in the bandanna before she shoved it inside her pocket. She looked around for a hiding place, but there was nowhere to run.

CHAPTER 20

The short-haired fox terrier with fist-size brown spots scattered upon its mostly white fur barked menacingly as it rounded the tree. Marty was grateful that, although it charged a few steps, then retreated, it did not attack her.

You have always been good with dogs. Try to calm the dog. If it stops barking, maybe then the woman will decide it is a false alarm and go away.

Marty stooped forward and held her hand, palm outward, toward the dog.

"Nice doggie," Marty said in soothing tones. "Let's be friends, okay? Good dog."

The dog ignored her. It continued to bark and dance in circles.

The woman stepped around the tree with the pitchfork raised, ready to attack. She stopped about ten feet away from Marty and began to cough. Marty straightened to her full height and faced the woman. Her eyes focused on the tines of the pitchfork that were wood, not metal. However, the tines were sharpened to points and dark on the ends as if they had been held over a fire to take all the moisture out of the wood to harden them. To Marty, they looked lethal.

When the woman made no further move towards her, Marty next looked the woman in the face while trying to use her peripheral vision to guess the time period of her clothes. The skirt was made of a brown coarsely-woven material. The bodice looked like it was a vest laced in front, but it was hard for Marty to tell for sure because it was mostly covered up with a shawl of off-white knitted wool that crossed in front and tied behind her back. Underneath it all the woman wore a white gathered blouse, similar to the frontier blouse Marty had on except that it was gathered at the neck with a self-fabric cord instead of the gathers being held in place by a neckband. Around her waist she wore a leather belt with a leather pouch suspended from it. At the top of the pouch Marty saw what appeared to be oversize metal scissor handles. The woman wore pieces of leather on her stocking-clad feet that tied at her ankles with leather laces. A white fabric cap covered most of her steel gray hair. The cap was gathered all the way around about an inch from the edge with a fabric string that tied on top.

The woman snarled something at Marty in a language Marty did not understand. At the sound of his mistress's voice, the dog barked more assertively.

"Hush, hush," Marty muttered to the dog, trying to make friendly clicking noises to calm it down while her eyes never left the woman threatening her with the pitchfork.

After a moment, with no response from Marty, the woman yelled louder, "Parlez-vous Français?"

The woman turned her head to the side, coughing into the shoulder of her blouse while her eyes glared at Marty.

Marty shook her head no. It sounded to her like the woman asked her something in French.

Where am I? The only place in North America I know of where the people speak French is around Quebec.

"Do you speak English?" Marty asked in a quivering voice.

The woman straightened up and gave Marty a hard appraising look.

"Aye, the king's own English," the woman finally replied. She then leaned forward and squinted at Marty. "Ye be no boy."

"No," Marty shook her head.

"Where be yer petticoats?" the woman demanded. "Why be ye wearing breeches and toting a medicine bag like a savage? Ye been with the Mingo or the Delaware?"

The woman burst into a coughing fit that doubled her over at the waist.

"Who? Delaware is a state."

Then Marty remembered. Cy had told her the Lenni Lenape were also known as Delaware Indians.

"Aye, the Delaware be in a sorry state, split twixt east and west, but I aren't nary a bit sorry for them," said the woman as she coughed up some phlegm and spit it off to the side. "As fer the Mingo, the most backwoods Colonist to the highborn English lords on the coast knows about the Mingos. They be some of the six-nation savages moved west to the Ohio."

Marty remembered what Green Corn told her about the tribes.

"The six nations? Do you mean the Iroquois?"

The woman raised the pitchfork a few inches higher and took a step towards Marty.

"Where be ye from, lass, that ye don't know the six nations?" she demanded.

"I'm from the United States."

"What tribe of savages be the United States?"

"I've lost track of time," Marty said with a sigh, now suspecting she was somewhere in time before the American Revolution. "What is the date?"

"'Tis I shall be asking ye the questions," the woman snapped, her response punctuated with a cough. "Wherefrom do ye come? Would ye have been with some western tribe? My thoughts be atwixt that or mountain folks."

"Yes," said Marty, resigned, as she leaned back against the tree trunk. She hoped that whatever the woman had that was causing her to cough was not contagious. "I have been with some Native Americans. I think they are from the west of here."

"Humph!" the woman responded. "Native savages, ye mean, what with them joining the French and killing off good Englishmen. Must be the Shawnee. There be no problem with the Shawnee in nary a long time. We dinna have trouble with nary the tribes 'til the French refused to give back our trading post they turned to a fort. Have ye been with the Shawnee, girl?"

"I don't think so," said Marty. "They called themselves Lenni Lenape. I was not with them long."

"Humph! They be the Delaware." The woman's eyes hardened. "Be ye adopted by the savages? Might that be why ye carry one of their medicine pouches on ye?"

"No, I was not adopted," Marty stammered. "I met this one woman and we treated to become friends. She gave me this medicine bag."

The woman gave Marty a suspicious look. Marty could tell the woman did not believe her.

"Ye treat with the savages, they expect gifts from ye. What did ye give?"

Something warned Marty she should not say anything about the earrings. If this woman thought she had valuable jewelry on her, she might forcefully search her and find her wrist screen. At all costs, she had to protect her wrist screen from being discovered by this woman. She looked down while she searched for an answer, then she looked back at the woman.

"My shoes," said Marty.

The woman's eyes twitched with a calculating glint.

"Ye had shoes? Ye had cobbled shoes, not moccasins?"

Marty nodded. Her eyes followed the dog as it continued to pace between her and the woman and occasionally sounded a warning bark.

"Who be yer people?" the woman demanded. "Where might yer family hail from?"

Marty wondered how she could explain Colorado to this woman. If she was correct, and she was back in Colonial times, there was no such thing as Colorado yet. In fact, most people in the eighteenth century and before had no idea at all what lay west of the Mississippi river.

"My family lives beyond the mountains," she finally said. "I was just trying to find my way home when I came upon your farm."

The woman stood there in silence for a moment, narrowing her eyes again as she studied Marty. Then she lowered the pitchfork and turned to the dog.

"Hist!" she ordered the dog. "Hunter, stop yer howlering. She be a friend."

The dog immediately stopped and wagged its tail.

"Come," she ordered Marty, as she motioned towards the cabin with her head. "I shall be getting ye some water whilst we talk."

Marty hesitantly followed the woman to the cabin. Once inside, the woman nodded towards a bucket of water on the split log floor that was just inside the door. There was a hollowed-out gourd hanging from a wooden peg stuck between the logs of the cabin wall. Marty dipped the gourd into the bucket and took enough to satisfy her thirst.

While sipping the cool water, Marty inspected the inside of the cabin.

While the log walls looked sealed with mud from the outside, from the inside she could see that the dried mud and straw chinking had been knocked out from between the logs at about eye level at certain places on each of the three walls. It allowed some light and a faint breeze to come into the interior of the cabin. The fireplace with its dying embers dominated the fourth wall that was to the left as Marty entered the cabin. The firewood was stacked next to one side of the great open hearth. Behind the door was a small section of log wall next to the fireplace. To her right, Marty saw a ladder that went to the loft that formed the ceiling for most of the cabin. She studied the squared cross beams. Across those beams, thick planks formed the floor of the loft. Above, other squared logs were set as rafters to create a steep roof over the loft. She could see bits of thatch sticking through the cracks between the roof boards.

"Sit," the woman ordered, pointing to a stool next to the side of the fireplace wall closest to the door. "Ye can knit or darn. There be too much to be done to sit idle."

"I can darn."

To Marty, darning was incredibly old-fashioned. She knew no one at home darned socks anymore. Yet, when she had ripped a hole in her favorite sweater years ago, her grandmother had shown her how to darn the hole so that it would not unravel. Her grandmother had also shown her how to crochet and do counted cross-stitch, but Marty had never learned how to knit.

The woman handed Marty an off-white woolen stocking with a hole in the bottom. She also handed her a needle made of bone with a large hole for the yarn at one end.

"Pull ye some yarn from the top of the stocking fer the thread. Be sure ye finish it off or ye'll be knitting it back when it unravels. Then ye can darn t'other."

Marty pulled out a length of the yarn and broke it off with her fingers. She slipped the end back through the top loop, just like she would finish off a crocheted piece. She wet and twisted the yard to thread the needle.

"Have ye no cutting knife or scissors?" the woman asked, as she tried to choke back a cough.

In spite of the woman's softened attitude and her invitation to come inside the log home, Marty still did not completely trust her. She said nothing about her pocketknife that was hidden in her boot. She would not take the chance that this woman would take it away from her.

"No."

"Tsk, tsk," the woman shook her head as she knit a new stocking. Then she broke into another coughing fit.

"Mayhap do ye have herbs for chest tightness in yer pouch?" the woman asked as she started to recover.

Marty struggled to remember what Green Corn had said about the purple flower plants in her pouch. Didn't she say it was for chest illnesses? She pulled some out and showed it to the woman.

"Would these help?"

"Aye."

The woman set the herbs on a wooden trencher. In the fireplace, a black pot on a chain hung from a metal tripod. The woman took some of the dried herbs and put them in one of the gourds along with hot water from the kettle hanging over the fire. She continued working on the new stocking she was knitting and Marty returned to her darning.

After the herbs had steeped into a tea, the woman used a wooden spoon to skim the leaves out. Marty watched as the woman then poured something from a crock jar into the drink. The woman held the warm gourd in her hands and inhaled the steam from the tea between sips. After several minutes, the woman ran outdoors. Marty heard her coughing and clearing her lungs.

The terrier trotted over and sniffed Marty before settling on her feet. Marty reached down and scratched him behind the ears. She decided it would be smart to become friends with the dog the woman called Hunter. Besides, he was pretty irresistible when he wasn't snarling and barking. The warmth of the dog's body felt good on her feet in the cool interior of the cabin.

"Good boy, Hunter," Marty said softly as she petted the contented animal.

The woman returned to her stool and resumed knitting.

"What be yer name, lass?" The woman asked after a few moments.

"Martha," Marty replied, deciding to use her real name rather than her nickname.

"Maggie. Mistress Margaret Grimsby," the woman replied. "Would ye have a family name?"

"My last name is Clark."

"Mayhap, be that yer husband's name or yer father's?" Maggie pressed. "Or be ye baseborn?"

"Clark is my father's surname," Marty said, wondering what being baseborn meant and why the woman wanted to know.

"Aye, good. And where might Goody and Goodman Clark live?" Maggie pressed. "When Mr. Grimsby returns from his trading journey, he shall be helping ye get back to yer kin."

"My parents are John and Shannon Clark and they live beyond the mountains."

"Mr. Grimsby be familiar with the territory beyond the mountains."

"I appreciate the offer, but I can get back there by myself once I get my bearings. Where did you say this place is?"

Maggie narrowed her eyes as she silently studied Marty again. She struggled to stifle another coughing spurt.

"Mr. Grimsby shall be helping ye when he returns, so don't ye be worrying about trying to find yer own way," Maggie said forcefully. "Twixt the French and their savage warriors trying to take the crown's own land from us God-fearing loyal subjects and the militia keeping a lookout, the land 'tis fraught with danger. 'Tis a sorry thing. 'Taren't nary the time fer a lone lass to be taking to the trails. 'Twould be asking to be captured by the savages, 'twould. Ye surely heard about the ambushment that kilt General Braddock. Routed them out atwixt our own Fort Cumberland west of here and the Monongahela whilst he be marching against the French to take back our trading post on the forks of the Ohio. Turned it into one of their forts, they did. Now we heard they be fighting fer the fort again. Even with the far savages going back north, t'other savages'll be all astir. 'Twill require us keeping a sharp eye out.

"By the far Indians, do you mean the Iroquois?" Marty asked, hesitantly.

"Ye sure ye dinna lose yer mind afore ye found yer way here?" Maggie shook her head. "The six-nation Iroquois be British subjects. 'Tis what our lordships say, though betimes they be still friendly with the Catholic Iroquois up Canada-way and be working fer what be best fer the Iroquois. The far savages be the northern tribes that fight aside the French. Atwixt ye and me, though, I trust nary a savage whilst there be war twixt us and the French. They all be fer plundering and scalping. The six-nation tribes been friendly with us in these parts fer years, except some that went west and turned to Mingo. Even so, when they go fer scalps, especially if they get aholt of spirits first, they mightn't be particular which Colonists their trophies come by. With Mr. Grimsby away, I keep a sharp eye out, I do. It dinna be a good time fer him to go, but with tobacco and wheat being our cash crops, their dinna be nary no other choice. 'Twas a necessity they go to market, savages or no."

Marty kept her head down and focused on her darning. She had no idea when she hiked down the mountain that the area was in the middle of a war. Was it the same war Cy told her about? Was it possible that the treaty between Green Corn's people and Pennsylvania failed and the Lenni Lenape were fighting the British now? It was hot like summer when she met Green Corn but it was obviously autumn now. She had to find out exactly where she was and what year she was in so Cy could get her out of here.

"So, do you really think they might be near here?"

"Aye, might be," said Maggie. "'Twould be a necessity fer them to cross the Blue Ridge first, though. Then again, we heard the Delawares be meeting with the Quakers in Pennsylvania, 'tho Maryland be not going this time. This land be bought years ago by Lord Baltimore. 'Tis the French and the western savages we be afearing. 'Tis said years back they visited frontier folks west of here at Fort Cumberland with indescribable ravages. 'Twould be they might follow the Potomac down, but pray they don't come up the Monocacy."

"Potomac! That is the river that runs by Washington, D. C., right?" asked Marty.

Maggie gave Marty another withering look.

"Ye be talking like ye be from the wilds of New France, lass," Maggie said, shaking her head. "There be no such place. If ye be talking about that upstart George Washington who be with Braddock, his family lands be down in Virginia. His brother married in with Lord Fairfax, I heard. 'Tis why he been surveying west of the Blue Ridge afore he signed with the militia, most likely to spy out choice land fer himself. All these lands north of the Potomac be Lord Baltimore's. Word has it Washington be trying to persuade General Forbes to build his army road through Virginia, instead of Pennsylvania. 'Twould have opened the way to the Ohio. The Virginia lordships be hoping to push the savages west and sell the land to us God-fearing British Colonists.

"Aye, Washington nearly got all his men kilt," Maggie continued. "'Twas at that make-shift fort, Necessity, 'twas called, a few years afore the rout that kilt the general. I heard, though, he disguised where the general was buried so's the savages dinna be able to sneak back to scalp and ravage the body. I shall give him that. Still, Fairfax connections or no, atwixt ye and me, that one won't nary amount to much."

Marty bit her lip. She wondered if Maggie Grimsby was talking about *the* George Washington who was the Revolutionary War general, hero and first president of the United States. Marty did vaguely remember that George

Washington started as a land surveyor. She wanted very much to tell Maggie that the "upstart" George Washington did amount to something. He amounted to something big. However, she knew she could not say a word about it.

"'Twas how me and Mr. Grimsby came to be here," Mrs. Grimsby reminisced. "Lord Baltimore put out his offer in '32. One hundred acres to any single male or female atwixt 15 and 29, 'twas. Well, I was getting close to being too old, but I had me eye on Mr. Grimsby. When I heard he be claiming his 100 west of the Monocacy, I knew the way to that man's heart. I claimed mine 100 akin to his."

"Oh, so you own 100 acres of land?"

"Nay, 'tis Mr. Grimsby's land now we be married."

Maggie's statement captured Marty's attention. She wondered if Green Corn was right about married women not being able to own land. She had to find out.

"But if something happens to Mr. Grimsby and he dies, you would get your 100 acres back, wouldn't you?"

"Nary speak such a thing about Mr. Grimsby," Maggie said in a panic. Then calmer, she continued, "But, nay, 'twould go to Mr. Grimsby's nephew, though I keep me dower's third whilst I live."

"His nephew? Wouldn't your land go to your children?"

"Nay, the Lord dinna bless us with such, fer which Mr. Grimsby holds me to blame," Maggie shook her head. "'Course, I darena be saying to him he had nary a child with his first wife afore she died of the cholera. 'Twould ease the burden if there be sons to help. But, there be no sons to work the farm or claim the land when Mr. Grimsby passes."

"What about your side of the family? Would they not receive the part that is yours?"

"Nay, ye be not hearing me, girl. The land be Mr. Grimsby's to do with as he wishes long's I get my dower's third whilst I live."

"Oh," was all Marty could say. Mrs. Grimsby went from owning half the land to having only a third, and then only while she was still alive. Otherwise, her husband owned and controlled all the land. It did not sound like a good deal to Marty.

Then, hoping to keep the momentum going now that she had Maggie talking, she asked, "So, the Potomac and the Monarchy are rivers that are close to here?"

"Monocacy. 'Tis the same river Mr. Grimsby be traveling to take our wheat and tobacco to Frederick, then on the Potomac to Baltimore to find a buyer and pay the quitrents," Maggie said, shaking her head. "He shall be back afore long. And you can kick that dog out the door."

"I don't mind," said Marty. "He helps keep my feet warm."

Maggie eyed Marty's bare feet and calves and let out a sigh.

"Well, 'tis best I find ye some civilized clothes afore Mr. Grimsby returns. There be the old petticoats from when I released Annie from bond this summer past. She be no bargain, that one. Did give her the new clothes and barrel of corn the contract called fer when her indenture be done. But, dinna let her keep the old, especially when the ungrateful wench took off fer Frederick to join t'other lout of a servant we had 'til the year afore. Mr. Grimsby offered her wages to stay 'til harvest be done. She was too much in love with him, she says. Humph! Though he be a good worker, the foolish wench shall soon learn how love be fading when he be growing tired of her. 'Twas a tight spot in which Annie left me and Mr. Grimsby. 'Twere good fortune we harvested most in time fer market afore the rains turned the roads all amuck."

As Marty watched Maggie cough again, she suspected that when Maggie spoke of love fading she was talking more about her marriage than she was about the woman Annie. Maybe Mr. and Mrs. Grimsby did not love each other anymore. Was that the reason why the older woman seemed so grumpy? Or was the reason she was cranky because she was sick?

Maggie heaved a sigh as she rose from her chair and slowly climbed the ladder to the loft. While Maggie rummaged around in the loft, Marty stood and stepped deeper into the cabin. She took the wrist screen from her pocket and turned it on. She covered it with both her hands, buried it in her bent-over body and faked a cough to muffle the jingle that signaled it was powering up.

"What be that sound?"

"Um, sounded like a bird. It's just outside the cabin, I think."

"Humph!"

Marty knew Maggie was not entirely convinced, but she could not worry about that. She quickly took two pictures of the inside of the cabin. One was of the fireplace and one was of the table and bed. She hoped that the light from the door and the fireplace were bright enough that they would turn out since she did not dare use the flash.

As the older woman slowly descended the ladder, Marty positioned herself to take a picture of the front of Mrs. Grimsby's clothes below her neckline. She snapped the shot and then quickly turned the wrist screen off, wrapped it and shoved it back in her pocket just before Maggie's head cleared the loft. Maggie clutched some clothing in one arm. She seemed surprised to see that Marty had moved from the stool, but said nothing. Once she was firmly standing on the cabin floor, she tossed the clothes at Marty.

"There be her old shift and petticoats. The corset be still wearable, too, though ye be likely needing to loosen the ties." Maggie returned to her stool and resumed her knitting.

What Maggie described as a petticoat looked to Marty like a long skirt gathered at the waist with a drawstring. It was made of a coarsely-woven brown fabric. The lighter-weight shift looked like an ankle-length nightgown with a gathered neck. The corset did not look like underclothing. It was made of a fabric similar to the skirt, but had something sewn between the layers to stiffen it. There were loops in which a long cord was laced.

"Mr. Grimsby and I decided there be no need fer a gown or stomacher fer that one whilst she be working here, so wear the corset over the shift. Then be sure ye wear a shawl crost over yer front and tied in back, especially when Mr. Grimsby be about."

"I'm sorry, but I don't see a shawl."

Maggie shook her head.

"'Twas ungrateful, the wench be. Left with her old shawl as well's the new. Will have to give ye me old one. And be sure yer hair be up under yer cap when Mr. Grimsby comes home."

Marty looked at the cap that was similar to the ones she had seen in Thanksgiving pilgrim pictures. It was once white, but now had a dingy yellow-gray tint. It was frayed and stained where the rim came in contact with Annie's head. Specks in the back looked like blood that did not completely wash out. One of the ties had broken and been knotted together.

"I don't see why I need to wear the cap," said Marty, wrinkling her nose at it. "It's still warm outside and this won't do much for shading my eyes."

"'Course ye shall wear the cap!" Maggie snapped. "Paul in the Bible preaches women will cover their heads. Mr. Grimsby will not abide an immodest woman."

Marty heaved a sigh and clamped her lips together so she would not say anything that she would regret. The woman's reference to the Bible surprised her.

"Besides, 'twill keep ye from scratching yer lice and head snow in the victuals and whilst milking," Maggie mumbled.

Marty wrinkled her nose in disgust. *Head lice!* Now she understood where the dried specks of blood on the back of the cap came from. If people in the olden days did not bathe or wash their hair very often, which Marty was pretty sure was the case, then maybe wearing a head covering served more of a practical purpose than anything else.

"Ye shall be covering yer legs with her old stockings, too, soon as they be mended," Maggie continued. "Ye be darning one. Ye can mend t'other next. 'Til then, ye can wear her old foot leathers. Mr. Grimsby and I don't believe in wasting cobbled shoes fer indentured servants, so 'twill be all we have fer now. They be about wore out, but ye can use some leather scrap to mend the soles. They be good enough 'til we get snow."

"Thank you," Marty muttered as she continued to darn the sock that she now realized was intended for her. However, she did not feel very grateful. She could tell Mrs. Grimsby gave the clothes to her grudgingly. They smelled musty, like they had not been washed in years. They were worn and frayed in several places. Marty could see where someone had attempted to mend several tears. As for the stockings, she decided to not mention to Mrs. Grimsby that she planned to be far away from this place before she needed them.

The moccasins were nothing like any she had ever seen before. Unlike the ones her mother usually bought her for Christmas, these were not cut and stitched to fit her foot. They were an oval piece of leather with holes punched through the edge so that the leather could be wrapped around the foot and tied at the ankle with a lace. What a difference from the beautiful beaded moccasins Green Corn had worn.

When Marty put them on, she could tell her feet were larger than the girl who used to wear them. She wondered if the clothes would fit.

"Ye kin chop and fetch us some more kindling wood whilst I make our noon repast," Maggie said. "The shorter logs be best fer now. Bring ye longer ones fer the night. Might ye be able to do that?" There was a hint of sarcasm in the older woman's voice.

"Yes, I think so," said Marty as she forced her voice to sound cheerful. She took an impatient breath and put her head down as she walked out the door to look for a wood pile.

It is only for the day. It is only for the day.

Although Marty had occasionally helped her dad with a chainsaw, usually her dad had always taken care of chopping firewood and kindling with an ax. Marty remembered watching him do it many times. As she found the small ax and reached for some of the narrower logs, the only thing that concerned her was that she had no practical experience with that particular tool.

At first, it was harder than she thought. But once Marty got the rhythm down, she split a nice pile of kindling. When Marty returned with the firewood, She could smell corn and bacon. For the first time she saw that there was a stone oven built into the one side of the fireplace.

"'Twill be no bread 'til Mr. Grimsby returns and takes some wheat to the gristmill," said Maggie when she saw Marty eyeing the oven door. "He shall be butchering a hog, too. "T'will have some good meat on a spit and hams set aside fer winter, we shall. 'Til then, 'twill be cornmeal mush and bacon."

The woman served up the mush in wooden bowls and handed Marty a spoon made out of an animal horn. Maggie took two gourds and filled them halfway with water from a pitcher. To that she added a few drops of the liquid she had used in her tea. Marty watched her stir her drink with the spoon. She did the same and took a sip. She could taste the flavor of maple syrup in the water. The cornmeal mush with small chunks of bacon tasted wonderful. However, when she felt a piece of solid fat in her mouth, she quietly took it out and slipped it to Hunter who remained at her feet under the table.

"'Twill milk the cow afore supper and be having ash cakes and milk with maple syrup," Maggie said.

"I will happy to wash the dishes," Marty offered after the meal. She did not want to eat from dishes that were not cleaned thoroughly after Mrs. Grimsby coughed all over them.

"'Course ye shall."

"Where do you keep the dishpan and soap?"

The woman looked at Marty as though she were crazy. Then she grabbed Marty's arm and pulled her out in the yard and pointed toward the stream that flowed on the other side of the vegetable garden.

"Be ye loony? Use sand in yonder stream to scrub the food off and rinse them good," she said. Then under her breath, Maggie muttered, "Wasting good soap on washing dishes! The wench be worse'n Annie."

"May I please have at least enough soap to wash these clothes you gave me?"

"Annie dinna wear them that many weeks atwixt the last time she washed them and she took them off," Maggie snapped.

"But she did wear them since the last time they were washed. I would prefer to start wearing them clean without her body odor on them," retorted Marty, struggling to remain polite. "Otherwise, I will make do with what I have on."

Maggie huffed with impatience and shook her head. Marty heard the woman mutter while she searched for some soap, "The wench must surely be from a high-born family. Trading cobbled shoes to the savages, she does, and wanting soap fer washing dishes. Her kin shall surely pay a fine reward for getting this one back from the savages, they shall."

Maggie turned and made a shooing motion in the direction of the cabin door.

"Wash ye the pot first and bring some water fer boiling whilst ye wash the rest of the dishes," she said. "'Twill be flaking some soap in the tub in the lean-to fer the clothes. And don't be like Annie and hang them to dry on the fence by the hog pen. The fence by the garden be the cleanest."

When Marty took the pot of water to the lean-to to heat, she looked at the small chunks of soap in the wash tub. They were gray with small black specks. Then she remembered that soap used to be made from animal fat and lye from wood ashes. She picked one of the largest pieces out to use on the cap stains. She finished the dishes and returned them to the cabin.

Once the water in the pot was hot, she poured it in the wash tub over the white shift and the cap she had put in to soak. She brought another pot of cold water from the stream to heat and add to it. After she washed all the clothes and wrung them out, she hauled them to the stream to rinse them.

Marty left the clothing on the fence rails to dry. She spent the rest of the afternoon with Mrs. Grimsby gathering pumpkins from the field. Maggie showed Marty how to clean the seeds out, cut the pumpkins into rings and string them on strips of leather. To dry, they tied the leather strips to pegs wedged between the rafters and wood planks forming the inside of the cabin roof. The seeds were set aside to separate from the stringy core later.

Marty could tell Maggie was impatient with her because she did not already know how to do the task.

Marty gained a new appreciation for pumpkins when Maggie told her that they would be used for food in the winter and spring until the new garden started to produce. She knew she could not tell Maggie that in her time period, other than using pumpkins for jack-o-lanterns, her only recollection of eating pumpkin was when her mother used canned pumpkin to make pies for the holidays. And, the only way she ate pumpkin seeds was in her trail mix.

Later, Maggie milked the cows and let the cream separate from the milk. She then skimmed the cream off and put it in what Marty recognized as a butter churn that Maggie kept stored in a shaded wooden box outside the cabin.

As the sun started to set, Marty checked her clothes on the fence rails. Only the shift and the cap were dry. The heavy fabric of the petticoat and corset was still damp, as was the one wool stocking she had finished darning earlier. The other stocking she had finished darning later. So now she had one clean but damp stocking and one dirty but dry one. Since it was starting to turn cold, Marty stepped into the lean-to and put the shift on over her blouse. She decided to wait to put on the cap until Mr. Grimsby arrived.

Back in the cabin, Maggie handed her a floor-length wool cape and a shawl knitted from the same yarn as the stockings.

"I suppose ye shall freeze afore wearing me old shawl and cape afore washing them," Maggie challenged Marty.

"Thank you, they will be fine," Marty forced a smile. She would have preferred to wash them first, but it was better to have them as is to help her stay warm. She wrapped the triangle-shaped shawl around her shoulders, crossed it in front and tied the ends in back at her waist.

When Marty brought the clothes back in the cabin at dusk, she found herself shivering from the evening air. She laid the clothes across the trunk next to the fireplace to finish drying.

After they ate supper, Maggie used more of the herbs to make another cup of tea. Her cough grew worse as the evening progressed.

Once it was completely dark outside, Maggie stripped out of her corset, gown and petticoats before she crawled under several heavy woven wool blankets on her bed. The bed frame was made of wood. Two legs held up one side and two pegs stuck between two logs that formed the cabin walls held up the other. From the dip in the bed once Mrs. Grimsby lay down, Marty could see that a woven rope platform supported the mattress. The mattress made a crunching noise as the woman squirmed around after another coughing spell. Marty suspected it was stuffed with straw or corn husks.

"Ye can sleep afore the fire or find ye a spot in the loft," Maggie said, just before she fell asleep.

Maggie had not offered Marty any bedding. Marty moved the stool so that she could feel the fire's warmth and watch the crackling flames. Several times she felt the clothes draped across the trunk.

Hunter curled up on the hearth next to Marty. He positioned himself so that it was convenient for Marty to reach down and scratch his ears. Marty smiled at the contented noises Hunter made as she gently petted his head. She could tell Mrs. Grimsby was fond of the dog, even though she spoke harshly and occasionally kicked the dog out of her way. However, Marty doubted the woman gave the animal as much affection as Marty lavished on Hunter.

Finally, the skirt and stocking were dry. Only the corset was still damp. For warmth, she put the skirt over the shift and pulled on the stockings under the makeshift moccasins. Marty draped the cape over her shoulders and tied it around her neck. She wrapped herself tightly in it as if she was preparing to make her bed in front of the fire.

Even though it had not been dark many hours and the fall weather told her it was early in the evening, she was tired from the day's walking and the work she had done around the farmstead. But she forced herself to stay awake.

She could not afford to fall asleep. She had to text Cy.

CHAPTER 21

Marty waited for the sounds of Maggie snoring. She knew that in order to get away without a battle, it was essential that the woman was in a sound enough sleep so that she would not wake up when Marty left the cabin. As she listened to the labored breathing, Marty realized with regret that Maggie's lungs were filling with congestion again.

Marty shook herself. *I cannot worry about Maggie. It is time for me to leave.* Marty silently stepped towards the door. Hunter instantly sprang his feet and stood by her heels.

"Shhhh!" Marty hushed the dog as she patted his head to calm him.

Marty eased opened the door and walked out of the cabin. She felt Hunter brush the side of her leg as he squeezed his body past hers on his way out. After she closed the door quietly behind her, Marty resigned herself to the realization that Hunter was determined to go with her.

Marty waited for her eyes to adjust to the darkness. Fortunately, the almost full moon was up. There was enough light for her to see as she crossed the yard to her hiding place behind the barn. She found her boots, but decided to wait until she was off the Grimsby's farm before she put them on. She caught the light of the moon on the face of her compass to check her direction and quietly walked toward the stream that she had followed down the mountain.

After she bit back more than one exclamation of pain when a sticker or sharp stone bit through her stockings the balls of her feet where the holes were worn through the foot leathers, she detoured long enough to pick several corn stalk leaves to line her makeshift moccasins. Hunter trotted several feet ahead of her, showing her the best path to take so that she did not trip.

Once she was surrounded by trees, Marty tried her wrist screen. She composed a quick text to Cy and hit send. She waited several minutes, but received no reply.

Hunter whimpered at the sight of the glow from Marty's cell phone screen. He leaped up, trying to capture it in his mouth as if it was a firefly. Marty held the phone high above his reach.

"No, Hunter!" she quietly commanded. "Down!"

Hunter responded by running a short distance back towards the cabin, then returning to Marty to give her a few short barks before he ran up the stream a ways and returned to her. At first, Marty worried that Mrs. Grimsby would hear the barking and come after her. Then she realized that she was too far away for the woman to hear, even if she woke up and found Marty and Hunter gone.

Marty tried to text Cy again. She waited, but still there was no response. She sighed with resignation. She needed to climb to the top of the mountain. She figured it would not be as easy as it had been to descend the slope that morning. Even with the light from the moon, the creek bed would be mostly pitch black where the trees were dense. She wondered how long she had before the moon slipped over the horizon and left her in total darkness. She now wished she had brought her flashlight.

Marty put her boots on and found the stream. Once Hunter realized the direction she was traveling, he kept in front of her several paces, sniffing the ground. Marty heard scurrying noises as small animals rushed away from them. Hunter frequently dove into the brush after them, but did not come back with any prey in his mouth. She hoped that they did not come across any large and dangerous animals.

Marty realized that Hunter could smell where she had traveled earlier that day. He was leading her back on the same path. Marty broke into a grin when, after they had climbed partway up the slope of the mountain, Hunter turned away from the stream and followed a jagged path through the forest trees and brush towards the top of the mountain. When it was too dark to see, she used the glow from her wrist screen to help light the way. If she got too far behind, Hunter either ran back to her to bark a time or two before going forward again, or he waited for her to catch up to him. She trusted him to lead her back to the group of rocks on the top of the mountain.

They finally reached the summit with its crown of boulders. The moon was still up but was low on the horizon. Marty sank onto a rock and fought discouragement as she viewed the rocky fortress. Everything looked so different from what she remembered.

It will be hard enough to find where I hid my daypack in daylight. How am I ever going to find it at night, even with the picture on my wrist screen?

Then Marty noticed Hunter nosing around a cluster of rocks. As she walked closer, and kicked up some dust that had the smell of burnt ash, she realized with excitement that the dog had led her to the site where she had spent the previous night. From there she started around the formation of stone in the general direction in which she had gone to seek a hiding place for her daypack. Once she moved away from the small cave area, Hunter bounded past her. Within moments, she heard his throat rumblings along with scratching noises as he started digging.

He found it!

Marty moved towards Hunter. *He probably smells the food.* She quickly located the pack and lifted it out. She held it high as Hunter jumped in the air, barking to let her know he wanted to eat some of the goodies inside.

Marty realized how hungry she was when she heard her stomach growl. She found a rock to sit on and pulled out one of the protein bars. Although Maggie Grimsby was a solidly-built woman, she was not nearly as tall as Marty. She did not eat as much food as Marty was used to eating. At suppertime, Marty finished what was set before her, but did not mention that the meal did not fill her up. The protein bar was a welcome dessert.

As Marty ate, she broke off tiny bites for Hunter who anxiously waited for anything she shared with him.

Hunter continued to nose around the daypack after Marty finished her snack.

"No, Hunter," Marty told him firmly. "You may not eat the beef jerky. I may need it before I get home."

Realizing that she was not going to share any more of her food cache with him, Hunter whimpered for a few moments. Then he settled down at her feet.

Marty checked the screen on her Sun Access to see if Cy had responded to her earlier texts. There was no message from him, so she resent him the message from earlier. Five minutes later, she sent her message again.

.

I have more info think im in colonial times several years after a general braddeck was killed in Ohio by French n Indians now Brits trying to take same fort from French George Washington wants to build a road thru va so can settle Ohio im close to Potomac and monokacee rivers there is a meeting with Delawares in pa soon please reply

.

Several minutes later, she heard the tone she was waiting for.

.

Almost gave up on u for tonite. Hope u r ok. Do u no what state or city u r in? If not let me do some research on what u sent

.

no city im in wilderness she said this is lord Baltimores land n her husband went to Fredrick then Baltimore to pay quikrents fort cumberband is to the west

.

At that point Marty remembered the other pictures she had taken that morning, although she was not sure if they would be helpful to Cy.

.

pix to follow

.

Marty sent all the photographs. After a few moments she received a reply.

.

Got pix but ones inside cabin hard to c. General Braddeck and other info helpful. Will brb.

.

Marty settled in as comfortably as she could with a rock for a back support. She wondered if she would be able to see the auroras again once the moon went down. Hunter curled up next to her and she scratched his ears. She was on the verge of falling asleep when she heard the trill. She immediately snapped awake. Hunter growled and she reached to comfort him.

.

U r in western Maryland Frederick County fall 1758 year of solar high one. Mtns to the west probably Catoctin Range. U r probably on Chimney Rock. Maybe Bobs Hill. Btw General Braddock n most his men were killed July 1755 in PA on way to Ft Duquesne now in downtown Pittsburg PA. Brits fought to get fort back from French Sept 1758. Indian warriors fought on both sides looking for plunder.

.

After three more texts with historical information, Marty shook her head in frustration.

I dont care about history rite now I will study it on my trip I want to get home colonial woman says natives may attack settlers scares me any ideas

.

Sorry re history n yes some tribes attacked settlers. Seven years war aka French n Indian war still going on. Indian tribes fought on both sides n very brutal. U should no Ft Cumberland in MD only fort left to protect area then. Frontier was dangerous. Lenni Lenape aka Delawares wanted peace w Brits but only if they could keep their land in west PA n Ohio.

.

Guess thats y maggie calls them savages

.

Whose Maggie?

.

Colonial English woman I stayed with today

.

She would think they r savages but tribes there had towns n societies. They were civilized but different than European people. Atrocities n savagery on both sides.

.

But these r innocent people who just want to farm n live in peace

.

From natives point of view European people invaded their land brought diseases like smallpox n many Indians died. British took best hunting grounds n always wanted more land.

.

Y natives attack these people now thought war was English vs French

.

Tribes had to trade furs for goods to survive because game n cropland was gone. Western Ohio tribes knew French wanted to keep British out of Ohio valley. British generals from England didnt listen to colonial militia leaders n were not willing to pay warriors with trade n gifts to fight with them so tribes fought on French side instead to get trade goods.

.

Marty realized that Cy was warning her that she may be in danger from the tribes that would not be able to distinguish her from the English people living in this era, especially if she was still with Maggie Grimsby. It felt strange to her that she was the history and social studies major, yet he told her more about this time period after just a few hours of research than she remembered from her high school classes.

Green Corn told her that her people wanted to set up trade with the British. Were they at peace or were they part of the war?

.

What about lenni lenape

.

Killed many colonists after Braddock failed in 1755. After attempt to retake Ft Duquesne in Sept 1758 Lenni Lenape wanted peace with Brits. Conrad Weiser told Iroquois it was time to let Delawares speak for themselves at council in Easton PA in Oct 1758.

.

Once more Cy gave her several texts of historical information until Marty fired off a text to him.

.

Does noing the date n place where I am help u get me home?

.

Donno til I figure it out. Til then im tracking everything. For now please stay where u r n stay safe.

.

Marty thought about what Cy told her. He was trying to get her back but he was not sure yet just how to do it. Even though she had her Sun Access with its solar battery, she began to wonder just how long she might be stuck here. If she was forced to live the rest of her life in this era, how was she going to manage?

Marty wondered if Maggie would let her stay with her. She shook her head at the thought. Maggie was a bitter person. She was not very nice to Hunter. Marty guessed that if she stayed at her place very long, the woman would start to treat her the same way she did her dog. Then there was the issue that Mr. Grimsby was due to come home soon. From what Marty gathered about Maggie's husband, she doubted she would like him very well.

Marty thought about the two women she had met since she went back in time. She knew that given a choice between Maggie and Green Corn, she would probably choose Green Corn. The problem was that Green Corn had been adopted by the Lenni Lenape. Marty did not know much about that society, but it sounded terribly violent, even though Cy said both sides behaved savagely. She was afraid the Lenape people were too different for her to live with comfortably.

The other thing that bothered Marty was the place women held in society in these times. She knew that women in the United States did not get the right to vote until 1920. But, how many other rights did they not have during Colonial times? Would she be able to adapt to being a second-class citizen, which was the status that both Green Corn and Maggie Grimsby indicated was the lot of most European women at the time?

.

Thanx cy btw would u please look up something for me in case im stuck here for awhile from what im learning I dont no if I would b better off with British or lenne lenape

.

What r u talking about? Im going to get u home please trust me

.

I do trust u but just in case it takes longer than u think I may need to make some decisions where to live

.

U look like u r of euro origin n u speak English. I would think u r better off with British if u r close to them. Y do u ask?

.

U would think id b better off with British but im hearing weird things about womens rites here green corn said British women must submit to n obey husbands

.

Whose green corn?

.

English captive adopted by lenne lenape I met in pa she said euro women dont own land n cant talk at meetings or help choose their leaders

.

Uno American women won rite to vote just last century

.

but lenape women do have a voice n they own land n they dont have to obey their husbands no matter what n the children belong to the mothers clan not to the fathers like the British

.

U worry too much. U dont have a husband or children. Think about it. English colonies have same language n heritage we r used to. Native societies r very different.

.

I no but green corn says lenape women have better life n more freedom than British women it sounds more like what we have now that I am used to uno me I wont b able to keep my mouth shut if I have limited rights just because im a woman I cant live where that gets me in trouble

.

I have noticed u can be pretty persistent n vocal. No offense I like that about u most of the time.

.

Most of the time?

Marty wondered exactly what he was suggesting with that comment. She would wait to ask him once she was home. Right now, she was not going to let him distract her.

.

Maggie said because she married all her land is now owned by her husband she only gets dower rights while she is alive whats with that can u please find out for me? :)m

.

Thought u did not want lots of history.

.

This is different I talked to these two women n I dont understand exactly what they r talking about but I need to no what im dealing with here if I cant get back home rite away

.

Uno im not a social science or history major but I will c what I can find out. Brb

.

Thanx cy :)m

CHAPTER 22

Marty fought sleep while she waited. She hoped Cy did not feel insulted because she asked him to research how things were for women in Colonial times. He might think she did not believe he could help her. If he decided that, he might stop trying. Marty fretted about that possibility for several minutes before she finally shook off the feelings of guilt and self-blame that threatened to overwhelm her.

Cy did not give up that easy. Besides, she was the one in a tight spot. If things did not go as planned, it was her life that was disrupted the most. She was the one stuck in an era where women often found themselves at a disadvantage. She had always preferred to be prepared for whatever situations might arise. If Cy could not get her home or if it took years for him to do so, she needed to develop a game plan rather than be totally at the mercy of circumstances.

At last she received Cy's next message.

Single English women could own land but the land became the property of their husbands when they married unless prenuptial. Prenupt usually to save land for sons of a first marriage. Men could not sell land without wifes ok because she was entitled to a third dower rites while alive but husband had full control over who got the property when both of them were dead. Married women got more property rights in 1860. In some states got property rights earlier. Women could not vote or speak at government or church meetings but if they owned land they still paid taxes

Marty reread the last line and tightened her jaw with indignation. *That's not right! What about no taxation without representation?*

Cy's messages continued.

Husband n wife considered one unit but woman under cover of husband n he had the right to make all decisions for the family. Women were subservient to men.

Marty fumed.

That does not sound very good for women. It sounds like some of the backwards societies still in the world today.

Marty realized that women probably lived happily enough with this arrangement if they did not know any better and if they had a loving father and at least a kind and considerate husband. But, if they ended up in an abusive family situation, they had very little legal recourse and few options for escaping to something better.

Marty felt relieved that she lived in a free nation in the twenty-first century where her society taught that men and women were of equal worth and they worked together as partners. Then she remembered. She was not in that century at the moment. She asked Cy her next question.

What about lene lenape were womens life better have more rights

Lenni Lenape were agricultural society n matrilineal. Different bands east n west but only three clans turtle turkey wolf. Could not marry someone in same clan. Chiefs were men chosen from mothers lineage. Sachems over chiefs. Women had more status because they owned the houses n land. They didnt need to obey their husbands. men n women were more equal.

That sounds a little more like it.

Warriors were chosen by merit. Men hunt n fish n help clear land but the Lenape thought plants were female n to grow well must be planted and cared for by women. Clans depended on food crops women grew so that gave their work value in the eyes of the clan. Women had more say about their children. Loyalty to clan strong so men with the most say in families were the maternal uncles n grandfathers. Same with the Iroquois which is y at that time period the Iroquois said they were the uncles to speak with the British on behalf of their nephews the Lenni Lenape.

Suddenly, a lot of what Green Corn had talked about started to make sense to Marty. She also realized it was a very different kind of society than what she was used to.

Native tribes could b brutal to enemies but usually saved young healthy captives. Those they adopted were accepted as full members of the family n clan. Especially indentured servants taken captive often preferred to stay with native captors. Often treated better by Indians than by the colonists who bought their bonds.

Marty shook her head when she finished reading Cy's short summary of Lenape society. It seemed to her that Green Corn might be right. If she was forced to stay back in the eighteenth century for a long time, maybe she would be better with the Lenape than among the English.

Then again, even though it had been only two days since Marty had seen Green Corn, she was now in a different decade. In Green Corn's lifetime, it was over ten years since the two of them met in Pennsylvania. Where was Green Corn now? Marty had no way of knowing how she would find Green Corn or if Green Corn would even remember her. And, although Marty was young and healthy, if any Lenni Lenapes other than Green Corn were to find her, Marty might end up being one of the "enemy" they decided to kill instead of adopt.

As Marty pondered the information Cy had shared with her, she received another text from him.

I thought u told me once u r a Christian. Keep in mind British had Bible and were Christians. Unless u find a tribe of Indians who converted to Christianity most r not. Uno because men r stronger physically than women in most societies women have had an uphill battle for rights all through history. No different among Christians. But do u want to b with people who do not believe in the same God u do?

Marty reread Cy's text twice.

For someone who was not a church-goer, he sure knows how to put things into perspective.

Marty knew the Native Americans were a spiritual people, but their religious beliefs were not based on the same Supreme Being she accepted as God. They did not believe in Jesus Christ.

Marty sighed with resignation. Even if she found herself living the rest of her life among the Colonial English where she could not enjoy the legal rights and freedoms of her era, she would at least still be able to read the Bible. She could still take every opportunity to work towards equality for all people as much as the society and customs of this era would allow. She had the benefit of knowing that things would get better for both women and the minorities who had few rights and limited freedoms in the current era. They will have made great gains towards freedom and equality within a few centuries.

Marty suspected Cy felt she would be safer with the British than with Native American people of the era because of language and cultural considerations. But, the best solution was for her and Cy to figure out how to get her back home.

Marty felt the fatigue of the long day catch up with her as she replied.

Thanx but woman I stayed with is really sick n needs help I will go back tomorrow but come back here at nite hope by then u have figured out how to get me home

Btw dont u leave for your history trip Thursday? Today is Monday. I suggest if u r not home tomorrow nite u text them to say u r delayed n will join them later.

Marty scrunched her eyes shut and leaned her head back against the rock in frustration. The trip! If Cy did not have enough answers by tomorrow night, would he be able to get her back home in time to go on the trip? If not, how could she explain missing the tour to her parents?

I cant I dont have anyones cell numbers in my cell all I have is a flyer for the tour in my car glovebox it should have the tour agency numbers if im not home Thursday will u please call them

Uno I will help u anyway I can

Lets just hope im home n ready to go by Thursday I didnt want to get this immersed in history I would rather c it on the tour

Uno I m doing my best

I no n thank u so much u r really impre im just worried is all I dont no y im here in 1758 or how to get back home y me here n y eddie in pa in different centuries is what I want to no

Im concerned too. I will not give up on u I promise. Need to check some things tonite. Now u mention it u actually r not very far from where Eddie landed.

In spite of her unease about her current situation, Cy's comment about Eddie sparked Marty's curiosity. She quickly pecked out a question for him.

Exactly where did eddie land

Quirauk mtn just north of u in the same ridge of mountains u r in.

She was in the same ridge of mountains as Eddie? Marty knew the Appalachian Mountains were formed differently than the Rockies. She struggled to remember enough geography about the Appalachian Mountains to picture a ridge and how many miles long a ridge might be. She wondered what Cy's theories were about why they both landed so close to each other. Was there something special about these mountains?

Y would we land so close to each other what do we have in common

He pushed to receive a cell call u pushed to call someone. Must b something to do with cell signals but donno exactly what yet. Solar highs n electmag flow r factors.

Who called eddie n where did his call come from

A friend of his in town.

What was the number

After Cy sent the number to Marty, she decided to enter it into her phone. She looked at the speed-call number next to Cy's. It was still assigned to her ex-boyfriend, Brian.

I sure don't need him on speed-call anymore.

She edited the screen to show Eddie's name and the cell number that Cy had sent. As she finished up, she heard the tone for another incoming text.

Who did u call?

U silly

Me? Y? I was standing rite there.

To tease u jokes on me I guess

.

There was a long pause before Marty received the next message.

.

Hard for me to believe all this because of a joke

.

U cannot worry about that just stay focused on getting me home we need to figure out what caused Eddie n me to go from rockies to appalachian mtns n lets hope its not a one way street

.

Finding a way to get u home has been my only focus since u left. Please b careful n stay safe. Prefer u stay on the mtn. I need to do some more research tonight. Will text u tomorrow my bff.

.

Thanx cy my bff I promise I will b careful tty tomorrow nite

.

Marty turned her cell phone off and wrapped it in the bandanna. She decided to put it in her daypack rather than back in her pocket. She had to feel her way to the pack because the moon had gone down and left the top of the mountain in darkness. She felt for the flashlight and used it to see as she rummaged through her bag to take inventory of what was left. She pushed Hunter away as he showed a renewed interest in the food smells coming from inside.

"No!" Marty spoke to Hunter sharply.

Hunter trotted a few paces away and lay down, resting his nose on his crossed front paws. Marty could barely make out the figure of the dog in the residual light of the flashlight beam, but she smiled at his forlorn expression.

Marty sat on her heels for a minute to consider what she should do. Cy suggested she stay on the mountain because of the danger of hostile attacks. Yet, she was not sure she could do that in good conscience. Mrs. Grimsby was not the most pleasant person Marty had ever met. But, she was sick. Marty felt she had to go back at least long enough to help her get well and warn her of the danger. Besides, she did not know how long it would take for Cy to find an answer and she was getting low on food. Maggie would feed her.

Marty looked over and shined her flashlight on Hunter. She saw the light reflected in the depths of his eyes as he looked at it in wonder. As fond as she was of Hunter, the dog belonged to Mrs. Grimsby. Marty had nothing to feed the dog. In spite of his name, Marty wondered if he could catch his own food.

Marty knew she was getting attached to Hunter. She wondered what would happen if she took Hunter home with her. Then she pushed the thought out of her head. Even though she had travelled back in time, she did not know what would happen if she tried to take another person or animal from an earlier time period and transport them forward in time. If she tried to take him with her, she might end up with nothing left of Hunter but a handful of dust and bones.

She needed to deliver Hunter back to his home with the Grimsbys first thing in the morning. She did not want to use up all of her flashlight battery to hike down the mountain in the darkness. Besides, she was too exhausted to make the trip again that night. Hopefully, she would wake up early the next morning and she and Hunter would get back in time for breakfast.

It was cold without a fire, but Marty did not bother with the solar blanket. With the shawl and skirt over own clothes, she wrapped the cape tightly around her. She found an almost comfortable spot to settle into for the night. Hunter cuddled next to her and added his warmth to hers.

She quickly dropped into a deep sleep.

CHAPTER 23

Cy looked at the clock on his BlackSlab. It read 9:11p.m. The internet café closed at 10 o'clock.

The information in the Eddie file was on the flash drive hidden under the garden pot on the roof, but Cy had no intention of using it on his old notebook computer. Plus, he realized that if he shifted the heavy plant container around too often, it would soon become obvious that someone was moving it. He did not want to draw attention to it. He decided it was better to use the flash drive at the internet café. He knew he needed to hurry in order to get anything done that night.

Cy raced down the stairs from the rooftop to his floor and flew into his apartment. He quickly backed up the information on his cell phone that he had just received from Marty onto another flash drive. Hopefully, he could get the information added to the Marty file on the flash drive at the internet café that night and the one hidden away on the apartment rooftop sometime before another raid on his place took this information from him.

Cy felt confident that Marty's concern that the movement from the Rocky Mountains to the Appalachians being a unique one-way pattern was unfounded. The other girl who disappeared from Dead Man's Drop had gone west, not east. He refused at this point to accept that once someone disappeared from the top of one mountain and ended up on another mountain in another time and place, it was a one-time, one-way event. If physical forces could get them there, the same principle of physics could bring them back. Cy was convinced that it was merely an issue of discovering the particulars of those principles of physics.

Marty brought up a good point that there might be a connection somewhere to explain why she and Eddie had ended up in localities so close to each other. Cy mentally kicked himself for not having thought of it first. He was the analytical one, yet it was fun-loving, curious, people-oriented

Marty who asked the question about why she and Eddie had each ended up in localities relatively close to each other. They each activated a cell phone call, and he now knew the phone numbers that were involved. He needed to investigate that further. To do so, he wanted to review the Eddie file again, including the latest text messages.

Cy grabbed a pair of disposable gloves and turned off the living room lights in his apartment. He locked up and then ran down the stairs, slowing to a brisk stride when he reached the walkway that could be seen from the street. He did not want to attract attention to himself by running.

The café was only a few blocks away. It was quicker and easier to walk than to drive over.

Cy reached the grocery store that was open until midnight. He started to walk past the entrance until something caught his eye. He double-backed and entered the store. A shelf unit standing in a nook tucked away in the corner held a variety of catalogs for real estate sales and rentals, car sales and other offers. He grabbed a local telephone book from the stack on the bottom shelf.

Cy thumbed through the front pages until he found what he was looking for. He hesitated a moment, looked around the front of the store to make sure no one was watching him, then he carefully tore out two of the pages. He folded the papers and put them in one of the side pockets of his pants. He returned the telephone book to the stack and left the store to continue towards the café.

In the men's room, Cy donned the gloves long enough to retrieve the flash drive from its hiding place. Next he bought an orange soda and settled in at his favorite computer. He added the latest information from the flash drive he brought with him from home to the Marty file before he reviewed the information in the Eddie file.

Only then did he pull the pages he tore from the telephone directory out of his pocket and smooth them on the edge of the table. He carefully compared the information on the pages to his notes in the Eddie file and added more notes.

The next thing Cy knew, the clerk working the counter signaled him that it was time to close up. Cy shook his head with annoyance. He knew the guy was trying to hurry him out so he could go home early.

Cy carefully saved everything to the flash drive that would remain in the café before he closed down the computer. He left his drink cup on the table ledge while he put the flash drive back in the restroom. Afterwards, he grabbed his drink cup and left.

Cy walked slowly back to his apartment and occasionally sipped on his soda as he thought about what he had reviewed that night. He had a feeling that he was on the right track. Still, something was missing.

CHAPTER 24

Lee Hardin was just about ready to call it a night and drive home to see if there was anything interesting on the ten o'clock news. Then he saw the lights go out in Cy's living room window. When the lights in Cy's bedroom did not come on within a few seconds, Hardin decided to wait.

He smiled with satisfaction when he saw the kid come bounding out the front entry of his apartment complex, then slow to a quick walk. Hardin waited until Cy was all the way down the block and had crossed the street before he started his truck and pulled forward. Rather than drive straight, which might draw Cy's attention to him, he turned right and circled the block with left-hand turns, intending to end up at the next intersection that Cy would cross. He had an idea where the kid was going. He had made a note of it in his journal the previous April before he left for New Mexico, plus he had watched him the night before. The kid was probably on his way to his favorite evening haunt—the internet café.

Hardin shook his head with amusement. After spending much of the day on computers at the university and no doubt a lot of his free time on his computer in his apartment, what does the kid do for entertainment? He goes to the internet café and gets on the computers there.

At the intersection, Hardin looked off to his right and saw Cy getting ready to walk past the grocery store. Then he watched Cy double-back, acting like he changed his mind, and enter the store. Hardin abandoned his original intent of circling the opposite block. Instead he turned right and pulled over to the curb in the darkness just before the glow from the store lights lit the sidewalk and street outside its windows. He stopped the truck and got out, hoping to see where Cy was going in the store.

Hardin quickly ducked in the shadows to stay out of Cy's line of vision. The kid had doubled-backed to the front corner of the store where they kept all the booklet advertisers that the stores tolerated as a service to customers. Doing his best to position himself so that Cy would not catch sight of him in his peripheral vision, Hardin watched Cy thumb through a telephone book, tear out some pages, put the book back and leave the store.

Hardin stepped back into the recessed entryway of the neighboring shop while Cy exited and continued down the sidewalk. He waited until the kid was over a block away before he left the shadow of the shop entryway and climbed back into his truck to follow him. He was relieved that Cy was so focused on whatever problem he was mulling over that he was not paying close attention to his surroundings.

Sure of the kid's ultimate destination, Hardin circled the block again so that he could use an alleyway to enter a narrow parking lot for a business on the opposite side of the street from the café. He parked in an unlit space bounded by a low hedge that obscured the view of his truck from anyone looking from across the street. He arrived just in time to see Cy leave the restroom and go to the counter to get a soft drink. He watched as the kid sat down at one of the computers and used his left hand to fiddle with something on the far side of the screen.

After a few minutes, Cy's left hand moved to the left of the screen again, then to his left pocket, then back to the left of the screen.

Hardin decided it was time to find out what was on the left side of the computers in the internet café.

Hardin continued to watch Cy. It was obvious that the kid was not there to play computer video games for relaxation. The kid was painfully intent about whatever he was viewing on the screen. Hardin watched with interest when Cy pulled out the papers he had torn from the telephone book at the grocery store and compared them to whatever he was studying on the computer.

Then he watched Cy type on the slab's hardwired keyboard, wondering why the kid did not use the high-tech holo stuff.

Lee Hardin watched Cy give a frustrated wave to the other kid working the café counter. Hardin checked his watch. It was nineteen minutes to ten, almost time for the store to close for the night. Evidently the guy on duty was pushing it a little so he could go home early. Hardin watched as Cy quickly finished whatever he was working on and closed down the computer screen. Then he saw Cy fiddle with the far side of the unit, stand up with his fist clenched and head for the restroom.

The kid sure has to use the john a lot.

Hardin waited patiently until Cy came back out, grabbed his drink cup and walked out of the door. He was not in as big of a hurry walking away from the café as he had been walking to it. Hardin guessed that the kid's thoughts were absorbed deeply in whatever he had worked on. He doubted it had anything to do with sports or what girl he wanted to ask to the show.

Hardin was almost sure Cy was finished for the night and going home. But, he waited patiently for the kid to walk a couple of blocks before he pulled his truck out into the street to follow him. Hardin made a right turn at the next block, circled around to the left so that he crossed the intersection behind Cy, then circled two blocks so that he ended up in one of his favorite parking spots in the shadows a half block away where he had a good view of the entrance to the building and the windows of Cy's apartment. Sure enough, the kid entered the building and a few minutes later, the lights in his living room window came on.

Before Hardin headed home to his own apartment, he drove back to the grocery store. He picked up the top telephone book and found the place in the front where Cy had torn out some pages. Then he picked up the next book and found the same spot. The two missing pages were the area code maps for the United States and Canada.

Lee Hardin tucked both books under his arm and walked out of the store.

Hardin checked his watch. If he hurried home, he might still be able to catch the tail-end of the sportscast. After that, he would update his notebook

.

CHAPTER 25

The sky was barely turning gray in the east when Marty awoke. The chill in the air cut through her cloak and other clothing she had wrapped around her. Hunter lifted his head and gave her an inquiring look.

"We better get back home, Hunter," Marty said as she struggled to her feet. "Your mistress will wonder what happened to us if we are real late. Besides, I definitely do not want to miss breakfast."

Hunter ran to the crevice where Marty had again hidden her daypack and began sniffing.

"No, Hunter," Marty said. "That stays here. The only thing I am taking back this time is my medicine pouch and compass knife."

Marty wished she had something she could take to Mrs. Grimsby as a gift to thank her for the clothes. It seemed like everything she had was modern and would not fit in the present era. Then Marty began rummaging around in the smaller pocket where she kept personal items like her comb and hand cream.

She pulled out a zipper fob and studied it with her flashlight. She had put it there after a previous hike. She remembered when it had snagged on a thorn bush and was yanked off the main zipper of her daypack. The metal ring holding it to the zipper pull had disappeared in the surrounding weeds. The pink, blue and aqua of the teardrop-shaped bauble cut from an abalone shell shimmered in the light. The coarse gray backing of the shell felt rough in her palm.

Attached to a thin rawhide cord, this will make a nice necklace, Marty thought. She put it in her medicine pouch.

Marty looked down at her boots. As much as she preferred to wear them while she hiked down the mountain, she had to admit they left a very distinctive print. She gathered handfuls of the broad leaves that were scattered on the ground and put them inside the moccasins to try to provide more insulation. That and the stockings would have to do, she decided. She stuffed her hiking boots inside her pack before she hid it.

In the dark shadows of the early dawn, Marty picked up a branch and brushed the ground to erase traces of her footprints and Hunter's paw prints. Afterwards, she cautiously started down the path she and Hunter had come up only a few hours before, erasing visible prints as she saw them. Once the dog realized Marty was traveling back down the mountain, he ran ahead of her to show her the path.

The sun had risen above the horizon by the time the two reached the bottom of the mountain. Marty knew they were getting close to the edge of the clearing. Once they could see the cleared fields between the trees, Hunter started to bark as he ran towards the cabin.

Marty continued to walk quickly, hoping she was not too late to help Mrs. Grimsby with the morning chores. About the time she reached the wheat field, she saw Maggie Grimsby walking towards her with a quick, resolute stride. She was carrying the pitchfork. As she came closer to Marty, Marty noticed she was frowning.

"Good morning, Mrs. Grimsby," Marty cheerfully called to her once she was close enough to be heard. "I was hoping to get back in time to help you with morning chores. I'm not too late, am I?"

Without a word, Maggie Grimsby strode past Marty, positioning herself so she stood between Marty and the mountains. Maggie raised the pitchfork and jabbed it at Marty, catching one of its tines on Marty's arm.

"Ouch! Why did you do that?" demanded Marty.

"How dare ye run away!" screamed the older woman. "Ye steal me dog and take fer the hills afore Mr. Grimsby returns. I already be telling ye, Mr. Grimsby will be finding yer kin fer ye."

Maggie doubled over in a coughing fit. Hunter barked and growled at his mistress as he danced protectively around Marty.

"I did not run away," protested Marty as she watched the woman struggle to clear her lungs. "I went for a walk. And I did not steal your dog. I tried to make him stay, but he insisted on following me. I was afraid if he started to bark he would wake you up."

Maggie frowned, and, unable to speak due to her choking on phlegm, shook her head and waved at Marty in denial.

"Mrs. Grimsby, you sound like you still are not feeling well. Perhaps you should get back to your house where it is warm."

"And do ye perhaps think the cows be milking themselves and the pigs be fixing their own slops, ye ungrateful wench?" She demanded in a shrill voice once she recovered her breath. "Get ye back and take care of the animals afore I run ye through. And ye shall be taking no more walks afore Mr. Grimsby returns. Then ye shall tell him who your kin be so's he can treat with them about returning ye from the savages."

"Mrs. Grimsby, I already tried to explain to you," Marty said, as patiently as she could. "Neither you nor Mr. Grimsby will be able to reach my family from here. I will have to find my own way home."

"Atwixt Mr. Grimsby and me, we shall get our money from ye one way or t'other," Maggie screamed as she tried to suppress a cough. "If ye'll not be helping Mr. Grimsby get the reward fer returning ye from the savages, then ye shall take Annie's place!"

"Annie?" exclaimed Marty. "You mean your former indentured servant? But, I'm not an indentured servant. You can't do that to me."

"'Tis I shall be telling ye what I can and canna do, ye ungrateful wench," said Maggie. "I feed and clothe ye, and this be the thanks I be getting from ye?"

Marty blinked in disbelief. She knew that indenture was a practice used as punishment for convicts or for people to repay their debts or their ship fare from England to the Colonies, but it was outlawed shortly after the Revolutionary War. She did not come from England on a ship. Did this woman actually believe that a day's food and some hand-me-down ragged clothes entitled her to enslave Marty for several years?

"You said your husband went to sell your harvest," said Marty. "Perhaps he will use some of the money he receives to purchase another contract for a new indentured servant."

"Mr. Grimsby already said 'twill be new taxes to raise fer the militia to fight the French, so trade 'twill nary be good this year. 'Twill be nary a cent left to replace Annie. He'd be preferring a lad, but a wench 'tis better than no. If ye'll not help Mr. Grimsby get the reward from yer kin, ye'll be pressed into service."

"Indentured servants have a contract," Marty protested. "You do not have any contract saying you have the right to make me your servant."

Maggie smiled slyly.

"Mr. Grimsby writes a fine hand, if need be. And out this far, nary a soul pays much mind to reading contracts or seeing how long it be afore they be up. Now, get ye milking the cow afore she starts to bawling!"

Maggie Grimsby raised the pitchfork, threatening to jab Marty again.

Marty turned and walked quickly towards the farm. She fought to hold back her tears. How could this be happening to her? She came back to make sure Maggie was getting better and to warn the Grimsbys of the danger from the hostile tribes to the west. Instead, Mrs. Grimsby threatened to turn her into their servant. She knew then she had to leave as soon as possible and never come back.

Marty also realized she needed to escape before Mr. Grimsby arrived home. Once there were two of them, it would be even harder to get away.

At Maggie's insistence, Marty laced the now-dry corset tightly over the top of her shift and then crossed the shawl across her front and tied it in back. She twisted her hair up and secured it with her leather clip. Then she shoved the cap over her hair, hoping the hot water and soap killed any lice eggs that may have clung to the inside of the fabric.

Marty did the chores Maggie Grimsby directed her to do, patiently putting up with the woman's verbal abuse. Marty did not know how to do many of the things the woman expected of her. This earned her the woman's complaints about her laziness and stupidity. She could not help but think that Maggie had a lot of practice being a jailer to Annie. She could understand why the young woman had been unwilling to stay to help the Grimsbys with their harvest.

Marty forced herself to not respond to the woman's tirades. The only rest she had was when she sat down to the noon meal. Between bites of cornmeal porridge seasoned with bacon, she used a piece of leather from the barn to mend her makeshift moccasins. She repeatedly told herself that it would only be this one day. She was leaving that night.

As the day progressed, Marty could tell that whatever was causing Maggie's congestion, it was not getting better. Maggie repeatedly grew red in the face as she struggled to breathe and keep her lungs clear. By late afternoon, the woman settled on her stool and leaned her shoulder and head against the wall of the cabin while she directed Marty on how to prepare their simple supper. Her tone was just as demanding but Marty noticed that her voice gradually grew weaker.

"Mrs. Grimsby, let me get you some hot water and more of my herbs for your lungs so you can make your medicinal tea," Marty offered after they finished eating. "Then I think you should probably go to bed and get some rest. I'll wash the dishes and I promise I will come right back."

"Ye'll nary be going out of my sight," Maggie commanded in her weak voice. "The dishes shall be waiting 'til morning. 'Twill have some of that tea, though."

Marty used the light from the fire to find the right herbs in her pouch. Then she poured the water and the herbs into one of the gourd cups and brought the molasses jug to the table. She watched Maggie's weak hands shake as she fixed the tea and raised the cup to her lips to inhale the steam and drink the brew.

Marty reached for her cape and started to tie it on.

"Where might ye have a mind to be going?" Maggie demanded sharply.

"Since you do not want me to wash dishes, and the evening chores are done, I am getting ready to go to bed," said Marty. "There isn't enough light to darn by. Was there something else you need me to do?"

The woman closed her eyes and shook her head.

"Take the cape and yer shawl off, afore ye step outside to do yer business," she demanded. "And don't ye be taking all night about it or I'll be coming after ye with the pitchfork."

Marty knew that last was a hollow threat. She doubted the woman had enough strength left to even lift the pitchfork. However, she did not want to raise any suspicions about her plan to leave that night, so she complied. She returned to the cabin shivering because of the cold night air. The extra clothing enveloped her body with its warmth.

"Up in the loft, wench," Maggie Grimsby ordered.

"What? I would prefer to sleep by the fire," protested Marty.

"Nay, ye shall not be sneaking off with me dog again," said the woman. "Get ye up above 'til morning."

Marty climbed the ladder to the loft. Hunter, unable to follow her, stood at the bottom of the ladder and whimpered. Her feet were no sooner off the top rung of the ladder than she heard a loud thud. She turned to look. Maggie had pulled the ladder down and let it drop to the floor.

"Hist! Shut yer whining, ye good-fer-nothing mutt," Mrs. Grimsby ordered. Marty heard a soft thud and Hunter's yip of pain. The old woman had kicked him. Marty fought back an angry retort.

Marty found a clear spot at the edge of the loft floor and laid down where she could peek over and see the fireplace and the section of table closest to it. She saw Hunter curl up on the warmth of the hearth with his head resting on his crossed front paws. His eyes locked on hers.

From the sounds she heard Maggie make below, Marty guessed the woman was taking off her corset and petticoats, as she called them, and was preparing for bed. She heard the ropes of the bed frame creak as the woman settled in for the night.

Marty rolled back away from the edge and sat up with her back against the hard side of a chest. She waited in silence. It was early in the evening, and would be dark soon. But Marty was exhausted. Mrs. Grimsby had overseen her all day, making sure she had put in a hard day's work. She fought sleep as she listened for the sounds that would tell her that Mrs. Grimsby had finally settled into a deep slumber. She knew she needed to leave for the safety of the mountaintop once the moon was up.

CHAPTER 26

Marty woke with a start. She realized she must have fallen asleep even though she had propped herself up in an uncomfortable position in an effort to stay awake. In the dark of the cabin with the fire burning low, she tried to figure out how late it was.

Marty carefully leaned over the edge of the loft, hoping to see through the cracks between the cabin logs to figure out if it was light outside. Then she remembered. One of the day's tasks had been to create a mud and straw mixture which Mrs. Grimsby had directed her to use to fill in the cracks between the squared-off logs, inside and out. She had told Marty it was time to chink the logs to keep out the cold of the coming winter.

Marty knew there was no other way to check on the time of night except to go outside. She flipped the edges of the cape back over each of her shoulders to keep it out of her way. As carefully as she could, she swung her legs over the edge of the loft floor, and scooted her body until she hung from the ledge with her hands.

Marty felt grateful for her height and long arms. The loft was only a little over seven feet above the floor of the cabin. She felt around with her toes for the ground beneath her. She froze in place at the sound of ladder scraping against the split log floor. Her head jerked in the direction of Mrs. Grimsby's bed. Was the woman still asleep or had the noise awakened her? The woman's labored breathing remained steady, assuring Marty that the noise had not disturbed her sleep.

The next thing she knew, she felt Hunter's cold nose touch her left leg just above where the scrunched-down edge of the wool stocking left her skin bare. Using her toes, she felt around for the posts and rungs of the ladder, working to place her feet so she would not trip or lose her balance when she let go. As she dropped to the main floor, Marty maintained a crouching position until she was sure the movement had not disturbed Mrs. Grimsby. Hunter whimpered at her side.

"Hush, hush," Marty whispered to the dog as she felt for him and scratched his ears.

"I pray thee, bring me some water afore ye step outside to do yer business," Marty heard the feeble voice. "And ye'll be needing to stir up the fire afore ye put on another log. 'Tis freezing cold in here."

Marty froze in place, tempted to fling open the door and run. Then something about Maggie Grimsby's weak and raspy voice caught Marty's attention. Mrs. Grimsby was even worse than before. Also, the inside of the cabin was warm. She knew the woman should not be freezing cold under all her blankets.

Marty stirred the embers of the fire to create enough light so she could find the squatty candle in its holder on the table. She brought it to the fireplace and used the tongs to pick out an ember to light the candle. Then she filled Mrs. Grimsby's gourd with water and took it to her.

The woman was too weak to raise herself to drink, so Marty slipped her arm under the woman's shoulders and helped her sit up far enough to take a few sips. Afterwards, the woman collapsed back into her bed.

The neckline of the woman's shift and her bedcovers were soaked with perspiration. Marty guessed that during the hours of sleep, Maggie had run a fever. But while Marty held her, Maggie was shivering violently and clutching the blankets tightly to her body.

Marty placed the still half-full gourd into Maggie's empty porridge bowl with its dried-on remains of supper. Then Marty stirred the embers again and put a few smaller twigs and another log on the orange embers. She tended it until the smaller twigs burned long enough for the thick log to catch on fire.

Marty wrapped her cape around her and started for the door. Hunter was at her heels. Marty turned to hold him back as she prepared to swing the door open.

"No, Hunter, stay," Marty ordered. "You cannot come. You stay with Mrs. Grimsby."

Marty eased her way out the door and closed it behind her. She stepped a few feet to the side of the door and leaned against the squared logs of the cabin. She tried to ignore Hunter yipping and barking inside. She could tell he was scratching the other side of the door, trying to follow her outside.

The moon was up. It was waning, so it was not as full as the night before. Yet, it gave off enough light for her to be able to see to get across the fields and into the forest beyond. She would not have Hunter to guide her up the dark paths of the mountain but, hopefully, the moon would provide her enough light long enough for her to get back to the top.

Marty could not shake the uneasy feeling that grew inside of her. A sense of apprehension prevented her from dashing across the fields away from the cabin and the mean-spirited woman inside. Then she realized what was bothering her. Mrs. Grimsby was really sick. Marty was afraid that if she left Maggie alone, the woman might die.

Marty did not know what was making Maggie Grimsby ill. She guessed it was something like bronchitis or pneumonia. However, she knew enough after listening to her mother over the years to know that if the woman was having chills, she probably would break into a high fever before long. The fever might help kill whatever virus was attacking Maggie's body. But, if Maggie was too weak or too sick, then without help, the virus and the fever could kill her.

Marty's mother considered her position as a registered nurse a calling as much as a job. Marty had never seriously thought about becoming a nurse. But, she now realized that some of her mother's healing values had rubbed off onto her. Even though Marty was not trained like her mother, she was the only hope Mrs. Grimsby had for help to get her through her illness. Marty also knew she would not be able to live with herself if something really bad happened to Mrs. Grimsby because she did not stay and take care of her.

Then Marty argued with herself. She had no obligation to help Mrs. Grimsby. The woman had told her just that morning that unless she and her husband could get a big reward from her parents—something Marty knew was impossible—they were going to force her to become their indentured servant for life. That was so unfair and so wrong. Marty would not let that happen.

Marty also realized that she had not warned Mrs. Grimsby about the hostile warriors that might be in the area. At the direction of the French who traded with them for guns and household goods, they might come to Frederick County. After being threatened with forced servitude, she had been too angry with Mrs. Grimsby earlier that day to pass on the warning.

Besides, if she did not leave now, she would not be able to receive Cy's text message telling her how to get back home. She might miss the departure of her history immersion tour—all because she was already more immersed in history than she wanted to be.

Marty ground her thumb joints into her eye sockets as she agonized over her dilemma.

What should I do? What is the right thing to do?

I cannot leave her like this.

But this is not my era. I need to get home to my own time and place.

CHAPTER 27

The following day, Lee Hardin reported to the office as usual. Mid-morning, about the time most of his fellow special agents were ready to take a break, he made an excuse to get away for an hour. He drove to the internet café.

Trying to puzzle out what Cy was doing hiking up Dead Man's Drop Mountain on Sunday was why Lee Hardin found himself sitting outside Cy's apartment on his own time when Cy hurried to the internet café the previous night. That was also why Lee Hardin parked his government-issue sedan a block away and walked to the internet café this mid-morning.

There were a few customers, but it was not as busy as it had been earlier in the morning or would be at lunchtime. He nodded to the young woman behind the counter and walked into the men's restroom.

A college-age guy was washing his hands when Hardin entered. Hardin stepped over to the mirror and checked the spot on his neck where he had nicked himself with the razor that morning. The two men made a point of ignoring each other. The college kid dried his hands and left.

Once Lee Hardin had the restroom to himself, he stepped to a corner and surveyed the room with a practiced eye. Something was drawing Cy to the men's room. He had watched Cy visit the internet café twice in the previous two days. He saw Cy exhibit the same pattern of behavior both times the kid was there. Shortly after arriving, he entered the men's room. Within ten minutes before Cy left the café, he paid another visit to the men's room.

Instinct told FBI Special Agent Lee Hardin that there was something that was worth knowing about in the men's room.

Hardin reached over and locked the restroom door. He took off of his suit jacket and flung it over the door of the handicap stall. Then he pulled a pair of white latex gloves from his pants pocket and stretched them over his thick fingers. He always kept several pairs handy since he never knew when he would be called on to handle evidence that needed to be protected from contamination. Either that, or he might need to protect himself from being contaminated by the evidence.

Hardin felt around under the edges of the sink. He double-checked by bending over to give the underside a thorough inspection. Including a few wads of old gum stuck under the rim, there was nothing unusual. He checked around and under the urinal.

He looked at the ceiling. The air vent was securely screwed in place. He doubted that Cy had stashed anything there. The kid was never in the restroom long enough to remove the four screws and then replace them. Plus, if he had been fooling with the ceiling vent when someone else was using the john, it would have been noticed.

Hardin checked each of the toilets in the two stalls. They were the style that had tanks, so he lifted the lids and checked inside each one. He felt with his fingers to see if there was anything wedged between the tanks and the wall. Both tanks were set flush with the wall with no space between.

Hardin stood in the handicap stall and walked from side to side, unable to see anything of interest on the sides and the back of the bowl. He reached down to the back of the neck that channeled the water from the bowl to the underground plumbing and felt nothing out of place. He made a face at the yellow stain that the swipe left on his glove. He left the stall and grabbed a paper towel. After he wiped most of it off, he washed the outside of the gloves with soap and water just to be safe and dried them carefully. He did not want to leave any unsavory souvenirs of his exploring for the restaurant customers to find.

Now I know for sure why I always wear these things.

Then another thought occurred to him. He walked to the doorway of the other stall and looked inside, studying the toilet. He realized that the stall was very narrow, probably as narrow as the building code would allow. He knew that if he had the need, he personally would opt to use the handicap stall rather than cram his large frame inside this one, especially when he took into consideration the prospect of closing the door while trying to straddle the bowl.

When Hardin tried to see towards the back of the toilet bowl, all he accomplished was to bang his head on the sides of the stall. Heaving a sigh of resignation, Agent Hardin stepped outside the stall long enough to grab a fresh paper towel. He then threw his tie over his left shoulder, and squatted down. Doing his best to not let his suit pants or shirt touch any part of the toilet, he contorted and wedged his body into the narrow space between the bowl and the divider on the right side of the of the stall. He reached until he could feel the back of the toilet bowl.

In spite of his discomfort, Lee Hardin smiled with satisfaction. His hunch had been right. There was something in the men's room. It probably was something that was worth him knowing about.

Hardin pulled the clump of white tape off the back of the toilet. He stood up and stared at the flash drive wrapped in the plastic that was stuck to the half-cocoon of white cloth tape.

Hardin carefully considered all of the ramifications. He had no business searching the premises of this business or removing possible evidence without a search warrant. Nothing he found here could be used in court if it was known that he just walked in and took it without going through proper channels. The way things stood with his boss, he would not be able to convince him at this point in time to give him the search warrant he needed to obtain the flash drive through "proper channels."

On the other hand, he knew the flash drive did not belong to the owner of the internet café. Neither the manager nor any of the employees knew it was there, of that Lee Hardin was almost sure.

The flash drive belonged to Cy. Hardin knew it without a doubt. But, the internet café was open to the public. Cy did not own or lease this building or business being conducted here. He had no legal claim to anything found inside. If he tried to claim legal protection from unlawful seizure of the flash drive, he would need to explain why he had it hidden away like he did. Cy would not want to do that.

Lee Hardin knew that whatever was on this flash drive was something Cy wanted to keep to himself. Whatever was on there was information he did not want the Bureau to get their hands on if they came back to his apartment with another search warrant.

Lee Hardin needed to know what was on the flash drive.

Just then Hardin heard someone pound on the door.

"Hey, unlock the door!" Hardin heard a loud male voice shout angrily. "What do you think this is, your own private head?"

"Sorry, Pal, I guess I locked it automatically without thinking," Hardin called back. "I'll be there in a moment."

Lee Hardin quickly took the flash drive out of the plastic and slid it into his pants pocket. Then he wadded the plastic back up so that it fit within the hollow of the tape cocoon. As carefully and quickly as he could, he returned the tape minus the flash drive to its place behind the toilet. He stood, threw the soiled paper towel in the bowl and flushed. Then he peeled the gloves off of his hands, turning them inside-out in the process, and quickly wrapped them in a fresh paper towel. He jammed them into his pants pocket. He did not dare try to flush them in case one filled with air and floated back up in the bowl. He grabbed his jacket and turned the knob on the lock.

Hardin pushed past the younger man waiting to get into the restroom.

Behind him, Hardin heard the man grumble in disgust, "You didn't even wash."

Lee Hardin went to the counter and returned the smile of the pretty young woman serving customers. He ordered something to drink. He did not want to be remembered at all, let alone as the man who created a ruckus in the restroom and then left without even placing an order.

While he waited for his drink, Hardin studied the left side of the computer unit closest to him. He saw the flash drive ports built into the side of the holo-projector unit.

After he left the café, Hardin called into his boss to let them know he was chasing a lead. He did not clarify what case the lead belonged to, but promised to be back after lunch. He drove to his own apartment and hit the "on" button of his computer as soon as he entered the door. He went to the kitchen to grab a snack while the computer started up.

Hardin smiled as he thought about what Cy might think of his antiquated all-in-one desktop. With his paper notebook routine, he probably had the kid convinced he was so technologically inept that he did not even know how to turn a computer on and off let alone how to use one. After all, he was more of a field man than a desk jockey. He subscribed to the attitude expressed by some of the old-timers that "real men don't type." Unfortunately, Lee Hardin was the first to admit that he could not do his job if he did not use a computer. The days of turning in hand-written case reports or developing cases without filing reports to be stored and shared electronically within the bureau were long gone.

He was well aware, more than the average special agent, of the limitations of computerized records. Sometimes it seemed that technology had all but taken over the Bureau. He had never learned to type well, which was why he used voice recognition software on his own computer. Still, he could read a computer screen with the best of them. Even though he preferred to read real paper and ink books any day of the week, he had done his share of onscreen reading and investigation.

And that is what he intended to do with the information on Cy's flash drive. He wanted to read everything on there and see where the evidence led him. He put on another pair of gloves before he took the flash drive out of his pocket and plugged it into the USB port.

Hardin took a moment to decide how he wanted to handle the situation. Rather than copy the information from the flash drive to his own hard drive, he set the machine to make a back-up copy directly onto an old-fashioned compact disk. Once the transfer was complete, Hardin put the CD in a jewel case and locked it in the closet floor safe where he kept his collection of handguns. He shut the computer down and drove back to the internet café.

Hardin left his jacket and tie in his car when he went inside. The place was packed with customers wanting to relax in front of a computer on their lunch break. He walked directly into the men's restroom. He grabbed some paper towels before he locked himself inside the small stall.

Hardin fought a wave of claustrophobia as he donned another pair of latex gloves and squeezed down to replace the flash drive in its protected hiding place. Once he finished, he carefully removed the gloves and wrapped them into a clean paper towel before he shoved them into his pocket. He waited a few minutes to allow the occupants of the restroom to cycle in and out before he flushed the soiled paper towel down the toilet, left the stall, washed his hands and then left the internet café.

CHAPTER 28

Marty knew she could not change history. Yet, something told her that she could not abandon someone she had met personally to a fate like Maggie might be facing. She had to try to help her get well. She had to at least warn the Grimsbys to flee to safety.

Marty sighed with resignation as she made her decision. She was going to stay with Maggie for now.

Hopefully, if she did not make it home in time, Cy would be true to his word and contact the tour agency to tell them she would join them later.

Marty stepped a few paces further from the door, hiked up her skirt and relieved herself. Never again will I not appreciate flushing toilets, no matter how old or dirty they are, she thought.

Marty tip-toed back inside of the cabin. She put some water on to heat while she searched in her medicine pouch for more of the purple flower herbs. She also found the herbs that were good for fevers. She put them both on a clean wooden trencher.

Then Marty went to Mrs. Grimsby's bedside to check on her. The woman was still shivering violently in her bed as she clutched the blankets tightly around her neck. Marty could see the reflection of the fire in the woman's eyes.

"Here, Mrs. Grimsby," Marty said quietly. "Drink a little more water. I will build up the fire again. In a little while I can have some more of the tea for you."

After Marty added another log to the fire, she sank onto her stool. Leaning into the table, she rested her head upon her folded arms. She willed herself to not fall asleep until she had finished fixing the tea for her sick patient.

Marty thought about how she had not slept very long or very comfortably the night she and Hunter had been on the mountain. She had only slept a few hours in the loft. She thought about how tired she was after the full day of work. She knew it was going to be a long night.

Marty tended the sick woman, catching only short snatches of sleep in between. She fixed and offered tea to Maggie throughout the night. When the chills turned into a raging fever, Marty coaxed her patient to drink as much cool water as possible. She rummaged around in the heavy chest downstairs and found some pieces of cloth which she used to wipe the perspiration off the sick woman's face and neck. One cloth she repeatedly dampened with cold water and placed on Maggie's forehead to cool her. She only let the fever last what she estimated were a few hours before she made another tea out of the herbs for fever. She laced it well with the molasses, and coaxed it down Mrs. Grimsby.

Towards dawn, the woman's fever broke. Marty pulled a clean shift she had seen earlier out of a chest. The woman was too weak to protest when Marty told her she needed to change out of the damp, clinging shift which, at that point, was rank with the perspiration. Marty helped Mrs. Grimsby put on the dry one.

After digging around in the loft, Marty found only one other blanket that was unused. The beautiful two-color pattern of blue on white with the main design like a medallion in the center of the coverlet impressed Marty as being a work of art. She brought it down, intending to use it to replace the bottom bedding.

"Nay," Mrs. Grimsby protested weakly. "'Tis my good cover. 'Tis for company."

Marty persuaded her to use it on top of her other wool blankets, at least long enough for Marty to move one of the drier blankets to be a bottom sheet so she could take the one saturated with perspiration out to be washed and dried. She rearranged the blankets so that Mrs. Grimsby had only dry bedding next to her.

Finally Maggie Grimsby slept soundly. She was still weak from straining to breath and her lungs still rattled with phlegm, but she had improved since the previous night.

All Marty wanted to do was to lie down and sleep herself. Instead, she forced herself to haul several buckets of water to the lean-to in order to heat it for the wash kettle. She chipped off what she hoped was enough soap and let it dissolve.

While she waited for the wash water to get hot, she fed the animals. Marty's fingers fumbled as she milked the cow. She prayed the animal would not take offense at her inexperience and kick her.

Never again will I complain about needing to make a special trip to the store for a container of milk, she thought.

Marty washed the sick woman's bedding and clothes. She used a long pole she found in the lean-to to stir them.

After she washed everything, she hauled even more water until she had enough to rinse everything in hot water. Then she set everything out to dry on the fence rail like she had been taught. She drew more water from the stream and put in on to heat. She cleaned the dishes from the night before in the wash kettle, even though she knew Mrs. Grimsby would not approve. Marty understood the need to thoroughly wash everything with soap and hot water, but she knew that in 1758 people had not yet figured out the importance of cleanliness in order to prevent the spread of germs.

For breakfast, she made some cornmeal mush and ate it with milk and molasses.

Marty checked on her patient several times. Since the woman seemed to be resting peacefully, Marty left her alone. She figured that sleep would heal Mrs. Grimsby better than anything else.

After finishing the chores she felt were necessary, Marty collapsed on the stool and once more rested her head and arms on the table. She slept until the ache in her back woke her up.

For the noon meal Marty fixed plain cornmeal mush again since she did not want to use up the Grimsby's store of bacon. This would be her last meal here. She made enough to last Mrs. Grimsby for the rest of the day.

Marty hoped to get back to her Sun Access and find a message from Cy telling her what to do to get home. She promised herself that once she was back in Colorado, she was going to go to the nearest restaurant and buy a cheeseburger with all the trimmings.

Marty checked outside. Judging by the position of the sun, she estimated it was mid-afternoon. She took the clothes and the still-damp blanket into the house. She did not want Mrs. Grimsby to be forced to go outside at night to bring them in. The blanket she secured to the edge of the loft using the weight of a chest and two wooden crates she found in the loft. They hung suspended in the main room of the cabin to finish drying before the fire.

She looked over and saw that Mrs. Grimsby was awake and watching her. Marty fixed a bowl of the mush for the woman, thinning it with water and molasses and only a little milk. She helped her patient sit up and turn in the bed so the woman could lean against the wall of the cabin. Although weak, Maggie was able to hold her own bowl. Slowly, without a word, she ate the gruel.

Marty made more herb tea. When Maggie handed back her bowl, Marty offered her the hot drink. Before Maggie could say anything, Marty ran down to the stream with a chip of soap. She washed and rinsed the bowls before she returned and put them in their place. After she finished straightening the cabin, Marty sat on the stool and faced her patient.

"Mrs. Grimsby, I think the worst is over," Marty started with an encouraging smile. "I think you are well enough to take care of yourself. I am going to leave now. I will not stay any longer and allow you and your husband to force me into becoming your indentured servant."

Marty waited for an explosion of protest and threats from the woman, but it did not come.

"I milked the cow and took care of the animals this morning. I left more mush in the pot and two more servings of tea herbs for you on the trencher," She continued. "I'm sorry I cannot leave more, but that is all I have."

"Why did ye stay?" Maggie Grimsby asked quietly. "Ye coulda run away last night."

"You were too sick. Besides, I have a warning for you. Do not ask me how I know this because I cannot say."

The woman narrowed her eyes with suspicion, but she did not say anything.

Marty continue. "If your husband comes home soon, you must tell him to pack up as many things as you can take with you and go to a fort or a city for protection. Some of the warriors who were fighting with the French may attack the English settlements in the Frederick area. If your husband does not come home soon, then you need to go by yourself."

Marty rose and felt the blanket hanging from the edge of the loft.

"It will be dry soon," she said. "Your other shift is already dry. I folded it and put it on top of the chest. I brought in extra firewood and have enough in the fireplace to give you a warm fire for quite awhile."

"Ye be a good God-fearing woman, Martha Clark," Maggie said.

The compliment startled Marty.

"Please take care of yourself, Mrs. Grimsby," Marty said softly. "And, remember what I told you. In the war between the French and the British, the Delaware, the Mingo and the Shawnees are caught in the middle. They will fight for whoever will trade with them so that they can provide for their families. Right now, that's the French. It makes it hard for settlers like you and your husband. Be careful and protect yourselves."

Marty started for the door. Hunter leaped to his feet, eager to follow her. She turned to hold him back.

"No, Hunter," she ordered. "You stay here and take care of Mrs. Grimsby. She needs you. Stay!"

Marty pointed her finger at the hearth as she repeated the command. The dog whimpered, but sank to the floor in obedience.

Marty remembered her gift for Mrs. Grimsby. She debated about giving it to her. Then she decided that just because Mrs. Grimsby chose to be abusive and inconsiderate was no reason for her to not show appreciation for what she had received from the woman.

"Mrs. Grimsby, before I go I have a gift for you to say thank you for the clothes and food you have shared with me. It is not much, but it is what I have. It is carved from the shell of an abalone. I cut a length of rawhide to make a necklace for you."

Marty helped the woman lean forward so she could slip the necklace over the woman's head. Maggie picked up the shell pendant and studied it in the light of the open cabin door. Then she looked at Marty with tears in her eyes and her mouth quivering with unspoken words of thanks.

"Fare thee well," Marty said, repeating the same words she had heard when she and Green Corn had parted just days before.

Marty turned and closed the door behind her. Then she hurried in the direction of the mountain. She still had a few hours of daylight. She wondered if she could get back to the top before nightfall.

She hoped Cy had not worried too much about her since she had not connected with him the previous night. She would be able to text him later, as soon as she got back to her Sun Access.

The hike towards the mountain took longer than Marty thought it should. She decided it was because she was tired. She had to search a little before finding her footprints and Hunter's paw prints that told her where she needed to break away from the stream to travel back up to the top of the mountain. She felt confident that no one was following her. She would be climbing on top of the boulder peak and home before long.

Then she realized, she better worry about protecting herself, just in case Cy could not get her off the mountain that night. She knew the Native Americans were excellent trackers. She raced back down the path to the stream and followed it back for several yards, searching for where her footsteps from that day or even the two days before may have left imprints in the mud or soft dirt. She was still wearing the foot leathers since she had not worn her boots back to the Grimsby's farm.

Marty found a broken limb with dead leaves and used it to brush at anything that looked like a paw or boot print. She brushed her footsteps as she double-backed to the stream again. Then, she took off the foot leathers and stockings while she waded in the water upstream.

She did not know how far she traveled in the stream, but it felt like it was over a mile before she climbed out on some rocks that were part of a cascade of boulders from higher up the mountain. She only knew that from her knees down she felt numb from the cold. The soles of her feet felt raw from stepping on the wet stones in the streambed. She used the hem of the cape to dry her feet before she put the stockings and moccasins back on. She hoped that the few drips that remained on the rocks would disappear before anyone came along and saw where she left the stream.

Where she traveled now was unfamiliar terrain for Marty. She had to continually reorient herself using the setting sun and the compass in the handle of her pocketknife as she made her way to the top of the mountain. Her journey slowed as she climbed and the day was soon gone. She struggled to see in the growing darkness. She soon wished she had brought her flashlight.

She finally felt like she was nearing the summit. The higher she trudged, the more she worried that she had taken a wrong turn and was not climbing the right mountain. If she had miscalculated, she could be in serious trouble. Her Sun Access was hidden in her daypack on top of the mountain Cy thought was Chimney Rock. If she ended up on a neighboring peak, she did not know how long it would take to find her way back.

In the deep shadows of almost total darkness, Marty's peripheral vision caught a movement off to her right. She froze in place. A few moments later, she silently eased up to a tree with a large trunk and pressed against it while she waited for her heart rate to slow down. The woods remained quiet. Too quiet, Marty realized. Without making a sound, she slowly leaned her head around the tree trunk to see if she could spot whatever had caught her eye earlier. It was too dark. She was blind under the canopy of leaves.

Then Marty closed her eyes as a wave of discouragement washed over her. She smelled smoke. Someone had built a fire. Someone was on top of her mountain. When she built her fire two nights earlier, she had realized it had been eons since the last time someone had camped there. Why had someone come here now, of all times? Were they friend or foe?

At this point, Marty decided, they were foe. Anyone who would keep her from finding out how to get back home had to be avoided.

How was she going to get her daypack so she could contact Cy? What if whoever was up there had found it first? She had worked hard to cover any tracks leading to her hiding place. But, she realized with regret, it still had been mostly dark that morning. She might not have caught everything. Had her boot prints and Hunter's paw prints lead whoever was up there right to her daypack?

Maybe she could wait until the intruders were asleep so she could creep up the back side of the mountain unnoticed. If the pack was still concealed in its place, she could sneak away with it and hide until morning. If necessary, she would hike to the top of a neighboring mountain and text Cy tomorrow night.

Marty's thoughts were interrupted when a huge paw of a hand clamped over her mouth and nose and jerked her head back. Another strong arm wrapped around her waist and yanked her until her back pressed tightly against the rock-hard chest of a man who was at least a head taller than she was. She smelled leather and sweat and another strong odor she could not identify. Instinctively, she tried to scream as both of her hands grasped at the hand smothering her face. She tried in vain to pull it away. Instead, the grip on her mouth tightened, shutting off her breath.

She struggled with every ounce of strength she possessed, but was unable to break free of the vice-like grip of her captor. She felt herself being dragged between the trees and up the mountain.

CHAPTER 29

Cy sat at his desk waiting for the darkness that would tell him it was time to contact Marty again. Would she be there tonight? He felt uneasy that she had not answered him the night before.

He had asked her to stay on the mountain for the day. But, he knew, Marty had a mind of her own. Problem was, Cy mused as he shook his head, she tended to follow her heart at times instead of staying focused on the logical considerations.

He wondered if she had gone back to the Colonial farm like she said she might. Okay, Cy had to admit, that logically was a place where she knew she could get food for the day. Unfortunately, being there exposed her to danger. He suspected her real motivation was to warn the woman there about the hostile tribes in the area.

Cy tried to force his concern about Marty from his mind. He had work to do. He had spent every spare minute of the day researching and mulling over cell and tower technology.

What has changed in recent years? How could those recent changes cause these disappearances? He also studied telephone numbers and pondered how they fit in all this. He knew he had to keep working at it until he broke through to a solution.

He studied the area code map torn from the telephone directory two nights before. Every few minutes he turned to his notebook computer and checked locations against the terrain maps on Google Maps and the east coast of North America pages in the printed textbook atlas from his geography class.

If connecting electronically with an incoming or outgoing cell phone call was the trigger to the time travel, how can it be controlled?

The answer eluded him.

It did not look good. All the calls that were involved in Eddie's and Marty's situation originated in Colorado, yet Marty and Eddie ended up back east. On the other hand, both of Marty's calls put her close to where Eddie went, but in different time periods.

Cy wished he knew the telephone number of the person who had called the girl who disappeared from Dead Man's Drop the previous year. The sister of the girl whom he talked to did not know. Because the girl's cell battery was dead, there was no way to find out now.

The knock on his apartment door startled Cy. He momentarily froze in place.

"Who is it?" he finally called out.

"Special Agent Lee Hardin from the Federal Bureau of Investigation, Cy," Hardin's voice boomed through the door. "Open up, please. I have something to give you."

Cy groaned and closed his eyes. Then he shut down the map site on his computer and slammed his atlas shut. Only after he cleared his desk of obvious signs of his research did he rise to answer the door.

He did not want whatever the fed offered because he was sure it was another search warrant. However, he knew the man's loud voice would attract the attention of his neighbors. Their suspicious glances and attempts at innocent-sounding questions would make life for him even more miserable in the days to come unless he acted to prevent it.

As soon as Cy opened the door, Lee Hardin walked into the room without being invited. The tablet and slab he had balanced on his arm looked familiar.

"Brought you something, Cy," the agent said without bothering with a greeting. "You see, after we talked in the parking lot the other day and you said we still had your reading tablet and slab, it got me to thinking. I said to myself, you know? The tech guys should already have gone through all your equipment twenty times over. They got what they need off them. There was nothing to justify an arrest warrant in anything they found. So, why are they keeping this stuff? Just so you don't have the use of it?

"Well, like I told you the other day, I've been gone out of town on another case," Hardin continued. "So, after talking to you, I decide to pay the techies a little visit to see where we are on this deal. They don't think they need it for evidence, but they want to hang onto it, just in case. That's what they say to cover their backsides. Truth is, they should have turned it back over to you, but your stuff got set aside and slipped through the cracks. Other cases came up, you know?

"So I say to them, hey, we got us a college kid who needs his tablet and slab for his schoolwork. What can we work out here? So, this is what we came up with, Cy. Here's your gear back. Now, I won't lie to you—the slab doesn't have the original hard drive. The tech guys kept that for evidence.

But, they put another one in exactly like the one they took out and they transferred over all your programs and files from your old one. I even told them you were a math genius, so to be nice, maybe they could add a program or two you might like for school. They said they did.

"So, here you go," Lee Hardin concluded as he handed the equipment to Cy. "It should be better than new. Sorry you had to wait for it so long but it wasn't my doing."

Cy slowly reached out and took his belongings.

"Thanks," Cy finally said. Then the muscles of his face tightened and Cy gave Hardin a skeptical look. "And I suppose you want me to believe that you did all this out of the goodness of your heart. I suppose I am to believe I don't have to worry that your tech guys stuck something in there to make it easy for them to get at anything I put on the computer."

Lee Hardin took a deep breath and shook his head.

"Look, Kid, you can believe what you want to believe," Hardin said. "I'm telling it to you straight what the deal was I made with the tech guys. If they set you up, I wouldn't know because that is not my thing. Besides, if they want what's on your computer without a warrant, they know how to get in without you knowing about it. And, if there's something hidden in there, you got the brains to find it, anyways."

"Okay, I'll accept what you say, Agent Hardin," Cy said. "I do appreciate having my equipment back. It has been hard going back to my old notebook computer."

"Now, I didn't push the issue on the cell phone," Agent Hardin continued. "Like you said, you got yourself another one and don't need two. You'll get it back once this is cleared up, even though, like you say, it may be outdated."

The two stood looking at each other. Cy was afraid to say much. He did not want to create an opening for Agent Hardin to ask him more questions. He set the returned tablet and slab computer down on a fairly level pile of papers on his desk.

Cy watched as Lee Hardin stepped further into the room and picked up a framed photograph from Cy's overloaded bookcase.

"I thought you told me Martha Clark is not your girlfriend," Hardin said as he studied the photo.

"She's not. She broke up with her most recent boyfriend around Christmas, so she asked me to her senior prom. Since we happen to be good friends, I agreed to take her."

"Good picture of you two. She's a pretty girl. You don't look so bad yourself in a tux and a decent haircut, Cy."

Hardin set the picture down on the shelf and angled it so the light did not create a glare. He snapped a picture of the prom photo with his cell phone.

"Ah, Special Agent Hardin, don't you need a warrant or something to do that?"

"Is there a reason I should need a warrant, Cy?" Hardin asked pointedly as his eyes bore into Cy. "You did invite me into your apartment."

"I suppose not."

To Cy, allowing him to enter as the lesser of evils was not the same as inviting him in, but he decided to not argue the point. He just wanted the man gone.

Lee Hardin looked over at Cy's desk and saw the area code pages Cy had ripped from the telephone book the night before stacked on top of the closed atlas. He walked over and picked up the loose papers.

"Brother, there sure are a bunch of area codes these days, especially back east and on the west coast. You trying to figure out what one you need to make a phone call or something?"

Hardin looked at Cy, waiting for a response.

Cy shrugged, forcing himself to not reveal the tension building up inside of him. Hardin was getting too close.

"Well, you might as well just bite the bullet and call information about it rather than trying to figure it out yourself," Hardin finally continued. "That would be my advice. I remember when there was a time you could always tell an area code because the middle number was either a zero or a one. They never used those two numbers in the middle of a local prefix. And, they never used the numbers two through nine as the middle number in an area code. Now there are so many areas they need codes for, they use any number they can find. When a telephone number comes across my desk these days, especially if some of the numbers are missing, I can't tell anymore if the first three are an area code or a local prefix."

Lee Hardin dropped the pages back on top of the atlas.

It sounded like a casual conversation to Cy, something that the man might say just as an excuse to stay longer in Cy's apartment. At the same time, a sense of excitement energized Cy's brain. He had a feeling that what the agent had just told him about area codes deserved more analysis.

***

Hardin studied Cy face, wondering what was going on in the mind behind the mask. He had not yet started looking at the information he had copied from Cy's flash drive. He knew he was holding back on Cy about that but he had told him the straight truth about getting the computer back from the techs.

On one hand, Hardin knew that if the Bureau ever needed to get the information on the flash drive legally, it would be best to find it in Cy's possession in his own apartment. On the other hand, if Cy was really searching diligently to find Eddie Burrows, having his newer computer returned to him might help the process along. It was time for Cy to bring his flash drive back home. Hopefully, the having his own slab would serve as the lure.

"Good night," Agent Hardin finally said as he turned towards the door. "Been a long day and mine ain't over yet. Take care, Kid."

***

There he is calling me "Kid" again.

Cy fought resentment as he closed his door behind Lee Hardin.

Cy looked down at the tablet and slab that had been returned to him. He wanted to believe that Lee Hardin was telling him the truth about why they were being returned. But, Cy was not sure if he could trust him. Even if Hardin was telling him the truth, who knew what the technological experts at the FBI did behind both their backs?

Cy did smile as he thought over the agent's assumption that the techies could hack into his computer if they really wanted to. All he had to do was get online and they could backtrack right into his information. Well, he knew how to hack. He could play their game, too. If they had inserted something, he would find it. Agent Hardin knew that, but maybe the FBI techs had egos too big to accept that an eighteen year-old student could outsmart them.

Something was going on, but Cy was not sure what. It was out of character for Hardin to go out of his way to do him a favor. Cy decided it was time to dig a little deeper into FBI Special Agent Lee Hardin and see what really made the man tick.

But, Cy knew he would not do it from home. He would not use his own computers. He would wait until tomorrow and start at the university library.

Right now, it was time to go up on the roof to try to make contact with Marty.

CHAPTER 30

Marty was startled by the soft owl call that issued from the throat of her captor. As they approached the top of the mountain, she watched as the native warriors around the circle of light cast by the fire raised themselves to a crouched position. Each grasped either a knife or tomahawk as they silently watched Marty and her captor approach.

The men before Marty were dressed in leather hunting shirts and leather leggings to ward of the cold autumn air. Designs in black covered their faces. The heads of most were bald except for ornamented scalp locks. Blankets and capes were bunched on the ground around the feet of many of them as if they had slipped from the men's shoulders when they stood up.

The big man holding her tightened his grip across her mouth, securing her head firmly to his chest while he moved his other arm from her waist long enough to signal to three of the men. They slipped silently into the darkness, each going a different direction. Then the man hauled Marty closer to the fire.

Marty shook uncontrollably with fear. She had no doubt about her situation. She had been captured by hostile warriors.

The lone woman in the group stood from her place next to the fire and stepped towards Marty. The woman moved gracefully even though she was thick around the middle. Marty suspected she was pregnant. Then she came close enough for Marty to see her face in detail. Right away, Marty noticed the woman's earrings.

It was Green Corn. Green Corn's face was older than Marty remembered. The firelight softened the appearance of her smallpox scars. There was no doubt in Marty's mind it was the same woman she had met just a few days earlier. Only, in Green Corn's mind, Marty knew, it was over ten years ago. Would she remember Marty?

"Others are with you?" Green Corn asked in English.

Marty did her best to shake her head no in spite of the grip on her face.

Marty realized Green Corn could not see her well enough to recognize her. Her cap had been pushed back and to one side, and several locks of hair had fallen over her eyes. Marty watched her through the hair strands, hoping once Green Corn saw who she was that she would protect her.

A few moments later the three men returned to the fire circle. With the faintest movement of their heads, they told the group they had not found anyone else.

"You must not scream," Green Corn warned Marty. "If you call out to warn others, Stalking Bear, as he is known in your tongue, with kill you. Do you understand?"

Marty strained against the man's grasp to nod her head yes.

"Will you pledge your word to not scream if we free your mouth?"

Marty closed her eyes a moment and again nodded. Green Corn spoke briefly to the man who held her. He slowly moved his hand from her mouth. Marty did not dare twist her neck to look at the warrior who had captured her. Instead, she looked into Green Corn's eyes. She stretched her lips to return blood flow, but was afraid to say anything for fear the man would think she was preparing to scream. Through strands of her hair that served as a screen to hide her face, Marty watched Green Corn study her.

"If you will not run, Stalking Bear will release you. If you run, he will strike you down."

Marty swallowed and took a deep breath before she choked out her response. "I will not run, Green Corn."

Green Corn jerked her head back and her eyes widened.

"How do you know the name of Green Corn?"

"We once treated to be friends. My name is Marty. We exchanged presents. I gave you those earrings and you gave me a beautiful beaded medicine bag."

Green Corn spoke a few words in a language Marty did not understand and nodded to the man holding Marty. He released his grip around her waist. Marty carefully took a deep breath, grateful to no longer be squeezed around the middle. She wanted to show Green Corn that she still had the medicine bag. However, it was tied to her belt and tucked under her skirt, or petticoat, as Maggie had called it. She was afraid to make a move that might be interpreted as reaching for a weapon. She definitely did not want them to search her clothing and find her pocketknife that she had put back in her knee pants pocket once it grew dark.

Although she tried to stand still, Marty started to shiver. She carefully pulled the cape tightly around her body to both ward off the chill and hide her adrenalin-induced shaking.

Green Corn stepped back to the same fire pit Marty had used three nights before and pulled a burning brand from the flames. She held the glowing tip so she could study Marty.

Marty cautiously reached up and straightened her cap. She stuffed her hair under the brim so that her face was exposed.

"You look well, Marty. The years have not changed you," Green Corn finally said.

"Your words warm my heart, Green Corn. How is your other baby that I saw last time?"

"My daughter grows strong and will choose a husband in a few years. She brings power to the Turtle Clan. Since we met, I have born two sons who will grow to be strong warriors."

"I am happy for you, Green Corn."

"Do you still have the medicine bag, Marty?"

"Yes. It is inside my skirt. May I show you?

At Green Corn's nod, Marty shrugged the cape back and reached inside the waist of the skirt. She noticed the men stir and grow cautious as her hand reached inside the gathers of fabric. Green Corn spoke a few words, and the men relaxed. Marty pulled out the medicine bag still tied to her belt and balanced it on the palm of her hand for Green Corn to see.

"I have used the herbs you had in the bag, Green Corn. I am hoping to find more."

"This mountain is not a good place to find the purple flower herb, Marty. You will need to search in the meadows to the north. Have you eaten?"

Marty shook her head no and let the medicine pouch rest on top of her skirt as a reminder she was Green Corn's friend.

"Come." Green Corn motioned for Marty to follow her. She led Marty to a place behind the rock and next to where Green Corn had been sitting while she tended the fire and prepared food.

Marty sat and kept her eyes focused on the ground. She carefully arranged her skirt and cape to keep her legs covered. She silently sighed in gratitude that she had left the boots in her backpack and only wore the foot leathers and stockings Maggie had given her. She was also grateful that she was sitting in a place that was partially in the shadows.

Marty sensed someone watching her closely. She glanced up, and then quickly returned her gaze to the ground in front of her, hoping her fear did not show in her face.

The huge man who had captured Marty and brought her to the camp sat cross-legged across the fire from her. His dark eyes set in an expressionless face bore into her. Even with Green Corn there, Marty felt extremely uncomfortable. She sat back deeper into the shadows and stared at her lap, attempting to be inconspicuous. However, she each time she glimpsed upwards, she saw that he still studied her.

Marty noted the sharp angles of the warrior's face with its classic Native American cheekbones and strong brow and chin. Like the other men, his copper skin was decorated with what Marty now realized were tattoos, not war paint. A pendant of European design hung from a leather string around his neck and oval loops cut from bone dangled from his ears. He sat with the dignity that comes from knowing he was an important man among his people.

As Green Corn continued to talk to the men, Marty's occasional upward glance told her that everyone's eyes were either on her or on Green Corn. She guessed that Green Corn shared with them the story of the first time she and Marty met.

As she spoke, Green Corn continued to poke charred oblong objects around in the coals on the edge of the fire. Gradually, they dented when she nudged them with the end of a stick. As they softened, she pulled them from the ashes and rolled them on a nearby rock. Marty guessed that they were a root vegetable.

Once they were all out of the fire, each man reached to grab a vegetable. Green Corn picked out a medium-size root and handed it to Marty. They all ate in silence. Marty followed Green Corn's lead as the woman peeled back the charred skin and ate the fleshy inside. They were not potatoes, but they tasted good.

Afterwards, Green Corn shared some jerky with Marty. Marty recognized the flavor right away: venison.

It was after they had all eaten and Green Corn had shared some water with Marty that Marty's captor stood tall and majestic. Once he had the attention of everyone present, he began to speak. His determined eyes never left Marty. The others in his party listened in respectful silence. Marty felt the dread build inside of her. She feared what this man may have in mind for her. The only thing standing between him and Marty was Green Corn.

Even if Green Corn did speak for Marty, would it be enough to save her from this man?

CHAPTER 31

"Please, Marty, please!" Cy muttered to himself. "Answer me tonight. I am so worried about you."

Cy forced himself to breath slowly in an effort to fight down the panic he felt threatening to consume him. It was two nights now with no word from Marty. Why was Marty not answering his text messages?

He had tried several times earlier with no response. Afterwards, in an attempt to keep from worrying, he had gone back to his apartment for about an hour to review some more of his notes. He had searched the radio sites on the internet to check on the status of solar activity and the atmosphere. He hoped that by trying again later at night, the conditions would be better for transmitting and she would receive his texts.

But now he had been trying for close to two hours with no response. It was late enough that it was early morning back east. Then again, he did not know if the times of the day or the days of the weeks stayed aligned as she traveled through the time and space. He only knew that their text messages seemed to transmit more consistently at night where he was.

What had happened to Marty? Knowing her, he thought, she wanted to warn the Colonial woman about the Indian danger. Had she gone back and run into problems with her?

Worse yet, was Marty captured by a war party from one of the hostile native tribes? Please no, not that, he willed with all the intensity within him.

He did not want to even consider that perhaps her cell phone had been broken.

Cy looked at his watch. It had been about ten minutes since his last attempt. He took a deep breath and started his final text message.

.

Text when u can. I have ?? re fone number u called. I will get info re your tour from your car n tell them u r delayed n will join them later. Waiting anxiously to hear from u. Your bff

After he pushed the send button, Cy reluctantly returned to his apartment. He knew he would not be able to concentrate on anymore research right then. It was time to give his conscious brain a break and let his subconscious work on the problems for awhile. He decided to play video games. He soon grew bored with them. There was nothing left he felt would accomplish much except to get some sleep.

Cy set his alarm for early in the morning and went to bed, hoping it would not take long for him to fall asleep. But he lay awake tossing about. He felt positively frantic that Marty had not responded to any of his text messages two nights in a row. Still, his only hope was to keep up the appearance that all was well. He had to keep working on getting her home.

He also knew he needed to get that information from Marty's car about the tour agency early in the morning. No one must be given a reason to suspect that Marty was gone.

He must retrieve the information from Marty's car while everyone in her neighborhood was still in bed. Marty's family was not due home until after July 4th, but the last thing he wanted was for a neighbor to see him and report him for breaking and entering.

Then there was Mr. FBI Special Agent Lee Hardin. Cy hoped the guy had to sleep sometime and that he could get the matter taken care of for Marty before the suit started his day.

Lee Hardin. Cy nodded his head with determination. *Yes, tomorrow is the day I am going to find out about Mr. FBI Special Agent Lee Hardin.*

CHAPTER 32

Standing proudly at his full height, Stalking Bear finished speaking. The other Lenni Lenape responded in unison.

"*Yo-heng!*"

Marty looked up to see Stalking Bear still watching her. Beyond the outward appearance of his face, stoic as a mask, Marty sensed his satisfaction. Marty leaned forward to get Green Corn's attention and spoke to her softly.

"Green Corn, I feel like he was talking about me. Are you allowed to tell me what he said?"

"Stalking Bear has claimed his right to you as his captive, Marty. The others have confirmed his right."

Marty's eyes grew round with fear as a flood of terrifying images flew through her mind.

"What will happen to me, Green Corn? Will I be tortured?"

"No. Stalking Bear wants you for himself."

"What do you mean? Does he intend to force himself on me?"

Green Corn replied in a disgusted tone. "No. Only European men force themselves on unwilling women. The Lenape know from birth that our bodies are our own. Our women decide when they wish to be with men. None of our men will force themselves on you that way. Stalking Bear wants you for his family."

"Will I be his slave?" Marty asked slowly. Marty now realized being an English indentured servant in many instances amounted to being a slave during the years of their contract. Had she just escaped being the Grimsby's slave only to be a slave to the Lenni Lenape?

"Stalking Bear wishes you to join his family. Both of Stalking Bear's sisters died a summer ago, as did a niece and two aunts this past spring. With so many women of his line gone, the voice of his family within the Turkey Clan grows weak. You will be adopted in the place of one of his sisters."

"He wants me for an adopted sister?"

"Yes, Marty. We all can see that for a European woman, you are tall and strong. You will bear strong, healthy children for your clan, especially since you are able to escape the European diseases. Is it not true what you told me years ago that you will not become sick with the smallpox or measles?"

"Yes, but...."

"Stalking Bear knows this and claims this power for his family. It is a great honor for you."

One thing that Marty had noticed as she had looked around the camp was that, except for Green Corn who had been born a European, the Lenape were a large and well-built people. At least the men were. Stalking Bear would have made a good guard or tackle on a football team if he lived in the twenty-first century, Marty realized. The others were not small people.

Marty knew that in her time, people had been growing bigger with each generation. Her own height of five foot eight inches was about average among her friends. Yet, she had been told her grandmothers were three to four inches shorter and much thinner than she was, and their mothers were shorter yet.

Size-wise, Marty could see that she fit in with these people more so than she did with people like Maggie Grimsby, who, although she was built on the stocky side, was several inches shorter than Marty. Marty suspected that due to diet and other reasons, the Europeans of this era were built more like her great-grandmothers. If Stalking Bear wanted a white woman who would produce large-framed warriors, she could see why they might think she was a good prospect.

But something puzzled Marty. If Stalking Bear was interested in her as a woman that would have children for his family who would grow to be large and strong, why did he want her for a sister to marry off to someone else?

"Smallpox swept through our town twice last year, Marty, killing many," Green Corn continued, disrupting Marty's thoughts. "I stayed well and three of my children survived. My infant daughter and my husband died."

"Oh, Green Corn, I am so sorry to hear that. And here you have another baby on the way, but your husband will never see it."

"My new husband is the father of this child. Voice-Like-Thunder is his name in your language. He sits two men to the right of Stalking Bear. He is the newest sachem of the Wolf Clan. My gift to hear the words and see into the hearts of the English adds power to him."

Marty sensed the happiness in Green Corn's voice as she spoke about her husband and the child she was expecting. Marty looked over at the man Green Corn pointed out as Voice-Like-Thunder. He was a well-formed man, smaller than Stalking Bear, but still a good six feet tall. He did not sport as many tattoos on his face as several of the others. Also, unlike the other men, he had a full head of hair that he wore in a single braid down the back of his head. He looked older than Green Corn by several years. Although he was not watching Marty and Green Corn directly, Marty suspected that his awareness was focused on the conversation between the two women.

"The Europeans brought their sicknesses to this land," Green Corn continued. "Many British, especially, cross the great waters and cover the land like black flies, bringing new waves of their diseases with them. It is only right that we claim captives from among the British to adopt and build our clans back up to our full strength."

"I do not understand what is going on here," Marty said quietly to Green Corn. "How will adopting me to be a sister build up Stalking Bear's clan?"

"He will find strong men for you to choose from for a husband, Marty. But, I promise you, he will not force a man you do not want onto you. Your children will make his clan, the Turkey Clan, strong."

"Would not my children strengthen the clan of their father and me?"

"No, Marty," Green Corn shook her head. "Our ways are not like the Europeans where there are no clans and the wife and children belong to the husband. European fathers bribe other men to take their daughters as wives by offering the men—what is it they call it, a dowry?—to marry their women. Among the British, a woman who comes to her husband with a small or no dowry for the husband to control is seen by her husband as having little worth. Among the Lenape, it is not so. There is no dowry because the women already own the land and the houses of the clan. A man or a woman always belongs to the clan in which he or she was born or adopted. A woman stays part of her clan whether she has a husband or not, just as her husband stays part of his clan. The children belong to the clan of their mother. Your husband will not be your relative or the relative of your children."

"You must be joking!" exclaimed Marty. "Are you saying a father is not related to his children?"

"No," Green Corn confirmed. "Your husband will be from a different clan so he will not be a relative. Stalking Bear will be your brother and your closest relative. He will see that your husband treats you and your children well. He will see that the women of his clan teach you and accept you as one of them. You will join the women of his family in the ownership of the clan homes and land. They will prepare you to speak good counsel to the matron. Because there are so few women in his clan now, the time may come that you or one of your daughters may be a matron in the Turkey Clan. Stalking Bear will be the uncle to your sons and teach them to be good men and strong warriors. Your sons will follow him, not your husband."

Marty stared at Green Corn as she tried to absorb what the woman told her.

Wow! Their understanding of family relationships is a whole lot different from what I have been taught.

Marty's initial reaction was that she preferred the parent-child family organization over that of a clan family. That was familiar to her. Then again, she realized, the more egalitarian father-mother relationship of her time and culture were much different than what often existed throughout many centuries and in many cultures where men thought they were better than women. She was now living in one of those centuries. Would she really choose the parent-child family unit of the Europeans over the clan family unit Green Corn obviously preferred if it meant that one of the parents dominated and basically owned and controlled the rest of the family?

Marty remembered learning the textbook explanations, written by those of European origin, that when English captives chose to remain with the tribes, it was because they could not bear the stigma they would suffer when returned to their own people. The women, especially, found they were shunned if they had taken an Indian husband and bore "half-breed" children. The English, and later the Americans, seemed to find it puzzling that these captives preferred to stay. The Europeans assumed the captives would want to return to the civilized society of the whites, even with the discriminatory treatment they often received afterwards.

Maybe the truth was entirely different. In one of his text messages, Cy mentioned that part of the 1758 treaty negotiations dealt with the return of prisoners captured by the Western Ohio Indians. Yet, out of 600 captives that were eventually allowed to return to the British, over half refused to leave their Native American homes.

After the dismal future Maggie had offered her, Marty could see where indentured servants, especially, who were captured and adopted would prefer to stay with their new Indian families.

Voice-Like-Thunder spoke and Green Corn turned away from Marty to answer him. Marty guessed she was repeating their conversation to her husband. Meanwhile Marty's mind raced as she thought about the fate Stalking Bear had in mind for her. He did not intend to kill her or enslave her. That was good. He still might make her run a gauntlet or prove her worthiness in other ways. He wanted her to be adopted into his family. It was not the worst of fates.

Yet, Marty was not from the eighteenth century. Family relationships among the people she knew as she grew up were based on love, respect and accepting each other as equals. People in 2024 Colorado had many personal freedoms and opportunities available to them as long as they stayed within the law. Given a choice between living with Green Corn's people and returning to the twenty-first century, there was no contest. She wanted to go home.

Marty gazed casually around the campsite. She did not see her daypack or any of its contents. She hoped that meant that they had not found her cache. She hoped they had no reason to search around the rocky mountaintop looking for it. But she also knew that was not her most immediate worry.

She could not escape by outrunning all these men. Once they moved her away from Chimney Rock, she did not know the area well enough to find her way back to her Sun Access. She knew that her only hope was to convince them to leave her there on the mountain.

As she considered her options, Marty developed a strategy. It would mean drawing on everything she had learned from Cy, Maggie Grimsby and Green Corn herself. She had always been a quick study in drama class and she had always been able to cram and pass her exams with impressive grades. But this would be the most important test of her abilities. If she failed, she risked losing her freedom. She risked losing a chance of ever returning to the twenty-first century and everyone who was important to her there.

CHAPTER 33

"Green Corn, you once told me when we agreed to be friends that if trouble crossed my path, you would speak for me. I am asking you to speak for me now."

"Stalking Bear has already spoken and claimed you, Marty."

Marty took a deep breath and willed herself to not lose her courage. She offered a silent prayer in her mind and hoped beyond hope that as she spoke, she would choose the right words to say and that the Lenape would not take offense if they did not understand something she said the way she meant it to be understood. She hoped that Green Corn would understand her heart and use the right words to share her meaning.

"I understand, Green Corn. But I still would like them to consider the possible bad consequences of taking me as a captive at this time when your people are preparing for peace talks with the British."

Green Corn squinted her left eye as she studied Marty's face. "You know the Lenape go to talk with the British soon?"

"Yes."

Marty wondered if she suspected treachery. Marty could claim with all sincerity that she meant no harm to these people. She hoped that Green Corn would sense that.

"If you wish to speak, stand and speak," Green Corn finally said. "They will listen."

Marty took another deep breath. She nervously pushed herself to her feet and stood as straight and dignified as she was able to. She slid the front edges of her cape back across her shoulders so that the medicine pouch, the token of Green Corn's friendship, was visible. She held her head high with an air of confidence she did not feel.

"Green Corn, please tell Stalking Bear that I recognize his right to claim me as his captive. Please tell him that I consider it a great honor that he chooses me be adopted into his family and his clan to take the place of one of his sisters who has died. But I also ask, is it a wise choice for the Lenni Lenape if Stalking Bear claims his right at this time?"

Marty could see the curiosity in the eyes around her. Green Corn turned to translate. Marty continued to talk slowly, allowing only enough time between every sentence or two for Green Corn to share her words. She was afraid she might lose her nerve if she stopped speaking too long.

"Is it not true that the Moravian minister, Christian Frederick Post, came with your chiefs Pisquetomen and Keekyuscung among the Western tribes of the Lenape? Did he not invite the Western tribes, including the Lenape, to meet with the British of Pennsylvania and New Jersey in Easton because the Lenni Lenape of both the Eastern and Western bands wish to treat for peace? Is it not true that the Eastern bands hope to regain their land that was taken by the Europeans at the time of the Walking Purchase?"

"This is true, Marty," Green Corn answered. "It is well-known that the chiefs among the Pennsylvanians obtained the land of the Eastern Lenape by fraud. However, that does not so much concern the Lenape in the West. Our warriors wish for peace because they cannot hunt and make war at the same time. Our towns grow hungry while we must fight on the side of the French so we can trade with them. Your General Braddock turned his heart away from the Lenape and the Shawnee. He wished us to fight with him but he would not treat with presents. In revenge and for our own survival, we have fought with the French and attacked many British in Pennsylvania these past years. Only the Quakers have we left alone. But now our revenge is stopped by hunger.

"This war is between the British and the French," Green Corn continued. "They should fight each other across the great waters where they came out of the ground and not bring it among the tribes who came out of this ground. The Lenape grow weary of the white men's wars. The hearts of the Lenape seek peace so our men may hunt instead of fight."

"Is it not true that your people also wish to make peace with the British so you may trade with them?"

"Yes. We have fought for the French to trade and live. But because of the British blockade of the French ships, few trade goods now come. The French ask too much for too little. Trade with the British would be better than with the French. The British also wish to drive the French out of our lands. To that we give our *Yo-heng*. But it must be that the British will also stay out of our lands. We offer peace for trade and a treaty that will keep the Europeans on the other side of the Alleghany Mountains."

"And will the British agree to peace or anything else when they learn the Lenape have taken a new captive?" Marty asked. "I will be missed, Green Corn. I have family waiting for me at home."

After Green Corn translated, Marty could see the look of understanding in the eyes of several of the men around the circle. Then Green Corn turned back to her and spoke without translating. Marty realized Green Corn was trying to persuade her of the benefits of going with Stalking Bear.

"Stalking Bear is a powerful warrior who offers you a place of honor among his clan, Marty," said Green Corn. "He will see that you will find a good husband among the Lenape. His clan lives with the same band as my clan, so you will still have a close friend in Green Corn. It will be a good life for you."

"Yes, I understand the honor he offers me. And I value your friendship, Green Corn. But I have a family."

"Do you have a husband, Marty?"

"No, not yet. I do have someone special waiting for me to return."

"Is this man your own choice or was he chosen as a husband for you by your father?"

"He is my choice."

Green Corn studied Marty's face. After a few moments, Marty continued.

"The British will regard the Lenni Lenape words of peace as a noise in the forest if they see what they think is an act of hostility so close to the time of the peace council. You understand the thinking of the men among the British, Green Corn. Even if I go with Stalking Bear willingly, will the British believe it was my choice? Is it not true that in their pride they refuse to believe that life is better among the tribes of this land than among the civilization of the English? Even if I say it is my choice, will they not say that I am but a foolish woman and I must have a man decide for me and speak for me? And if this man does not choose peace with the Lenape, will he not speak his own words instead of the words of my heart?"

As Green Corn translated for the others, Marty wondered how much of their conversation she shared with them. After Green Corn finished translating, her husband briefly spoke.

"You speak true words, Marty," Green Corn said when she turned back to her. "But who does not wish peace with the Lenape? Is it not better for the British that we no longer fight on the side of the French?"

"Yes, but the Iroquois—I mean, the Haudenosaunee—have considered themselves the rulers over all the eastern tribes for many summers. Before, they were your uncles to speak for your tribe. Is it not true the Haudenosaunee, not the Lenni Lenape, in the past have attended the feasts of the British to treat with them and received the presents from the British to brighten the Covenant Chain? Did they not have this power over your people and receive these gifts instead of the Lenape even when the covenants were about your people and your land?"

"It is as you say, Marty. At one time we were called the grandfathers, because we were the first tribe among the Algonquin. The Haudenosaunee were the enemy ones, not of the Algonquin people. But, when they defeated us, they made themselves our uncles. It is only in recent memory that we have become strong enough that we no longer pay them tribute. It is only in recent memory that the British have taken the skirt from the Lenape and made us men to speak for our own tribe at council."

"Does it warm the hearts of the Haudenosaunee that the Lenape now wear the breechcloth and treat for themselves?" asked Marty. "Does it warm their hearts that the tribes of the Ohio Valley will receive the presents and feast with the British in a manner that the Haudenosaunee once enjoyed alone? Is it not in their heart to still be your uncles and to still be the chief tribe in the lands of the British? Is it not in their heart to remain the uncles and the only way that the Lenape and others may enter the Covenant Chain? Will they not try to stop the words of the Lenape sachems by pointing to Stalking Bear's captive? Will they not claim that the Lenape behave as children and still need their uncles, the Haudenosaunee, to speak for them?"

Marty thought she saw a knowing look on the faces around her as her argument was translated.

"It is true that the Haudenosaunee turn their face away from seeing the Lenape as men who need no uncles to rule them," Green Corn replied. "The Haudenosaunee wish our voices to be as a noise in the forest with no power to make our own covenant chains. But the Moravian Christian Post says that the treaty is only for the Lenape of the East and for Western tribes of the Ohio."

"Yes, but Sir William Johnson of the state—I mean—the colony of New York has learned of the treaty council. For the Englishman Johnson to keep his power with the great king across the great waters, he must keep the Haudenosaunee hearts close to the British. The British eyes do not see the Haudenosaunee as a separate nation of people. To the British, the Haudenosaunee are British subjects. In the hearts of the British, they are the uncles to the Haudenosaunee. The British base their claim to the Ohio Valley, where you make your home, on the Haudenosaunee claim that it is their land by conquest, even though they never lived there. To prove to the Haudenosaunee that his heart is with them, Johnson has invited them to the council to oversee the other tribes who also claim the Ohio Valley."

Once Green Corn translated, Marty felt like she could cut the tension among the Lenape with a knife. Was this was the first time they heard that the Iroquois would be there?

Cy had put that information in one of his text messages. As much as she had been impatient with his history lessons, Marty was now grateful he had sent these details. She knew she could not change history, but the Lenape might as well know what they were facing when they went to Easton.

"Were your words not true, Green Corn," Marty continued, "when you told me that the Virginians used cunning and deceit against the Haudenosaunee sachems at the Lancaster council to trick them to put their marks on a new treaty? Was it not in the hearts of the Virginians to sell your land to European settlers to bring the powerful men of their colony many riches? Did not their great king across the waters, who is the father of us all, look at the marks of the Haudenosaunee sachems on the paper brought to him by the Virginians? Did he not believe the hollow words of the Virginians when they told him the Haudenosaunee gave them your land in the Ohio Valley by treaty? And now these past summers the Lenape have fought with the French against the British. The Virginians do not come to treat at Easton as they did at Lancaster. But, will they not have ears in the bushes to know the words spoken about this land of yours that they covet for themselves?"

Tense silence hung thick in the air as the men considered Marty's words.

"These things are as you say," Green Corn finally acknowledged.

Marty continued with more confidence. "Did not the Virginian George Washington go to the new General Forbes who wished to reclaim Fort Duquesne from the French? Did not Washington's words try to turn the general's heart so he would build his army road the long way through Virginia instead of the short way through Pennsylvania? Is it not true that General Forbes stopped the words of George Washington because he knew in his heart that Washington's heart was not for the British army? Did Forbes not see that it was in Washington's heart to have the road in Virginia so the Virginians could someday use it to bring English settlers to your land?"

After Green Corn finished translating, Marty sensed another wave of unease travel among her audience as they looked at one another. The men muttered among themselves. Was this also new information for them?

"How is it you know these things, Marty?" asked Green Corn.

"There is much talk among the English here in Maryland. This land of Lord Baltimore is between Virginia with its wealthy land-hungry men, and the Friendly Association who work for peace in Pennsylvania. But not all British seek peace with the Lenape like the Quakers of Pennsylvania."

"Pemberton of the Quaker's Friendly Association speaks of peace, but his is a voice in the woods that holds no power," said Green Corn. "We know we treat with the British of Pennsylvania and New Jersey who are not friends of the Lenape. But we have grown to be a strong nation in the west and the Shawnee and Mingo stand with us."

"Yes, but Virginia is a strong colony, too. Many of their mighty men have their hearts set on possessing your land. They do not fear to send their warriors to take your land so they may sell it to the European settlers who flood their shores. Would it not smooth their path for capturing your land in the west if there was no peace treaty between your people and the British?

Would it not serve these men well to point to a new captive among you? Would they not use it to show that your words of peace are hollow and you will not hold a covenant chain of peace with the British close to your hearts?"

Marty paused for dramatic effect.

Not for nothing have I taken drama classes.

Then again, she realized, this was not a make-believe drama where, in the end, everyone lives happily ever after and the audience goes home feeling entertained. This was real. The future course of her life depended on it. She forced herself to stand even taller as she gave her closing statement with as much force and conviction as possible.

"The Lenni Lenape must choose between the right of Stalking Bear to claim his captive or power for the tribe to show a true heart when they treat for peace at Easton. Which is the wise choice?"

After Green Corn finished translating, Marty sat down. She forced herself to keep a neutral expression on her face while she anxiously waited for their decision. She stared as the dwindling flames of the fire as though she was indifferent to the outcome. In reality, every sense about her, including her peripheral vision, was tuned into the people around her, trying to gauge their response to her words.

At first there was total silence. Apprehension built up inside Marty. Had she persuaded them? Would they let her go? Or, would they decide that she was one of the hated British who were cheating their people and, therefore, deserved no mercy?

Speaks-With-Thunder finally rose and spoke. Marty looked up and studied his face. She knew that, as a sachem, he would be at the Easton council to speak for his clan. She wondered what he was saying but Green Corn did not translate for her. The sachem's face did not betray his thoughts. Everyone listened in respectful silence. When he finished and sat down, the Lenape, all but Stalking Bear, gave him their *Yo-heng*.

Once again there was silence except for the occasional crackling of the fire.

A few minutes later, Stalking Bear rose to his feet. He stood tall and straight to speak. The man still frightened her, but Marty could not help but be impressed by the warrior's physical presence and air of dignity. After he finished, he turned to Marty, his face betraying no emotion. She studied his eyes. What did she see there? Anger? Determination? Disappointment?

"*Yo-heng!*"

Stalking Bear sat back down and looked off into the blackness beyond the rocks. Silently and without expression, Green Corn stirred the coals and added several more branches to the fire.

CHAPTER 34

"You will sleep between me and the high rock, Marty," Green Corn finally said quietly. She offered an opened deerskin pouch to Marty. "Do you wish bear fat for your face and hands to help you stay warm?"

Marty immediately recognized the strong odor as the same one she had smelled on Stalking Bear when he first grabbed her in the woods. She politely declined.

Marty began to doubt herself. Had she been foolish to try to talk her way out of accepting the honor of being adopted as Stalking Bear's sister? She knew she had a friend in Green Corn. If she had to be stuck in this era, would she not be better off with these people? Yet, she had just done her best to persuade them to let her go. If they forced her to stay with them, would they hold that against her?

Marty knew why she tried to persuade them to leave her on the mountain. She still believed that Cy could get her home.

Marty glanced in Stalking Bear's direction. He had moved outside the light of the fire to sleep. She saw the reflection of the flames in his eyes as he studied her.

The rest of the camp was just beginning to settle in for the night when one of the warriors assigned to guard the group silently appeared in the faint light cast by the campfire. He quickly spoke to Stalking Bear. The other men gathered around to hear what he said. They did not act as though they were in eminent danger but something had happened. There were several glances towards the northern sky. Marty looked up to see if she could tell what they might be talking about. The sky looked lighter than it had earlier, but she could not distinguish anything unusual in the night sky.

I wonder if there is another aurora like there was the other night, Marty thought. She grew uneasy with worry. Did these people have legends or superstitions about auroras? If so, would they consider one at this time as a positive or negative sign as far as she was concerned?

Green Corn rose and joined her husband long enough to hear the discussion before she returned to Marty's side.

"There are lights in the sky to the north," Green Corn said to Marty. "The night will be like a full moon. The men discuss the wisdom of posting more guards."

Marty wanted to see for herself. If it really was an aurora, then it meant that her chances of getting home the next day were very good. That is, they were very good if she could get to her Sun Access and make contact with Cy so he could tell her what she needed to do.

"Green Corn, could we walk towards the north side of the mountain to see?" asked Marty. "Besides, I need a little privacy away from the men for a few moments before I go to sleep."

Green Corn gave her a knowing look.

"Yes, Marty, I will come with you to find privacy. Then I also would like to climb the rocks away from the camp to see the lights to the north."

After Marty and Green Corn emerged from the depths of the bushes, they moved around the base of the rocks to the north. Marty grew apprehensive as, in spite of the shadows, she recognized that they were close to where she had hidden her daypack. She wondered if she had successfully brushed away her boot prints and Hunter's paw prints from two nights before. She did not know how long Green Corn and her party had arrived before she was brought into their camp. If it was still daylight when they came, they might have surveyed the area to be sure there were no signs of anyone being there recently. She dare not look in the direction of where she thought her hiding place for the daypack might be for fear of drawing attention to it. She felt somewhat relieved that nothing appeared to be disturbed.

Marty could see the glow above the trees, but the dense branches still held enough leaves to block the northern horizon.

"Come," said Green Corn as she held out her hand to Marty to help her climb the boulders. Marty gathered up her skirt and shift and draped them over her right arm while she reached out to Green Corn with her left hand. She was glad Green Corn started up a jumbled stone stairway that did not look like the cluster of rocks Marty had used to hide her pack.

When they reached the top, the two of them gazed in companionable silence at the blue and pink aurora dancing to the north of them.

"Among our tribes of the Algonquin, some have the legend that these lights come from Nanahbozho, creator of the Earth," Green Corn said. "When he finished his task of the creation, he traveled to the north to live. He built large fires. These northern lights are the reflections of his flames to remind his people that he still thinks of them."

"That is a wonderful creation story, Green Corn. I never heard it before. Thank you for sharing it with me."

They continued to watch the aurora.

A few minutes later, Marty learned her fate.

"We will leave in the morning, Marty. You will stay. For the good of all the Lenape at the peace council in Easton, Stalking Bear has chosen to not take you with him at this time."

"Thank you, Green Corn," Marty exhaled a sigh of relief. "You have proven yourself to be a true friend by speaking for me. I can never repay you."

"I spoke of our friendship only. The words of council you spoke yourself, Marty. Green Corn only put your words in their ears. The men heard your wisdom. They know your heart is good. But as I spoke for you because of our friendship, Marty, I now ask as a friend that you stop your words for us. We return from the Shawnee where we have learned their hearts and ours are as one about making peace with the British. We traveled these mountains to stay far from the French who may hunt for us in this land to try to destroy the British peace. Just as they tried to find and kill the Moravian Post before he could give our message to the Pennsylvanians, they will try to kill us if they know we are among those who will go to Easton. You spoke true words when you said there are those among the British who want our towns and hunting grounds more than they want our peace. They would keep us away if they knew we offer peace only in trade for keeping all Europeans from our land. When you return to your people, do not speak of us being here."

"I give you my word, Green Corn. I will say nothing to the British or to anyone who might slip up and say something that will get back to your enemies."

Marty continued to watch the auroras with a joy and amazement born of relief. She could not get over how beautifully the lights danced across the heavens. Then she became aware that Green Corn was no longer looking at the sky. Instead, she was studying Marty's profile.

"Marty, we have treated to be friends," Green Corn said solemnly. "But it has become more than a bright covenant chain. I feel in my heart you are a friend. I admire your bravery and, perhaps, too much foolish trust in your heart as you travel through the wilderness alone. But I am still Lenape. I speak as a Lenape woman when I tell you how it saddens my heart that you have chosen to not walk with the Lenape. It saddens my heart that you have turned your face from becoming Stalking Bear's sister and joining our band."

Marty turned to look Green Corn in the eye. How could she explain to this woman about Cy and her family and friends who belong to a different time and place? How could she explain all that awaited her in the twenty-first century? Green Corn would not understand.

"I appreciate what you are saying, Green Corn. I am sorry that I must disappoint you by not coming with you. I know your people have suffered at the hands of the Europeans. I understand that Stalking Bear bestowed a great honor upon me by desiring to adopt me into his clan. However, I do believe that it will be better for your people if the British and the Iroquois cannot accuse your tribe of destroying peace by taking another captive so close to the peace talks."

"You must hold this man who waits for you very close to your heart. It saddens my heart that you to choose for you and your children to be as captives to him if he decides to treat you as such. As a Lenape, it saddens my heart that you wish to live as a weak Englishwoman with little standing among your people when you could be an equal of all with a strong voice among us. You would bring much power to us, Marty."

Marty had learned enough from Cy and Maggie Grimsby to understand what Green Corn was saying about the status of Colonial women. On the other hand, based on what she had learned about the Lenni Lenape, there were things about their ways she did not like any better.

"It is hard to explain, Green Corn, but I am not from here," said Marty, choosing her words carefully. "What you say about how it is with the English Colonists, it is not like that where I come from. Men and women have equal status. Both men and women have a voice in society. The mother and the father have the responsibility of raising their own children. Even though they have different roles in the family, they both are related to their children. Aunts and uncles and grandparents on both sides of the family are relatives. It is more like we are all part of one big clan, not divided into different clans like the Lenape."

"Different clans are important. It is not good to marry in your own clan. For us, it is forbidden."

"We look more at not marrying too close within extended families when making marriage choices," Marty responded. "Besides, your talk of power feels uncomfortable to me. It sounds like it is important to you to be better than the other people around you. I believe people—both men and women—should see each other as being equal in value. Why can't both men and women have the same rights? Where I come from, being a man or a woman only partly defines who we are or what we should do in life. People have different talents and abilities but each one is important. It is not like only men have certain abilities so they must only do certain work and only women have certain other abilities and must do only women's work."

"The spirit of our earth mother would be offended if men instead of women were to plant and grow our crops, Marty," Green Corn said defensively. "She would turn away her gifts and not give us a good harvest. Our people would suffer great hunger in winter with only the food our hunters bring us."

Marty decided to not tell Green Corn that among the Europeans, the men successfully worked the farms. However, Marty realized that the contribution of the Lenape women towards providing food for the people must be part of the reason they were considered equal to the men in society. It did seem to her that so many societies throughout time valued people based on the material wealth they generated.

"Our hearts speak of the same thing with different words, Marty," Green Corn said, drawing Marty back to the present. "We also each have our own special power—what you call abilities. It does not make one Lenape greater than another. But I have lived among the English, Marty, and I know of no such place like the one of which you speak. Among the Europeans, men think they are better than women and look down on women's work and abilities as less important than their own."

Sometimes we run across men who still think like that.

Marty shook her head with regret, but decided she was not going to mention the exceptions to Green Corn.

"You make it sound like European men do not love their wives. They only use them."

"No," said Green Corn wistfully. "My heart tells me my English father and my English mother loved each other. My English mother came to this land as a child slave. Once the words on her paper said she was free, she was alone and she owned only herself. I once heard the words of my English father's heart when he told her he needed no dowry but her love."

"Did your English father love you?"

"Yes," said Green Corn quietly. "And I loved him. But, I often felt great sorrow in my heart because he turned his face away from me learning as my brothers learned. His words to me were that such knowledge was wasted upon a girl because I only needed to know how to care for my family and my home. All else was for the men in my life. My mother spoke for me but her words were stopped when my father said no."

"That is too bad, Green Corn. It is not like that where I come from. Boys and girls both have the freedom to follow their interests and develop their abilities. When men and women marry, they work out between themselves how each will use these interests and abilities to take care of their children and strengthen the family."

"If what you say is not just noise in the bushes, then this place you come from is a good place, Marty. If you will not choose the Lenape way, then you must get away from the British and go back there."

"I plan to as soon as possible, Green Corn."

"I hope it is as you say and that as the summers pass this man you choose proves worthy of your trust."

"I also hope I am not making a mistake," Marty said quietly as she turned to once again study the aurora, hoping she saw in it the power to take her home. "But, for now, since Stalking Bear has allowed me to stay here and not go with the Lenape, I must follow my heart."

Green Corn also turned to look at the Aurora. After a few more moments, she spoke again.

"Marty, I speak to you now, not with the heart of a Lenape, but with a heart of one who holds you close as a friend," she said in a low voice. "Your heart is an English heart, but it is good. I understand love for a man. So I speak words of caution to you. Do not come in the wilderness again to search for your herbs. Go to your family and the man you choose in this land you speak of. Stay far away from the lands of the Lenape and our allies."

"I hear you, Green Corn. I think I have learned my lesson. I know I was very fortunate that of anyone who could have found me, it was you and your people."

"Remember, Marty, it will only happen this once," Green Corn warned. "The Lenape know you are Stalking Bear's captive. They hold him close to their hearts because of his sacrifice tonight. If you are captured again after we meet with the British at Easton, he will not be denied."

CHAPTER 35

The sky was still black when the Cy's alarm sounded. He groaned at the thought of having to get up. Nevertheless, he forced his body out of bed.

He checked outside his window. Although the stars still twinkled bright in the sky, he knew that within an hour a thin ribbon of gray would form on the eastern horizon. He would have to hurry if he was going to get to Marty's house and get into her car before it was light enough for her neighbors to see him. He threw on his clothes and grabbed his shoulder bag. He brushed his tousled, uncombed hair out of his eyes as he ran down the stairs towards his car.

Once Cy reached Marty's neighborhood, he parked around the corner a block away from her house. He then briskly walked around the block, thankful it was an average-size neighborhood block instead of a long, winding street designed for aesthetic appeal as well as to discourage speeding. He approached her house from the opposite side of where he left his car. He craned his neck to double-check house windows and garage doors to be sure no early risers preparing to leave for work might be about to spot him. Satisfied that most of the neighbors close to Marty's house were still asleep and all was quiet in the surrounding homes, he moved up the driveway between the side hedge and the driver's side of her car.

Cy punched the code to deactivate the alarm, smiling in appreciation at how easy she had made it for him to remember the number. Once the car door opened, he quickly climbed in and closed the door to kill the overhead lamp. He searched for the light switch, and turned it off so that light would not come on again when he was ready to leave. He opened the glove compartment and shielded the small light inside with his shoulder bag while he searched through her papers for the flyer she had described.

A pair of headlight beams flashed into Cy's peripheral vision as a car pulled out of a driveway across the street and down two houses. It turned his way. He slammed the glove box shut and ducked his head below the window. After he heard the car drive past him, he cautiously peered through the windows to make sure no one else was around.

He opened the compartment again. Once he found the flyer he needed, he slid it into his bag. After Cy reset the alarm on Marty's car, he hurried down the drive and turned to walk the shortest distance to his own car.

Cy casually surveyed the neighborhood again to see if he could detect anyone on the street watching him. He nodded to a man out walking his dog. He silently sighed with relief when he reached his Civic. He turned back to check again as he unlocked the driver's door. The guy with the dog was already around the corner with his view of Cy blocked by a house.

As he arrived home, Cy noticed that the eastern horizon was a ribbon of pink below the gray. He knew he would not be able to go back to sleep. He showered, dressed for the day and ate some breakfast.

Cy read through the brochure from the tour company. He shook his head at the play on words: "Where West Meets East" by West Tour Agency. He looked on the back for the tour details that were printed above the picture of a middle-aged man wearing a white Stetson. A bolo tie around his neck set off a blue western-cut shirt. Mr. West himself was leading the tour.

Marty's group was to leave at 8:00a.m. Check-in started at 7:00a.m. Cy decided he wanted to be there as soon as someone arrived to organize the people as they showed up with their luggage. The agency was across town. He glanced at his watch. He realized he better leave right then in order to get there in time.

He left his shoulder bag in the apartment. He would bring the car home and park it afterwards so he could walk to the university as usual.

Cy only had to circle the block that housed West Tour Agency once in order to find the staging area. He quickly parked where his vehicle would not been seen by the agency employees or the tour guests. He did not see anyone fitting the description of Mr. West, but he spotted a woman with a tablet checking in people who were standing near the bus with their suitcases and backpacks clustered about them.

The woman was surprised when Cy gave her Marty's message. She expected to hear something like that directly from Marty or her parents. Cy smiled and, hoping to assure her, explained that Marty's parents were out-of-town on vacation. Marty was having trouble with her cell. Cy spun a story about how she had tried to call him but the connection kept cutting out. She had then contacted Cy by text message to say she was delayed. She did not have a cell number for anyone in the agency, so she had been unable to text them directly.

Much to Cy's relief, the woman seemed to accept his explanation. She told him she looked forward to Marty joining them as soon as possible.

She also gave Cy her business card with her cell number and told him to have Marty text with updates.

Afterwards, Cy drove back to his apartment and parked the car. He went inside long enough to grab a quick snack, some bottled water and his shoulder bag before he left on foot for the university.

Remembering that the FBI had shown up with a search warrant for the computer he used in his T.A. office, Cy decided to use the computers in the library to do his research. Thankfully, with summer classes in session, the library's computer services were available.

CHAPTER 36

Lee Hardin was in a foul mood that morning. The night before he had hoped to go through the files he had copied from Cy's flash drive. Instead, he had been kept at the office as back-up, waiting on a team that was in the field until late. By the time he arrived home, he had decided to call it a night. After grabbing something to eat while he watched the news, he went to bed.

He was doubly annoyed that morning because someone else was parked in the spot he liked to use for watching Cy's apartment. While he looked around and tried to decide where else he should park, he almost missed seeing Cy drive his car into the apartment parking lot.

The kid is out awful early for not being a morning person.

Hardin circled the block and parked out of the direct line of sight of Cy's windows but where he could see when Cy left the building. He had almost decided that Cy went somewhere else after leaving his car without returning to his apartment when Cy finally appeared and started walking towards the university. He followed Cy at a distance, long enough to know that the kid entered the campus.

Hardin knew what he was going to check on next. The girl, Martha Clark, was due to leave on a tour that morning. No one had seen her back in town and she did not answer her cell phone. He would stop by West Tour Agency to see if she showed up. He called the Bureau office to tell them he was following up on a lead and would be in later.

Hardin talked with the receptionist and discovered that the "Where West Meets East" tour left shortly before he arrived. The receptionist was reluctant to provide him with information about the agency's clients in the absence of the owner, Mr. West, who was leading this particular tour. A flash of his badge and some cajoling convinced her to confirm that Martha Clark missed leaving with the tour. Someone, she believed it was a family member or a friend, had come that morning to tell them Ms. Clark had been detained and would join the tour later. The receptionist was not at work when that took place. She gave him the cell number of Mr. West's assistant who handled all the check-ins.

Lee Hardin called the assistant as soon as he returned to the parking lot. She confirmed the receptionist's story. Her description of the young man who gave her the message about Martha Clark matched that of Cy Riverton.

Hardin knew without a doubt that something was going on and the kid was right in the middle of it.

Hardin decided right then that he had to get home early enough to have time to review what he had copied from Cy's flash drive.

CHAPTER 37

Marty woke the next morning to find Green Corn and her companions gone. The fire was dead and the ashes scattered. She waited for what seemed like hours until she was sure they were far away. Then she circled the rocks to find out whether or not her cache had been discovered.

She sighed with relief as she pulled the rocks away from the crevice. Her daypack was still in its hiding place. She pulled her wrist screen from its padded pocket and unwrapped it.

She had left it on in mute mode in hopes of receiving texts from Cy while she was with Maggie Grimsby. The screen was blank. She tried to activate it. Nothing happened. It appeared the battery was drained. Marty nervously sucked in her breath. Was that all that was wrong? Were her efforts to escape from Green Corn and the Lenape in vain? Was her wrist screen broken, which would mean that she was stuck back in 1758 after all?

Marty set the wrist screen in the sun and waited impatiently for the solar battery to have enough time to recharge. She climbed the rocks and once again looked in the direction of where she had seen the aurora the night before.

Her mind appealed to the now-invisible spectacle.

Aurora, are you still there? Cy always asks if I can see you. Are you friend or foe?

Back with her wrist screen, Marty closed her eyes and made one final plea for success as she turned the unit on. The trill told her she had a text message waiting. She pumped the air with her fist as she whispered a triumphant "Yes!" She closed her eyes and hoped that when she opened Cy's text, she would find directions for what she needed to do to get back home.

Marty found several messages waiting for her. They were all from Cy except for the one from her mother that asked her to please call.

Marty saw Cy repeated pretty much the same text message every ten to fifteen minutes for over an hour, assuming all of them came through. He evidently tried again to reach her a couple of hours later. The first several asked her to let him know if she was okay. The last message prompted her to give a sigh of relief about one of her concerns.

.

Text when u can. I have ?? re fone number u called. I will get info re your tour from your car n tell them u r delayed n will join them later. Waiting anxiously to hear from u. Your bff

.

It was so good to read that Cy had contacted the travel agency about her delay. That was the good news. But afterwards, Marty felt disappointed because he did not have any answers yet, only questions. That meant she would not get home today. She would have to wait until nighttime before making contact with him.

Marty decided that to be on the safe side, as long as she remained there, she would remain in period costume. Besides, she planned to go home that way. It would be so impre to see Cy's face when she showed up on Dead Man's Drop dressed in clothes from 1758.

As the sun climbed overhead, she moved the wrist screen away from the encroaching shadows to keep it in direct sunlight.

The hours of waiting for the day to pass started to wear on Marty. She missed her family. She even missed her brother Jason.

She missed Hunter. She almost wished she had brought him with her, although it was just as well she had not. What would Stalking Bear have done to him in order to capture her? It surprised Marty to realize how much she wished for the comfort of the little dog.

Most of all, Marty missed Cy. Even though they were texting back and forth, it was not the same as being with him in person. She wanted to be back on Dead Man's Drop helping him take his readings. She wanted to be anyplace other than in this strange, bygone era.

Marty paced around the base of the rocks. She felt restless as she waited for night to come. She still had some snack food and water in her day pack but it would not last much longer. Even though she did not dare wander far in case there were people traveling in the area who would present a danger to her, Marty decided to roam around the top of the mountain in search of anything edible.

Where did Green Corn find the root vegetables she had cooked the previous night, Marty wondered? Did she bring them with her? Or, were they somewhere in the area ready to be dug up and baked if only Marty knew where to look?

Marty found more berries and ate several. She soon returned to the top of the mountain. She carefully brushed away any visible footprints. It surprised and disappointed her when she checked the position of the sun and realized that it was only mid-afternoon.

Marty found a rock where she could sit in reasonable comfort while she used her wrist screen. She decided to study some of the files she had saved while she and Cy were on Dead Man's Drop Mountain. Several references were for internet sites which she could not access. However, the pdf and text files she had downloaded were available.

Marty read again about the solar winds being deflected by the earth's atmosphere and circling the earth in bands of electromagnetic fields. It was these electromagnetic fields that created the auroras at both the north and south poles. The fields were closest to the earth near the equator at noon. If that was part of the energy that was moving her through time and space, perhaps that explained why Cy wanted her to call him on the cell phone in the middle of the day.

Aurora power.

Is that what my wrist screen is using to move me?

Even though she could not see any auroras in the daytime, one of the forces that created the electromagnetic fields that interested Cy so much was the same phenomena that caused auroras. Aurora power was easier for her to remember than all those physics terms Cy liked to use.

Marty looked at the sky and felt her heart sink. It was starting to cloud over. Like the day she came to Chimney Rock, it looked like it was going to rain.

Will my phone still activate and carry me home if it is overcast and rainy, she wondered? There had been an electrical storm when she left Dead Man's Drop, but could a drizzly rainstorm with a thick cloud cover hinder the aurora effect?

Would the clouds interfere with the sound waves that transmit the text messages? She hoped it would be a brief, late afternoon storm that would be gone by evening. It was essential that she be able to contact Cy that night.

Marty wondered how long aurora episodes usually lasted. There was an aurora the previous night, but would the increased electromagnetic power be gone by the next day?

Marty gave herself a pep talk in an effort to keep any feelings of foreboding at bay. She had to keep a positive attitude. She had to stay convinced that the following day would be bright and sunny at noontime and she would have the answers from Cy that she needed so she could go home.

CHAPTER 38

R u ok? Im so worried about u please reply

.

So glad to hear from u been scary but im ok

.

What happened? U didnt answer last two nites. My messages not get thru?

.

Got your texts today I went back to grimsbys to warn mrs g of Indian attacks she was really sick I stayed to help also saw green corn her people r on their way to easton to make peace treaty

.

That is the short version. Knowing how frightened Cy was of the possibility that she might be captured by one of the native tribes in the area, Marty decided she would wait to tell Cy the whole story, including her narrow escape, once she was home. No sense worrying him now.

.

U had me really concerned. I told tour u will join them later

.

Sorry about that n thanx for help with tour I wud have sent text last nite but couldnt because surrounded by lenni lenape

.

No problem. Ditched cowboy ok. U still in Catoctin mtns?

.

Im on same mtn u think is chimney rock I hope u were nice to mr west n did not say anything re his western clothes im already embarrassed about joining the tour late

.

No I would not do that. All is good with Mr. West. Lets just get u home

.

Believe me I am ready to come home as soon as u tell me how to do it :)m

.

I think I figured out something important. When u called my number exactly what numbers did u enter?

.

I called using my speed call that I always use to call u

.

Did u include the area code?

.

Marty blinked after she read his message. Area code? She just used his speed-call number. She had no idea if it included the area code or why that would make a difference. All her calls except to her grandparents were local. Usually the seven-digit numbers went through just fine.

Marty checked the speed-call number for Cy on her Sun Access. It was only seven digits long. No, the area code was not included. Then she checked the number Cy had given her for Eddie. It was only a seven-digit number, too. Not only that, the first three digits of the Eddie number were the same as the first three digits of Cy's cell number.

.

No area code just your seven digit number is that y im here n not there your prefix is the same prefix as number u gave me for eddie is that y im so close to where eddie ended up?

.

Could b. The EM fields may pick up the signal of the first few numbers n treat first three numbers as an area code. Try with area code tomorrow. Lets hope that gets u back home

.

Do I still use the 1 before the area code?

.

Yes. That may be what keeps u in north America. Whatever u do dont enter the country code for any other country especially Siberia or Greenland. that would b bad

.

That is so funny u r so impre to come up with a joke like that

.

I was being serious. Use the number 1 before the area code n then my cell number. Then lets hope it gets u home ok

.

So that was it!

Cy figured out that the electromagnetic fields picked up on the first few numbers sent or received by the cell phone. That is what determined where the electromagnetic currents sent whoever was holding the phone giving off that signal. That made a lot of sense to Marty.

It solved the mystery of why she could not get back to Colorado using the number on her speed-call. Without the area code, the signal could not direct her to where she lived. She felt like jumping up and down with excitement now that she knew that Cy had solved the puzzle. She was going home tomorrow!

Then Marty laughed and shook her head. Cy was something else. Here he made a great joke, yet he could not see the humor in it. Did he really think she would enter the country code, whatever that was, for Siberia or Greenland or anyplace else, even if she knew what they were?

I am still laughing, even under the circumstances. That is a good sign.

She sent her reply.

.

Will do I am adding area code to your cell number rite now thanx cy u r so smart and downrite impre I new I cud count on u :)m

.

Even though she was caught up in the excitement of realizing that Cy figured out how to get her home, Marty could no longer ignore what was going on above her. The earlier cloudiness had cleared up and the night sky was clear and crisp. Her jaw dropped as she looked with wonder at the sky over her head. She had to tell Cy.

.

U shud c this impre aurora it is the britest red glow ive ever seen it fills the whole sky not just in the north like others it is everywhere will take pix

.

That is really helpful. There r not that many big auroras seen south of Canada except during solar cycle highs or when big solar flares hit earth.

.

U wud b proud of me I read that info about solar winds n electric mag forces u found for me pretty impre stuff I call it aurora power hope this aurora lasts n gets me home

.

Me too. Please stay there n away from people. Only go for water if u need to. Call my number with a one n area code tomorrow at noon. I will b on Dead Mans Drop. Lets hope this works.

.

Not to worry im not going anywhere until I call u tomorrow im so ready to come home I miss u n cant wait to c u again

.

Me too. I didnt no how much I would miss u until u were gone. I will b waiting for u tomorrow. U really r my bff

.

      Marty read Cy's last text over several times before she responded. She focused on the part where he said, "I didn't know how much I would miss you until you were gone" and "You really are my best friend forever."

      Maybe there really is hope for Cy and me. Maybe he does think of me as more than just a friend.

      Marty closed her eyes and wished it to be so with all her heart.

.

Thanx for being there for me I will hope n pray this gets me home tomorrow I will call n then u can come get me u really r my bff :)m

.

No calls. Text only. As long as u r back in 2024 I will come get u no matter where u r. promise

.

Ok gotcha will send text c u tomorrow :)m

.

CHAPTER 39

Cy slept in late. He was exhausted from the long day before that had started when he rose before the sun to get the tour information from the glove box of Marty's car and did not end until after he had exchanged text messages with her late at night. He took his time with his shower and a breakfast of pink-frosted toaster pastry and an over-ripe banana. Then he thought about what he could do while he waited to pick up Marty. Rather than pace his apartment, he decided to go to the internet café.

Cy retrieved his flash drive from the restroom but found it hard to settle down and concentrate. His stomach was tied in knots. Marty's response to his texts the night before bothered him. She seemed confident that he had found the answer. He was not so sure. There were so many other factors that could play into the situation that he had not figured out yet. He was so anxious to see her that he did not know if he could handle the disappointment if she did not make it back today. He could not face the prospect of failing Marty and leaving her back in time. She had not said much about what she was dealing with, but he knew he would worry about her until she was safely home.

Cy's thoughts kept coming back to Marty's questions the night before about Eddie. Something about her interest bothered him although she had brought up some good points that confirmed that he might be on the right track. She was close to where Eddie landed. However, she did not end up on the same mountaintop, or knob, as they called it back there. She did not end up in the same time period as Eddie. That left a lot of unanswered questions. That was why Cy decided he wanted to review the file on Eddie and compare it to the information he had gathered on area codes.

Cy grimaced with annoyance when he caught sight of Special Agent Hardin entering the café. It was Friday, no classes this morning, no students to tutor that day, and he wanted the day off for himself. He did not want to deal with the man. The only person he really wanted to see was Marty.

Cy closed down the file on Eddie and brought up his favorite search screen. He noticed that the special agent was dressed in his usual rumpled business suit. Hardin went to the counter to place an order. Cy waited until the fed had his back to him before he pocketed the flash drive.

Hardin walked over to Cy's table and plunked down the tall drink cup with its spill-proof lid and straw before sliding into the seat across from Cy.

"Good morning, Special Agent Hardin," Cy said coolly. "I am surprised to see you this morning."

"Why would that be, Cy? Friday is another work day, just like any other weekday," Hardin responded.

"I would think you would want to take it a little easier on Fridays so you could get ready to spend the weekend off with your family," Cy said, even though he now knew the agent would not be with his family over the weekend. Then he groaned inside himself as Lee Hardin slipped into his folksy story-telling mode and launched into one of his monologs.

"I would, if it was up to me, Cy, but my family doesn't live close to here," Hardin said. "My two kids live back east with their mother. But, my job brought me out here. Sometimes you just gotta go where the Bureau sends you, if you know what I mean."

"I suppose."

"I got a boy fourteen who plays sports," Hardin continued. "Don't matter what sport, he loves to play them all. And he's good at them, too, just like his old man was in his day. I try to get back to see him play when I can. Good kid, going to play freshman football this fall. I told him, though, there's more to life than sports. He has to keep his grades up or a sports scholarship to college won't do him much good in the long run. I think you know what I mean there, Cy. You tutor lots of kids who need to keep their grades up because they finally realize it is important."

Cy made no reply. He lowered his eyes and studied the blank search engine screen.

"Now my daughter, that's a different story," Lee Hardin continued. "No one needs to tell her to keep up on her studies. Now that she's a senior in high school, she knows how close she is to applying to college. She understands the need to have the right grades to get into the one she wants to go to. She's always hitting the books. She's on the computer all the time. Kinda like you, Cy. In some ways, you remind me of her, Kid. What do you think of that?"

"I think you should be talking to her instead of to me," said Cy with a shrug. He knew the fed was leading up to something. He wished the man would just say it and get it over with.

"Oh, I intend to," Hardin said after he took a long sip of his drink. "I try to talk to them every weekend that the Bureau doesn't pull me in on duty. Sometimes have trouble catching my son at home, busy with sports and his buddies and all, but I can almost always get my girl on the phone. She keeps me up-to-date. I got one of those family plans, you know what I'm talking about? So I let her have her own cell, one of those wrist things, on the condition she keeps up on her studies and does not go over her texting limit.

"Now my boy, I gave him a cell, but ended up taking it back. His mother complained he was messing up on his grades because he spent too much time with all that texting business and web surfing you kids like to do. The daughter, though, she stays up on her grades and under her limits, so she still has her phone. Makes it easy for me to keep in touch."

Cy glanced up long enough to see Lee Hardin gaze in the direction of the restrooms as he took another long sip on his drink.

Cy was not sure if the agent was just staring off into space and the door to the men's room just happened to be in his line of sight. Or, was he looking at the restrooms for a reason? Was the fed showing an interest in the flash drive's hiding place because he knew or suspected something? Cy fought back a quiver of nervousness.

Then Lee Hardin set his cup down, straightened in his seat and folded his arms on the table in front of him. He leaned forward and looked intently at Cy. The folksy act was gone.

"Why do you think that is, Cy?" he asked, his voice all business.

Cy's eyes met his glare.

"I have no idea what you mean, Special Agent Hardin."

"My daughter is a typical teenage girl who likes to do teenage girl things, like texting and talking on the phone with her friends. Why do you suppose my daughter can be responsible enough to stay up on her schoolwork and under her text limits when her brother kept messing up every month until I took his cell away? Do you think it's because she is older than her brother? Do you think it's because she's a girl? Is it because she is a more studious person who is concerned about her grades? What do you think makes her a more responsible person?"

"I would not venture to say, Special Agent Hardin," said Cy, confused about where this was leading. "I am not a psychology major."

"I know you're a math and physics guy, Cy. Me, I was a chemistry guy in college. Helped me out dealing with the drug busts and all, you know? But, even being a math and physics type, I thought you might have some insight on the matter," said Hardin. "Take, for instance, your friend, Martha Clark. She's a girl, no argument there, right? She has one sibling, and like in my family, she's older than her brother. And she must be a good student because she hired you to tutor her so she could get good grades. Yet, unlike my daughter, she doesn't seem to be very responsible."

Cy's gaze held while the agent's eyes drilled into his.

There it is. He is going to question me about Marty.

"I am not sure I agree with you, Special Agent Hardin," said Cy carefully as he brought up his hands to tick his responses off on his fingers. "I have always found Marty to be responsible. She was very good at keeping her tutoring appointments. If she had to miss, she always let me know in advance and there was always a good reason why she had to reschedule."

"Well, that confuses me, Cy, it really does," said Hardin as he leaned back and turned sideways in his chair. He rapidly tapped his almost empty drink cup on the tabletop several times. "You see, I have been trying to catch your friend all week now. I call her, but she does not answer her cell. She doesn't call me back. I call her parents. They say she has sent a text message, but she doesn't call or return their calls. I ask you last weekend why you are getting into her car and driving it to her home and you say she asked you to because she is in Pennsylvania even though she is due to leave on a big tour back east in a few days. So, yesterday I figure I'll check with the tour agency her parents said she was going to travel with. Guess what, Cy? She was a no-show. What do you think about that, Cy? Does that sound responsible to you?"

There were several moments of silence as the two stared at each other.

"Maybe something came up that detained her," Cy finally said softly. "Maybe she had a good reason for not being there."

"Well, that could be, Cy," Hardin said, as he turned away. "And I suppose you might know what that good reason might be. You see, I talked to the gal down at the travel agency and she said that someone came by and told them Martha Clark was delayed and would join them in a few days. Now, it wasn't her parents who told them. Her parents are still in California and didn't know anything about her missing her tour bus. It was a friend who told them. And, from the description, it sounded an awful lot like that friend is probably you."

Hardin turned back to look at Cy and demanded, "So what was her reason for not being at the agency in time to start her bus tour, Cy?"

Cy took a deep breath and let out a slow, audible sigh.

"Marty went back east and was not able to get back in time to catch her tour bus," Cy said. "That is why she asked me to tell them she would join them in a few days."

"So what is Martha Clark doing already back east if she was getting ready to take a big trip back east?" Hardin pressed. "And why is it you are the only person Miss Clark seems to call? Why is it she does not return her parents' calls or my calls? Is there a reason she is avoiding talking to her parents or the FBI? Why does she avoid talking to everyone but you?"

"She doesn't call me. She sends me text messages," Cy explained. "She says she is unable to make phone calls. She has one of those new Sun Access phones. It has new recharging battery technology. I think she is having technical problems."

In a sense it is true. Marty is having problems, and they are technical in nature.

Cy did not clarify that it was not the cell unit that was having the technical problems.

"Humph," Hardin grunted skeptically. "Just like that? No one hears from or sees the girl but you? When she needs help with something, the only person she asks is you? And all this is done with text messages? So, where exactly 'back east' is Martha Clark right now, Cy, and how did she get there since her car is still sitting in her driveway?"

"I assure you I do not know, Special Agent Hardin. I only know that she is trying to locate her tour and join them on the road."

"Well, you send her a text message and you tell her to find a pay phone and call me," barked Hardin, annoyed. "You tell her I have some questions for her. You tell her I want to know exactly where she is and that she's all right."

"Why don't you text her yourself, Special Agent Hardin?" Cy suggested calmly.

"I don't text," Hardin snapped irritably. "I don't have one of those a-b-c keyboards and my big fingers don't like pushing those tiny buttons. I only punch numbers, no letters, and only if I have to because who I want to call isn't on speed-call."

"They have had voice-activated messaging available for years, you know. Have you tried that?"

"That talky-talky thing is okay if you talk the same way as that snooty little computer in the phone, but my talky-talky words always come out more garbled than my typing," Hardin snarled. "You just tell Martha Clark to call me. Her cell gets to working, tell her to use her web-cam. I want to see her face. If not, I want to at least hear her voice."

"I will tell her, Special Agent Hardin."

"Anything else you think I should know?" Hardin asked, sarcastically. "You know, since it seems you are the only one she stays in touch with and all?"

Cy slowly shook his head no. It worried him that the agent was starting to focus on Marty. Cy knew he had to get Marty home soon or Hardin was going to cause a lot of trouble for him. He hoped Marty would be back in Colorado this afternoon and he could pick her up. That would solve everything, at least as far as questions about Marty were concerned.

The more Cy and Lee Hardin studied each other across the table that housed the computer, the more Cy realized that the agent did not intimidate him nearly as much as he had before. It's because I know things about him now, Cy realized.

"Well, you got my phone number," said Lee Hardin as he heaved himself out of the chair. "So, if you do think of anything, you call me, okay, Kid?"

Cy recalled what he had learned about Lee Hardin at the library the previous day.

Yeah, I have your number.

Hardin twisted as if to leave, then he turned back towards Cy.

"Ya don't mind if I call you Kid, do ya?"

Cy could not stand it any longer. He hated to be called Kid. He could not resist the impulse.

Cy looked directly into Lee Hardin's eyes with a straight face and casually replied, "Not at all, Cowboy. You don't mind if I call you 'Cowboy,' do you?"

Cy felt a surge of satisfaction as he watched the older man's head jerk up and his back stiffen. Then the agent relaxed his body and raised one corner of his mouth in his usual lop-sided grin before he responded.

"Sounds like you been doing a little investigating yourself, Kid."

Cy lowered his eyes to the still-blank search screen.

"In my field, Cowboy, we call it research."

CHAPTER 40

After Lee Hardin left Cy at the internet café, he found himself driving in circles. He could not pry Cy's retort out of his mind. The kid had done some digging and knew about Ohio. He actually had the nerve to call him "Cowboy." Hardin had no doubt that the kid was smart enough to know how that nickname was used Ohio. He shivered with fury at the very thought of it.

The kid has no respect for the law or for me as a special agent. He knew what he was doing when he shoved that into my face. I should bury him for that alone.

What Hardin really hated was that the kid had dredged up painful memories of a part of his life that he preferred to keep buried away in a far corner his brain. He had worked diligently through the years to keep the awareness of that time from imposing itself upon his consciousness. If there had been one thing that Lee Hardin had to name as the lowest point in his life, that year in Ohio had been it. It had changed his future, disintegrated his family and triggered the decline of his career.

Hardin called the office. He told his boss that unless they needed him, he wanted to take the afternoon off to compensate for the extra hours worked the previous two nights. He sighed with relief when his leave request was approved.

Knowing he would not be able to concentrate on the Burrows case or anything else until he had once again worked through the Ohio incident and buried it back into the depths of his memory, Lee Hardin ran the mindless personal errands he had been putting off the previous few days.

It was early afternoon when Hardin entered his apartment carrying an armload of survival groceries. He turned down the air conditioner temperature and turned on the computer. It was time to get the CD out of his gun safe to see what Cy had on his flash drive.

Hardin put the CD into the drive before he went to the kitchen. He slapped a piece of salami onto a slice of bread, spread a ribbon of mustard down one side of the meat and rolled the bread over. He knew it would be the first of three or four rolled sandwiches he would make that afternoon. He grabbed a paper towel and folded it in half to use as a blotter for any of the mustard that dripped while he was eating.

Hardin sat down at the computer. With his sandwich clutched in his left hand, he used his right hand to work the mouse so he could view the CD.

Hardin had his mouth wide open and was in the process of taking his first bite when he saw the name. He froze, staring at it in disbelief. Then, taking a deep breath, he opened the file labeled "Marty." The hand holding his rolled sandwich dropped to the desk next to the keyboard as he started to read the contents. He shook his head in disbelief. Then he felt the anger well up inside of him again.

Martha Clark was gone, too.

Cy knew she was gone and was trying to keep it quiet.

No one had reported her missing. No one had even hinted at the possibility. But, Hardin then realized, the warning signals had been there all along. He had been looking at them the whole time. Yet, he had not allowed even himself to see them. And here it was before him in the file.

Hardin slowly ate the sandwich without tasting it as he quickly skimmed the documents in the Marty file. He was so angry with Cy that he wanted nothing more than to strangle him. First, the kid had gone digging into his past and rubbed it in by calling him Cowboy. Now, Hardin realized, the kid had been playing innocent while he knew all along that Martha Clark, the girl Hardin had asked him about just that morning, was missing.

Pages of notes that looked like text messages filled the file. If he could have convinced his boss that keeping an eye on the kid was important to an ongoing investigation, he could have gotten a search warrant and gotten the same information from Cy's internet provider. But, even without that, here it was laid out for him on the information taken from Cy's personal records.

The messages appeared to Hardin to be a jumble of nonsense. In some of them, he got the distinct impression they were discussing history lessons. Other texts talked about Ed Burrows.

Hardin realized he was not in the right frame of mind to concentrate on any of it. What he needed to do was find the kid and squeeze him until he got some decent answers out of the smart-aleck.

His thoughts swirled as he leaned back and stared at the ceiling. Then he got up and paced the floor for a few minutes before he sat back down and forced himself to carefully go through the information in the Marty file.

Hardin reviewed all the notes written by Cy. They were dated and had times noted, like journal entries. He shook his head in disgust when he read the ones where Cy supposedly tells Marty not to tell anyone because he cannot help her if the FBI knows she is gone. Cy's lack of trust in and respect for law enforcement really annoyed him. Then again, Hardin admitted to himself, of all people, he knew why a few in the FBI deserved little respect.

Hardin shook his head as he realized the storyline that was being developed in Cy's notes. Maybe the kid was certifiably crazy. Didn't they say that sometimes there is a fine line between genius and insanity?

He tried to ignore the thought that crept into his mind that, if by some wild stretch of the imagination, everything Cy was leading up to was real, then the kid was right. He would have good reason to not have faith that the Bureau or anyone else would figure out the truth. The whole scenario the notes and messages described was too far-fetched. It was impossible. Intelligent people in their right minds, especially trained special agents, would never believe it.

He gritted his teeth with resentment when he came across Cy's notes about him. However, he could not help but smile when he read Cy's comment about how he hated to be called "Kid."

Yeah, I got to the kid genius, Lee Hardin thought, nodding his head. Throws him off-balance just enough. One of these times it will slip him up so I can get the truth out of him.

Then Hardin read Cy's commentary on why he hated the nickname. A thought ran through his brain that dropped his anger level several notches.

Okay, Hardin had to admit to himself. Maybe when it comes to this throwing around nicknames, the kid and I have more in common than what I thought. He doesn't like being called something that he feels is a put-down any more than I do. Maybe he wasn't trying to shove the Ohio debacle at me so he could grind me into the ground with it. Maybe he just picked up on the nickname and decided to give as good as he got. Perhaps he was hoping I would take the hint and stop calling him Kid.

Hardin realized then that he did not start calling Cy "Kid" to deliberately annoy him. It just came out. Maybe the kid did kind of remind Lee Hardin a little bit of his own daughter. That was not necessarily a good thing, considering the special feelings he had for his girl. It could cloud his judgment and hamper the investigation. It annoyed him to realize he actually liked Cy Riverton and enjoyed the challenge of sparring with him verbally.

Yeah, but that will change real quick if Martha Clark doesn't show up safe and sound real soon.

Whatever was going on with her and the Burrows kid, Lee Hardin knew that Cy was somehow right in the middle of it.

CHAPTER 41

As Cy drove to Dead Man's Drop Mountain, he could feel the excitement build up inside of him. He realized it was more than getting Marty back safely. It was being able to see her again. It was knowing that he would actually be with her. It was knowing that he would be able to talk to her in person instead of just exchanging text messages. He had told her she was his bff—his best friend forever. More than ever, he knew how true that was. He did not have much experience around girls, but maybe she would someday be more to him than just a best friend. He would really like that. Why had it taken her disappearance for him to realize that?

Marty had told him to wait at home until she arrived and sent a text to tell him where to meet her. However, Cy later worried that if he and his cell phone were not physically present on Dead Man's Drop Mountain, a place he knew the subsurface electromagnetic forces were strong enough to allow a person to transport through time and space, Marty might end up anywhere within the region covered by the area code. Worse yet, she might come to the area in a different era. He decided he needed to physically be on Dead Man's Drop with his cell in his hand and turned on when she made her call to him.

Cy also hoped that Special Agent Lee Hardin would back off once Marty was home. One of the first things he planned to do once he got Marty off the mountain was to call the fed and invite him to meet him and Marty at the café. Once the man realized Marty was safe, maybe he would stop following Cy around with his endless questions and folksy tales.

Yes, Eddie was still missing. Cy would still continue to work on a way to find Eddie and bring him home. And Marty gave good, practical feedback. That would help him, too. But, it would be so much easier without Lee Hardin relentlessly pursuing him as if he was responsible for the disappearances. Maybe Marty could get through to the man and convince him that Cy was not the bad guy.

That thought prompted Cy to review in his mind what he had found out about Hardin.

***

Cy missed his lunch the day he researched Lee Hardin at the university library. Although he did not find Hardin's life story, by the time he finished he had a fairly clear picture of the fed, or G-man, as Cy learned FBI special agents used to be called.

The more he thought about it afterwards, the more Cy realized how the events that had taken place in Ohio revealed a lot about the man. It explained why he tended to work alone and perhaps why the other agents were not buddy-buddy with him. It also explained his attachment to the old-fashioned paper notebook he carried in his pocket.

Cy had used his favorite search engines to look for information about Lee Hardin. He found quite a bit about a couple of men named Lee Hardin, but they were not the FBI special agent. He could not even find old online white pages listings for him. A few links referenced old news articles, but the links were no longer active. Even when Cy used the "Way Back" site, he could not find much.

The FBI must take steps to keep information about their personnel private, thought Cy. Either that, or Hardin himself made the effort to keep his information inaccessible.

However, using the name of the newspaper in which some of the now-unavailable sites once appeared, Cy followed the suggestion of the reference librarian and found the old newspapers on the library's subscription to the newspaper database, *News Bank*.

There, starting about nine years earlier, he found articles written about Special Agent Lee Hardin in the northern Ohio newspapers.

Hardin's name first showed up when he was the head of a multi-agency task force involving both the Bureau and several local law enforcement agencies. He had been the spokesman to the press about a successful operation that resulted in the breakup of a major drug and money-laundering ring whose activities crossed two state lines. Several arrests were made. Millions of dollars worth of drugs and currency were confiscated.

The bust also resulted in three deaths. One of the men killed was an undercover police officer.

A few days later, the tone of the local news stories changed as the identity of the undercover officer became known and it was determined that Hardin had fired the fatal shot. Lee Hardin was placed on administrative leave. The public outcry swelled, demanding justice for the slain officer.

As he read, Cy began to notice that once or twice a week there were long investigative reports published in one of the newspapers, all with the same by-line. Based on "confidential sources within the FBI," the reporter seemed bent on glorifying the fallen local police operative while insisting that the FBI special agent running the task force, Lee Hardin, had deviated from Bureau procedures during the bust and should be held accountable for the policeman's death. Hardin maintained that he had worked the taskforce operation according to plan and that it had been a righteous shoot. Hardin claimed he caught up with the undercover cop trying to get away with the cash during the take-down. When the undercover cop pulled his gun on Hardin, Hardin fired back in self-defense.

The local police department was infuriated that Hardin would accuse one of their undercover operatives of being dirty. Special agents from the Bureau, some he worked with as well as his immediate superior, denied that he had warned them of his suspicions about the man.

The newspaper reports over time told the story of the internal investigation. They seemed to be trying to protect the image of the FBI while subtly laying the full blame on Lee Hardin, the "cowboy," who shot from the hip and asked questions later. He was not a "team player." He was a special agent who often operated on his own. The reporter wrote a persuasive argument claiming that in this instance, Hardin had gone too far. In doing so, he ended the life of a top undercover officer while concocting the self-defense story to protect himself.

Even with his limited experience as a teacher's assistant dealing with the workplace politics at the university, it was obvious to Cy that one or more of Hardin's co-workers were out to get him. The question Cy had was, why? Was it because he really was not a good agent? Or, was it because he was too good and made the others around him look incompetent in comparison?

The results of the FBI's internal investigation led to Hardin's suspension. Although no criminal charges were filed, the family of the fallen police officer filed a wrongful death suit against Hardin.

Cy almost missed it, but it was at that point in his research that he found a legal notice announcing that Mrs. Hardin filed for divorce.

More information about Hardin's side emerged during the trial. At first, there were only occasional short statements by Lee Hardin or his attorney maintaining his innocence. Otherwise, they refused to say anything else. During the trial, the same investigative reporter, flush with statements fed to him by his anonymous sources, continued to discredit Lee Hardin.

Certain members of the Bureau who were involved with the operation took the stand and testified that Hardin had acted on his own without the Bureau being made aware of Hardin's suspicions about the undercover policeman. Two witnesses provided copies of progress reports on the task force investigation obtained from the Bureau's computerized files. All showed a noticeable absence of any reports of suspicion about the detective.

The reporters covering the trial had, at first, ridiculed Hardin for using his paper journal as part of his defense. They made fun of it for being an antiquated method of recording investigation notes.

Hardin demonstrated that he faithfully made notes of his interactions with the undercover cop. He detailed all the man's activities once Hardin grew suspicious that the man was on the take and had been hampering the efforts of the task force all along.

In that bound journal, Lee Hardin had also listed dates and the names of his superior and co-workers to whom he had made his verbal warnings or to whom he had submitted written memos and reports about the case he was building against the local operative. He had consistently dated and initialed each entry. It was established that his journal entries were in date order, they had not been altered, and that no pages had been removed.

When Hardin's attorney started bringing in his technical witnesses to provide testimony, the reporters started to back off.

First there was the special agent who was close to retirement and no longer concerned about advancing his career. He testified that Hardin had indeed warned the others about his suspicions of the undercover cop. But, because of the potential political fall-out with the local police department that could result if the suspicion proved to be wrong, some of the special agents on the task force preferred to ignore Hardin's warning and continue with the operation. They were afraid the controversy could break apart the task force that they had worked for so many months to pull together. They pressured the special agent in charge to ignore Hardin's suspicions, insisting that if Hardin was right, they could deal with it later.

Hardin's attorney had subpoenaed the Bureau cell phones used by two of the agents to record their notes. The recording feature on the cells was the original digital sources of the reports that ended up being filed in the FBI's computer. His technical expert testified that he had thoroughly gone over the recording media in each device. He established that there had been information entered that was later erased. He had been able to get date stamps and enough data to show the agents had recorded comments about Hardin and suspicious activity and a cop and then later deleted it. Enough was retrieved to show that the transcribed report entered earlier into evidence was not an exact transcription of what had been originally recorded.

The jury found for the defense and Lee Hardin was exonerated.

Several weeks later, a different reporter managed to get a short article about Hardin published in the middle pages of the paper. Lee Hardin had been reinstated as a special agent in the Bureau with full seniority and back pay. He had been reassigned.

As much as Lee Hardin annoyed him, Cy realized that the man had gotten a bad deal back then. It almost seemed to Cy that because the Bureau in that region ended up being publically embarrassed because of the incident, the powers that be in the Bureau had not forgiven Lee Hardin for being right.

Cy thought back to the day he had been served with a search warrant and the special agents invaded his apartment. Lee Hardin did not head that task force. Cy remembered how the other special agents acted around each other and how they had ignored Lee Hardin.

Then Cy told himself to stop feeling sorry that Lee Hardin was wrongly accused back then. The man really was a cowboy. He was the only one regularly following Cy while the rest of the Bureau had decided to "cold case" Eddie's disappearance and focus its attention elsewhere. Lee Hardin being a cowboy had accomplished nothing except to interfere with Cy's attempts to help his friends.

But, Marty will be coming home. Hardin will be able to see her face-to-face and talk with her all he wants. After she is home, with a little bit of luck, Cowboy will hang up his spurs and stop digging them into me.

Cy sighed with relief at the thought.

CHAPTER 42

The sun climbed to its zenith. Marty strapped her Sun Access on her wrist, making sure the clasp was securely fastened. She put everything into her daypack and tried to pull it on her shoulders. It did not fit comfortably over the cape, so she slipped it on under the cape.

Marty barely started to climb the rocks to the top when she heard barking. She immediately recognized that it was coming from Hunter. Had Mrs. Grimsby let him out of the house and he decided to follow her up the mountain?

Marty froze with apprehension when she heard the man's voice. She could not make out his words at first. Eventually, she realized he was speaking English.

"Aye, Hunter, she be at the top of the mountain, eh? There'll be nary a chance of her escaping us now, eh, boy?"

Marty looked for the biggest crevice in which she could hide. She had barely scrambled over a few rocks on her way to an opening when Hunter bounded out of the bushes and ran to her. She could tell by his bark that he was excited to see her.

"Go away, Hunter," she ordered in a whisper, afraid that the dog would lead the strange man to her.

"Aye, thar she be, Hunter, my boy," said the man with a satisfied expression on his broad face as he burst through the trees surrounding the small clearing. "Here, Boy. Now!"

Marty assumed that the man before her was Mr. Grimsby. She felt her heart sink once she saw that he held the abalone shell necklace she had given Maggie. That was how he had prompted Hunter to follow her scent. Had Maggie turned on Marty after all? Marty now wished she had not given the gift to the woman.

The man was middle-aged, with salt and pepper-colored hair. He was thick around the middle with broad shoulders. His small dark eyes were close together and sank back into a fleshy face that was flushed from the climb up the hill. He was dressed in breeches, stockings, and a leather hunting shirt. A powder horn and water bag were slung across his chest. A leather box was attached to a leather belt around his waist. He gripped a musket in his hand.

Even though he was a few inches shorter than she was, Marty realized that the man was strong and would be hard to break away from if he ever laid his hands on her.

Hunter ran back to his master, dancing around his feet in excitement. However, when the dog started back towards Marty, the man caught him on the belly with his boot and flung him off to the side.

"Nay, ye cur," he roared in anger. "Stay away from the wench."

Then the man turned his attention to Marty. She felt extremely uncomfortable under his lecherous scrutiny. He narrowed his eyes as a wicked grin spread across his face.

"So, ye be the ungrateful wench what been stealing the clothes from the mistress and leaving her to die?"

"I did no such thing," Marty retorted indignantly. She moved her arm with the Sun Access behind her and hid it in the folds of the cape. "Maggie gave me these clothes. I took care of her while she was sick. I left only after she was better."

"She gave ye the clothes with the understanding ye'll take Annie's place," he insisted. "Ye took them with false pretenses of stealing them."

"Absolutely not!" Marty insisted. "She gave them to me before she ever said anything about forcing me to become your servant. I never would have accepted them if she had told me what she had in mind."

"Ye lie!" he bellowed. "The proof be in ye wearing them. Now, unless ye whilst prefer to be hung fer thieving ye shall come with me and do what ye be told." Then, with an evil chuckle, he continued, "Aye, ye shall make a fine replacement fer Annie. And every few years we'll rewrite the contract to where ye can plan to spend a long, useful life with me and Mistress Grimsby."

At the threatening tone in his voice, Hunter began to pace in circles at the side of his master.

Marty felt a chill course up and down her spine but forced her voice to remain calm and determined.

"I will tell you what I told your wife. I am not going to stay and become your slave. But, I also think you may be in danger of being attacked and burned out of your home. You would be smart to take Mrs. Grimsby and as much as you can carry and go away to somewhere safe."

"Aye, she spoke yer prattle. 'Twas forced to beat the truth out of her afore she'd tell about ye and how she let ye sneak off. But, ye'll not get away so easy from me as ye did that poor, sick woman. Now, get over here, wench. Ye and me shall be going home now. Anymore back-talk and ye'll be feeling the back of my hand."

"I told you, I am not going with you."

Mr. Grimsby lifted the musket and cocked the firing pin.

"Me musket says ye will!" he yelled.

Marty fought the panic rising inside of her.

I have to get away now!

It was the middle of the day, the time that Cy said the electromagnetic fields were the strongest and would take her home. She had already edited his speed-call number to include the area code with the numeral one in front. All she had to do was call his cell.

Marty lifted her hand to press the speed-call number for Cy.

"What have ye there, wench?" Mr. Grimsby demanded. "'Tis mine now. Hand it over or ye'll rue the day ye crossed me."

At the sight of his master aiming his musket at Marty, Hunter yipped in distress. Then he ran and leaped into Marty's arms.

Instinctively, Marty grabbed Hunter with her left arm and clutched him close to her. With her right hand, she reached again and tapped the speed-call key.

This is going to work. It has to.

She pushed the send button on the wrist screen.

Marty held Hunter tight in her arms as she felt the two of them caught up in the cocoon of light. The flow of electromagnetic energy swirling around her to take her home and away from this horrible man. She knew that the next thing she would see was Cy at the top of Dead Man's Drop waiting for her.

I am coming home, Cy. I can hardly wait to see you again, my best friend forever.

CHAPTER 43

Marty raised her head from the rock pressing against her cheek. A few moments later, Hunter wriggled out of her arms and stumbled several paces away. He shook his head in dazed confusion. Other than that, he appeared to be all right.

How interesting! Not only did I travel back in time, but Hunter was able to travel forward in time.

Marty briefly felt sorry that Maggie had lost her dog, but not enough to regret that Hunter had come home with her. Marty sat up and softly called Hunter to her. When he climbed into her lap, she scratched his ears while she looked around.

"You are one lucky dog, Hunter. You are going to get to meet a very special guy. His name is Cy. You will like him."

Hunter climbed out of her lap and started nosing around, curious about his new surroundings.

Cy was nowhere to be seen yet. Marty was too happy to be home to be worried that he was running late. Besides, maybe with the time zone difference, it was she who running early. All she knew was that he had come through for her the whole time she was gone. She was confident he would soon find her and take her and Hunter home.

Then she remembered. She needed to send him a text to tell him she was back so he knew where to come and pick her up. She decided to not take any chances. First she was going to get off the rocks and hike partway down the mountain before she sent her text. Then she would wait patiently for him to hike up the slope to her.

A smile lit Marty's face at the thought of seeing Cy again. She had missed him terribly. From his text messages she felt she had every reason to believe his feelings for her had grown stronger while she was gone. She couldn't ask for more.

Marty also realized that they both had learned so much from this challenge in their lives. They made a good team. Maybe together they could figure out how to find Eddie and get him back home, too.

Wait until Cy sees me in these old-timey Colonial clothes.

Marty chuckled at the thought of how much fun she was going to have teasing him about how she was almost adopted as a Lenni Lenape warrior's sister.

Marty stood up and stretched. It was time to climb off the rocks that formed the crest of the mountain. She called to Hunter to follow her.

The End

ABOUT THE AUTHOR

Robyn Echols has been writing since she was in junior high school. The mother of six children, she has pursued a varied education and several employment paths. She enjoys learning about family history and teaching it to others. She looks at history from the viewpoint of a family historian, focusing on the details of the everyday lives of those who lived in the past. Now Robyn resides with her husband in California and has fun researching and writing the books that she hopes will interest and entertain her readers.

Coming Soon

Watch for the next book in the Aurora Series

Aurora Redress

by

Robyn Echols

The saga continues as Marty makes a startling discovery about the mountain on which she and Hunter land. As she searches her cell call history and realizes what went different than planned, her disappointment turns to anticipation over the possibilities. Can she find Eddie and help him use aurora power to return home, also? Cy agrees that she needs to try to find Eddie, even though it means he must somehow continue to fend off the increasing threat to his own freedom as a result of being pursued by "Cowboy" FBI Special Agent, Lee Hardin.